An Unclean Act

An Unclean Act

by

Dean Burgess

THE PERMANENT PRESS
SAG HARBOR, NY 11963

Library of Congress Cataloging-in-Publication Data

Burgess, Dean
     An Unclean Act /by Dean Burgess
       p. cm.
     ISBN 1-57962-046-9 (alk paper)
     1. New England--History--Colonial period ca. 1600-1775--Fiction.
     2. Puritans--Fiction. 3.Adultery--Fiction. 4. Divorce--Fiction.
     5. Quakers--Fiction. I. Title

     PS3602.U847 U53 2002
     813'.6--dc21   2001036613
                                     CIP

Manufactured in the United States.

THE PERMANENT PRESS
4170 Noyac Road
Sag Harbor, NY 11963

To the late
Ann Heidbreder Eastman
who once said to me:
"Librarians know about so many things,
and are so interesting when they talk
about them. Why aren't more of
the writers?"

I am doing my best, Ann.

1

MY EARLIEST MEMORY is the sea. I do not mean the sea as you look out upon it from the shore. What I remember is being on the sea, but as if I were in it like a womb. Sometimes I think it is my real mother. As I say, it is the first thing I remember. No, what I remember is being tossed in a ship's hold like half a barrel end in the midst of the sea. Yes, like Mary Hamilton's babe in the old ballad, set to sea in a "pyder pig." Even though I was very small the under decks of that ship seemed not as large as a room. It was filled with people: knee to back and shoulder to chest. I cannot remember what they looked like now in that utter blackness. It was dark beyond belief except when the little half round door was opened and then the sunlight was so bright it blinded me with painful light. I might have been in a furnace like the little Hebrew children but the fire was outside and the heat of it within. Beyond that door black faceless bodies moved in silhouette against a piercing white day. When we went sailing on the *Good Cheer* I must have been six or seven and my brother a baby in arms.

I don't remember my mother and father, although they surely were there, but I do remember a young man reading from the Bible in a fine, high, thin West Country voice. Trying to understand what he read was difficult, not just because I was very little and many of the words unknown to me, but because the moving beams of light made him lose his place so that the phrases never quite knit together. Those beams of light seem alive in my memory: the pain as they struck my eyes and then the red patterns on the back of my closed eyelids shaping and reshaping, tangling themselves up in the words that young man read. Since that time, although I have often gone to sea, I have never been seasick. That crazily slanting world turning this way and that *was* the world, you see.

But what I mean to tell you was what happened on the deck. It was early in the morning, I think, the ship sliding and rolling about in some deep ocean swells. All the crowd in the hold was groaning and praying like the prophets of old and not watching what might happen to a silent sallow little boy, as I must have been. I got to the hatch and opened it; it was held only by a bit of rope looped over a hook, and there I was, all at once slipping and sliding on the gray deck. The wind was so fierce it threw me across the deck, striking me against this and that as though it would break my bones before it swallowed me up. Surely this is God, I thought, and I was looking into that fierce face alone. The gale was such that I could barely open my eyes, and my mouth was so full of wet salt and mouthfuls of wet wind I could neither breathe nor cry out. I could see no one when I grabbed hold of a davit, but there was someone there and he had seen me. He came reeling like an acrobat hand over hand down a sheet to where I lay sprawling, hugging my head against that little hooked piece of wood. He grabbed me by a leg and an arm and thrust me under his coat. Now I knew there were men on deck as we could hear them singing; the good matrons would hold their hands over our ears so we would not hear their song. The young women would sit nearer the door laughing, and giggling to each other until they were quieted and the Bible was read very loudly to drown out the evil songs. You can understand why I was much more frightened of that man than I was of drowning in the sea. He pulled me up the short flight of steps to the high brightly painted aft and tethered me to him. He was himself lashed to the mast like a dog on a rope. He drew my head out from under his coat, cupping it in one of his hands and with his other arm held me close to him, looking at me with a hard squint, his stubbly face only inches from my own. He smelled of urine, tobacco, sweat, wet wool, and what I now know was rum.

He pulled my ear close to his mouth and shouted out of the whirlwind, "What is your name, boy?"

"Thomas, sir," I shouted into the storm with all my might. "I am the son of Thomas Burge."

"And I am the son of no man, boy." He felt me shivering beneath his arm and looked down again. "You shouldn't be out here, but back in your wooden nest. Your mother, whichever of the goodies she may be, will skin you alive when she finds you with this one."

"It's all right, she told me to," I lied.

He gave me a long look and then began to laugh so hard I thought he would let me go. "A man who can speak up for himself like that belongs up here with the men, not down there with the yeomen of God. If you choose to sign on this ship, boy, I will vouch for you."

We sat for a long time in the blinding wind and water, with him looking out into the whiteness as though he could see something there.

"Where do you come from, boy?" he said at last.

"From my mother, sir."

"Well, that's true enough. We all do come from there. I mean what county do you come from at home?"

"I am a Cornishman, sir, I come from no county."

"Ha, there's another good answer. I should have known you for a Cornishman right off by the way you talk and that look in your eye. You belong to no county, and no man, do you, boy?"

"Do you know where we are sailing to?"

"You're not as smart as I thought then, after all. Everyone knows where this ship is going."

"Well, I don't."

"We are sailing for Virginia."

"Is it far?"

"Why, not as far as you might think. I was watching for it out there just now. Don't want to run into it, do we?"

"And what if we should miss it and sail on past?"

"Oh, don't worry, little prayer. I am told it is quite a large place and we aren't likely to miss it."

I hid my head in his coat, hoping to find a dry breath there. "But it is God will carry us there, will He not?"

"God, ah well, I am not surprised they have told you that. No it is I will carry you there, John Cutting, and at no small risk to myself. I think of myself as the boatman who carries damned souls across to hell. That is Virginia, you see," and he began to laugh again. "You know about the boatman, do you not, boy?"

"No sir."

"When you die they will put a penny in your mouth, just like this" (and he pantomimed putting something large into his mouth), "and that will be to pay the boatman who will carry you across to hell. That will be your John Cutting then. That lucky sailor gets payment in advance, you see."

"I have not read of that in the Bible. Are you sure?"

"Nor will you. It is a story a Greek man told long ago. Not one of your Jews."

"But God will be in Virginia, won't he?"

"Who told you that? No, he most certainly will not. Now, as I see it, God was himself once somewhere in France, or Somerset. Yes, he was in Somerset, somewhere near Taunton I would think, and all of us are children of that god. But God was never in this new land at all. But the Devil was. He lived there all fat and foul, belching and cursing, and full of children's gizzards, don't you know? He lives beyond those rock cliffs you will see. His heart is cold as the stone and he eats people like you for his supper. He hates all that is good and holy. You hear me, boy? He paints his face like a whore. And all the folks who live there, they are the children of that old devil and they have no souls left in them at all. Now when you get there, you look sharp for your soul that they do not take it from you, boy. That they do not cut it out, don't you know, or pull it out your mouth and cut it off with a knife."

I remember John Cutting, that sailor, but I don't know what ever was to become of him. I can remember everything he said to me, and how that slick deck looked, just as though it were yesterday.

I don't remember much about Saugus Plantation. No, I am wrong. It must have been there that I remember walking along a beach, the clouds very dark and so low you would think you could touch them. I was with other boys, picking up fish from the surf. We carried them like cords of wood, dropping some and then trying to pick them up again and then as we bent down, dropping more. Were they frozen and was it a winter beach? I don't remember. But now I will take you into the real world.

2

WHEN WE LEFT Saugus I cried, and my brother cried, and my mother loved us so much as we wept into her skirts, she cried too. Or perhaps she didn't want to leave, either. But my father had a grant of land among the Plymouth men and so we would have to go.

Now, my father was a man of some learning. He could read and write. So could my mother. His father in his time had been mayor of Truro and his father's father had sat for Truro in the House of Commons in the Long Parliament, in the time of old King James. They were not inconsiderable people in that time of the world when few could even read the Scriptures and fewer still could scratch out their names on a legal document.

My mother's greatest worry about leaving her friends in Saugus and going south among the Plymouth men was that their beliefs were not as ours were: not as steadfast, not as homely. But she never questioned what my father willed. "If that is God's plan for this poor servant of his," she would say, with her mouth drawn up and not looking at him. Making it very clear that father's will was quite a different thing from God's, and that if they should diverge at some turning in the wild wood there was little question which of the paths she would follow.

There were no fine carriage ways as now stretch out through the forests as far as New Amsterdam, so you either went by small boat, wrapping up well against the cold sea wind and the likelihood of a good drenching in saltwater before the trip was ended, or you followed the tracks the Indians had made here and there in the forest, steering by the sun when you could see it, or by your wits. These trails, I must tell you, seemed to have been made by Indians in their cups and wound in an unhurried way between their villages. You would lose them now and then in a stand of birch trees, perhaps the site of some aboriginal lovemaking, or some forgotten battle, or where the trees were so thick the underbrush no longer marked their verges.

For all that and the fear of wolves which were then thick on the land, these walks were magnificent for a little child who could see faces in the moss on the ancient trees, learn the songs of the birds, and take joy in the enclosed proportions of the place, its dim light shot through with beams of sunlight so clear and bright you felt you could grasp hold of them and swing away into fairyland. We always traveled in company and were armed for fear of coming upon an unknown band of Indians unaware, and they carrying out some secret rite they would rather no white man ever see. There were ferrymen at each of the rivers and they would greet you as long lost friends, with embraces all around and congratulations that you had survived as long as you had with only the minor wounds apparent. You would share all you had seen on the trip, and then pay them for their help across the river with whatever you had in your pack to share. The ferries were just flatboats which the men pulled across the current on a rope stretched from a tree on one side to a tree on the other. There was a closeness in travel then, as though everyone was equal for that time, under the strange laws of the forest and all taking part in the same adventure.

It was spring and I was as green a sapling as any that sprouted that year in the Old Bay Colony. Everywhere there was the sound of peepers and your feet sank into the mulch of a thousand years of leaves filling those dark open spaces with its sweet perfume. I remembered in my heart what the sailor had told me, but I didn't doubt that we had brought God with us from Somersetshire just as surely as if we had tucked Him away with the things in our packs that cool morning at Saugus Plantation. There was redemption in us, and no harm, we thought. We had prayed a good hard prayer full of simple sternness among the men of Saugus and set out for Duxbury side as though the devil were nowhere to be found in those woods.

Now I will tell you how we lived in Duxbury in those days, because it is really there that the part of my story you may be interested in begins.

3

THE MEN OF Plymouth lived differently than they did in Saugus. The land was almost clear of trees. Whether it had always been so or recently cleared by them I do not know. Each man lived in his own small house set in the middle of his own plot of land, and around it he had thrown up bastinados. These were great fun for us boys, particularly in the winter when they were the ramparts about a castle, or the high road, Wattling Street, taking us to our martyrdom at Tyburn cross, or just a secret passageway from a dinner we did not want to eat.

Now, these bastinados had not been thrown up just for our pleasure. They were raised to defend against the heathen Indians so the man whose land it enclosed would be safe if the savages should take it into their heads to slaughter him. Should this happen and their wild war cries ring out from the forest, the little family would band together behind their bastinados, lying belly down on them with their guns at the ready. This way they would be in the open, rather than greet the war party in their cabin, where they might then be roasted like a crab in his shell if the savages should fire on them with flaming arrows. Well, no Indians came, at least in that way, and so after a time the people built no more and those that were there grew covered in briars, buckthorn, small dogwood, and wild grapes that had a bitter musty fruit bursting with a delicious taste. There were even hickories marking this high ground, and when the nut time came you quickly learned where the windfalls were likely to be, before the squirrels might find them. You learned which would be of the sweet shagbark and which of the mouth-rasping bitternut. And in the spring the bastinados gave out great clouds of bluebirds like torn pieces of the sky. There were little chipmunks you could catch in your hands and now and then a bold fox would stop on his rounds and stare at you, his tiny mind trying to match you with all that he had seen and nowhere finding the like. I tell you it is the secret highway we went swinging and singing along, safe from the eyes of our elders. We were the children of a new age and a new place, and it is still the place I will go back to in my mind even now.

It was usually all of us boys there, of course, although Elizabeth was there too as you will hear, but usually we boys would keep to ourselves and our own ways in the bastinados.

We had no home waiting for us when we got to Duxbury side.

We had the land and that was that. It was up to us to build something on it and father was none too eager to get started on that project. We knew we would be living with father's friend William Bassett who owned the land which adjoined ours. I sometimes wonder if I can tell all of this, or if I should. But now I have started I cannot turn back anymore than we could have gone back to Cornwall.

The Bassett's house was one large room of wattle and daub with a wooden chimney and a fine, full, rich new thatch of grasses like a new blond head laid down there in the middle of a field of wild flowers. Like the head of Elizabeth Bassett resting there, now I think of it. Resting in that Duxbury field and looking out at me across all these years.

The inside of his large room was dark, for candlelight was dearer than anything and, if you had candles to burn at all, you burned them only on some special day, or when visitors came. However, there were few visitors in those days and with the labor of the new land, little time to visit. The Bassett house had two windows in it, uncurtained and, of course, without glass, or any other covering, for who was there to look in but a passing deer? I can see in one of those windows Elizabeth Bassett sitting in russet with her golden hair loose in a breeze as though she were the sunlight itself. One of the windows was near a great fieldstone hearth hung with pots and utensils. Up above was a loft where the children slept. The adults had real bedsteads with rope netting pulled tight on their frames and mattresses full of husks of Indian corn. We ate all together at a real trestle table, sometimes with linen on it. We made linen then in the colony, but this was beautiful embroidered linen which had been brought from the old land.

I must tell you now about Elizabeth: Elizabeth Bassett I mean, not my sister Elizabeth. We had come running in out of a storming night, shedding water like old dogs who had been swimming in the creek. We were with William Bassett, who had met us at the lane's turning as we had planned. He had stood there in the driving rain with only an oak protecting him, the water sheeting off his hat's broad brim. We were drenched through and through and the mud had been up to our ankles for miles. My brothers Joseph, Jacob, and John and I were frightened, exhausted and fighting with each other. Coming into that large room with the firelight, the warmth, and the smell of animals and dinner in the pot over the fire was what the dear Savior must have felt when His Father called him at last from the cross to join Him. And there by the fire was Elizabeth Bassett with the firelight behind her and her long golden hair with a little cap on it. Her mother was by her, of course, and all of us were struck dumb. I was twelve then, or thirteen, and cared very little for girls, but I was ready to embrace anyone my age and she smiled at me. With bright blue eyes and dimples, she was a sun which warmed me more than the fire. Even with all the mud and rain I hugged them all, strangers that they were.

"You may sleep with me in the loft, Master Thomas Burge," Elizabeth said, "and if you are good I shall introduce you to the animals tomorrow." Ah, what an age of innocence!

But to give you a better idea of Elizabeth Bassett, I think of one hot day with the sunlight across my path making the trees cast sharp black shadows and the sounds of wild things all about us, Indians for all I knew. I thought I was alone, walking silently toe in, in Indian fashion, when suddenly there was Elizabeth sitting in the bastinado almost at my feet.

"You may come in, Master Thomas Burge," she said, as if this were her own room and I stumbling into it from someplace outdoors. "We are having a nice dinner here and you may join us if you will be very quiet, listen to us, and not talk and shout as you so often do. We are having raspberries and a good grape wine. Now

Goodie Frye is sitting there, just by you. See that you do not step on her with your great feet. And Goodie Walker is there by the chokeberry. Ladies, this is Master Thomas Burge you have heard me speak of in the past."

"Elizabeth, I didn't expect you here."

"Thomas, say hello to my friends. Don't ruin it."

"Oh, hello," said I to the empty air.

"We have been waiting for you, Thomas, do sit down. When will you have your own house, Thomas?" she said to me, and I knew from her earnest look that now there seemed to be something different between us. "Do you think I am pretty, Thomas?"

"I don't know, Elizabeth. I don't think about that. I don't think it is right for us to think about that, do you?"

"You are a good boy, Thomas Burge. Isn't he, Goodie Frye?"

As she served imaginary cups of broth to her imaginary friends I thought how light and little she was and that, right or wrong, she *was* pretty, white cap glowing in the last bits of daylight. We talked about Indians, and meetings, and her imaginary friends until finally I could not keep myself from taking her hand. That was all I did. We both knew it was time to go home, but she did not draw away as I thought she would.

"Why, Master Burge, what is this?"

"May I kiss you, Elizabeth?"

"Of course not, Thomas, what are you thinking? Who has put such a thing in your mind?"

"Come on, let us kiss, just here in the bastinado. No one can see us."

"God is here, Thomas, God is always here, and will see us." Then she ran away. I think she was crying, but all I did was hold her hand. I swear it.

My sister Elizabeth was born there in the house of William Bassett, in that one room in the firelight. Mother called out many times lustily to her Savior, as we were never allowed to, I can tell you. They named her Elizabeth for grandmother Elizabeth Pye. I heard much about this grandmother; although, of course, I would never see her in this life. She was a considerable person in Truro and, with her father and brother, the spirit of the pure religion in that place and time. My father was a quiet man and I heard many stories from mother. During the Protectorate the Pyes were sequesterers and great correctors of the unholy, and in those misguided congregations they said "From the fury of the Pyes, dear Lord, deliver us." Well this new Elizabeth, her namesake, later on spoke just as loudly for virtue in this new land as our grandmother had in the old. I watched her come into this life from my vantage point in the square opening to the loft with Elizabeth Bassett lying beside me.

I should tell you now about the elder Bassetts. Goodie Bassett was also blonde like Elizabeth, but not so pretty, her face being pockmarked and drawn. She was thin and ill; her skin seemed yellowed like last year's leaves, and she coughed every night. Everyone knew she would not live long. She would bear only one more child, another girl, and die in the process. William Bassett was older, or at least he was gray, even then. He was a tall, hard man, but fond of rich clothes, for which he was often criticized at meeting. Sumptuary was a sin then. I think, however, that Goodie Bassett secretly liked how grand he looked. My father liked William Bassett and they walked long hours across the fields to where it was planned we would build our house. They would stand in the fields watching over their land in silence. They were also very interested in the news from the General Court at Plymouth which came slowly up the Indian trails. My father was eager to see Plymouth and it was often the subject of their evening discussions. They would sit at night with their great creased boots up on pots by the fire talking of faith and law, still wearing their broad-brimmed hats. Elizabeth Bassett and I would lie peeking over the loft door rim, side by side, listening to them until their words blurred like smoke as we fell asleep. I believe the two men agreed there on one of those evenings that Elizabeth and I should marry.

And now Elizabeth says:

You must know that everything Thomas has told you and will tell you about me and my family is a lie.

4

MY FAMILY CHANGED that rainy night when the Burge family burst in upon our quiet life on the Duxbury side. It was the beginning of a punishment God has chosen me to live.

We were spread out on Duxbury side and the land was remote. We were latecomers. Most of the others were those who had come up on the land like children let out of meeting when it was apparent the picket walls around the little Plymouth town were no longer needed, and the wives and children could dare to follow their men into the wide world without fear of murder by the savages. We had driven these dark folk back into their woods where the spirit of their vice lived, where it dwelt almost within our hearing: only a step from where we lived in our little islands of civilized life. The time had come to spread out into the land we had driven them from. We were making that wild land into farmsteads with wholesome grains and fruits as God intended. We wanted roads and rail fences, and stacks of English hay, and cattle, and orchards white with the blooms we had dreamed of, and holy hymns of grace caroling up from the thankful land which now was relieved from bringing forth vipers.

My father is a handsome, large man full of laughter and fond of soft cloth. When he would hold me in his lap it was like being cradled in the land. He always smells of fresh things growing. My mother not only bore me in pain, as is a woman's lot, but I watched her die on the day I had expected to be a day of joy. She struggled almost a full day with Death and snatched my sister from his black arms, but lost herself in the folds of his cloak. I wish she had been less brave. I watched her shadow and death's struggling in the fire-light all around the walls of our house that night. I had thought the struggle would pass as it did with Goodie Burge when her girl came and she slept at last. I lay that night with my dress clenched between my teeth, suffering with each of my mother's cries, and when I woke my mother was cold and silent as stone. What a price there was for that one apple and that one sin! What a price for our weakness! We named my sister Trial for the trial she had given mother in her coming.

My mother had labored until her hands were sore. She fed us, clothed us, loved us in our sorrow, kept me as clean as any English lady's child must be, and all the time she would spend the day grubbing up great stones in the fields as I watched her. She swung the sickle in harvest time under a yellow moon and, as God must love her as His own child, stood to the traces of the plow, when she must in the spring, like a draft animal to get the seed in before the rain.

I remember holding her rough and broken hands in mine when I was very little and she saying to me, "Would God had made us men, dear Elizabeth; the burdens of a woman, and the chains of nature in which we must stand make me weep for you." I would cry with her, but I did not know then what for. Thomas Burge taught me that lesson if none other.

I remember the night they came clear as clear can be. We had brought in cheese, my mother's best cornbread made with some of last year's good crop of rye, and pints of father's best black barley beer. On the crane we had a pot of barley porridge with some of the English peas which were scarce that year because of the summer sun burning them. There were four boys: one my age and the others very small. They ate and drank as though they had had no food all the long way from Saugus Plantation.

The girls at the meeting had teased me about what he might look like, this little Saugus man, and I was mightily afraid he would look like a great hairy hog as they had said, with his teeth all curly out around his mouth, little squinty eyes, and hobbling in on feet like the Devil's. In the firelight with him all wet and his clothes and hair all wild as marsh grass when I first saw him, I drew in a good long breath and thought what Becky might say when I had to lead this thing on a string through a ring in its nose into the meeting house. Then he put up his hand, shy and quiet, with big, deep, dark eyes and wiped his wet hair back, and I saw he was a great beauty. I knew Becky would have nothing to say. When I first saw him that night he was tall and so thin it made you want to cry out and hold him to your breast like you would a weak wild animal after a storm. He seemed lost. His nose was thin and straight as I have never seen in a man and his hair I loved from the first: black as a very dark night with no sign of any other color in it and his skin so light it seemed to glow. Then an amazing thing happened. This shy boy almost seemed to collapse, as if a shell had broken, and then he threw himself into each of our arms in turn. We were amazed and laughed, but it was sweet to me beyond all imagining.

Things, however, are not always what they seem. I was still a young girl when they moved in with us. He has probably told you that I am cold. God knows I am not that. He was not tender as he should have been.

I knew every little bird that grew in our fields from the time it fledged. I had held all the little animals and birds he and his brothers would throw stones at. I would go out in the morning fields, damp as they were, and fall down on the grasses and feel all this good earth where I was born lean against me like a lover. You see, it is my land in a way. It will never be Thomas's for he was not born here. I would look out of that nest of grasses and yellow and blue flowers into the farthest reaches of the sky, find the faces in the clouds, and dream that I was looking into the face of God and He was looking down into mine as if He were my father telling me about the Hebrew girl Ruth in a strange land.

Then there was Thomas Burge. I won't tell you that I hated him then. I was incapable of hate. I loved him in a real way, but my love was in the eye, and in the ear. He had a sweet voice and in the flesh I could hold him in my mind as a shield against what might come to harm me. We would play at fighting lions, though neither of us had seen one, do our work together, and knock down English hay and slide down it, pick berries, and many other homely things, as if he were one of the girls at the meeting. We laughed secret laughs and I can remember our bodies touching as we lay side by side in the loft in bitter weather. With our covers drawn as close as we could bring them to the loft door, we looked down into the real world of our parents where it seemed like some pageant was being played out below us for our edification, or some story I might have thought and acted out with corn husk dolls in the fields. Particularly, I remember Thomas's father and mine with their big boots tied with a thong and their great coats and wearing their hats in the house, God help them. They put their boots up on mother's best pots, like little boys, looking into the fire.

Now, Goodie Burge was always good to me, and though a fine woman all her life she was coarse as mother was not, and spoke to the men as if she were master of the house which she certainly was not, while my poor mother was always biting her tongue and cleaning, or spinning while Goodie Burge had her say.

I will tell you now what I have never told anyone before. I was a child, but matured very early. For all that, I still cared more for the girls at the meeting house than any others and loved my dolls and the little animals of the field, but I was becoming a woman all the while. To my great mortification, my breasts grew as if I were a wanton and I tried to hide this with all my heart. I feared that Thomas might see it and mention it to father. I went off sometimes into the bastinados and cried. I began to bleed and knew nothing of it being God's curse on all my kind for listening to the whisperings of the serpent, but thought that I would die soon, somewhere alone and in shame as I had seen little animals die and their own kind turn on them in their death. I hid it, but mother knew somehow and took me in her lap once. It was a sunny day and I remember it well. She held me in her lap in a chair even though I was almost as big and tall as her and my feet dangled down to the floor. We sat there a long time saying nothing, but mother weeping and me holding her tight, telling her it was all right.

And in that time I ran away into the bastinados and brought all of my friends of the woodland about and we had a council: a council of women and all that is female in the world, a council of how we would have all this world for our own. I can see it now, with the wind and the sun just so low that it shines in your eyes among the trees. Here came Thomas Burge, then, with dark stealth like an evil shadow in those quiet places, like Lucifer. He sat down and said something sweet to me. My heart leaped out of my body to him and I felt a great longing for him to touch me, not as we had often touched as playmates in a game, not as we touched in the loft, but not as men and women touch either. He held my hand as the darkness came and it was as if this small place was our home: his and mine. But when the light was almost gone and he felt himself safe in the evil darkness he attacked me; and for the first time I was afraid of him.

5

MY FATHER NEVER built his house on Duxbury side, but the cattle and hogs we had brought with us from Saugus multiplied and fattened on the good grass there. We also had horses. Horses were still uncommon in the colony, and all of those beasts required fences.

One fall day when the leaves were starting to turn and the air full of the ripe smell of the coming fall, the smell of stumps and corn stubble burning, and the sky that intense blue, I was splitting rails for father who would come back to where I was working, hitch them to a horse, and drag them to the end of the new fence. I was sweating and the sweat sent a chill down my back as it met the first cold breezes of the fall. I looked up suddenly and saw two mounted men not ten yards from me. How long they had been there I could not know, their horses were so still. The leader wore a beaver cap with the fur turned in and black wampum around it like an Indian. Wampum was still legal tender in the colony and the black the more valuable. His coat had wide sleeves and was laced with gold in a rich manner I had never seen before and his breeches were as smooth as velvet. Both their horses were large with shaggy white hair around their hooves. The hooves were as large around as pewter plates. The older man in the gold lacings said, "You are Thomas, but I am sure you will not remember me."

The second man was round-faced and cheerful and might have been any yeoman of the Duxbury side, but for the pheasant's feather in his hat.

"I am a friend of your father's from Saugus," the man in gold lacing said, "come here to offer you both a grand future. Where is he? Oh, I should have asked, is he still alive?"

"He is beyond that clump of trees, sir, working at the fence end and alive the last time I saw him."

"William, bring our friend here along while I ride on ahead." He gave his horse a kick and was off.

The other man dismounted and offered me his hand. "We knew you as a child. I am William Almy. We knew your family at Saugus. I hope your mother is still well, and there were brothers, too, I think."

"What is it like now in Saugus?"

"I have not been there for many years now. I am a wanderer. We come here from Plymouth town."

"Who is the other man: an Englishman?"

"No, that is Edmund Freeman, deputy governor, since about a week ago, of Cape Cod. He is a wealthy man and confidential agent for the adventurer Thomas Beauchampe. We plan to open a new land there and be the first to take the fish and fur. The best in the world we think. We are looking for others to join us. We rode here from Plymouth to recruit your father."

"Is my father to go to Plymouth?"

"Not for our sake. We were issued license there to settle sixty families on Cape Cod in the village we shall call Sandwich. We have ten families of Saugus men went there last year and now we are eager to find the rest."

"There is nothing on Cape Cod but Indians and sand beaches, I have heard."

"There is a great fortune in fish for the taking. A man need only wade out and get them. There is a fine pond in this new town which

I have seen myself and land beyond counting, with no neighbors to hem you in as you have here."

"Have many of the people you talked to been interested in joining you?"

"This is not a good time for us to be beginning this project," he said, resting a hand on my shoulder and leading his horse behind him. "Plymouth was almost empty."

"How can that be? Plymouth is the largest village in the colony."

"Haven't you heard? There is a great war being fought in England, against the king."

"Against the king?"

"Yes, because he is a Papist."

"But will God allow a man to fight against a king?"

"God can allow whatever his providence can conceive. Many have gone back there to fight for our faith and against the French and the forces of Popery, and those who used to come like geese this time of year from England to settle among us will not fly this way for many years again, if ever. But we must build this town in the Nausets while we can. There are none but Christian Indians there and a wide land for the taking."

"My father is not an adventurer, Mister Almy. Father will not move again," I said, as we entered the little grove of trees.

Moving to Sandwich was the hardest and strangest voyage in the wilderness I have ever taken, for there were not even Indian paths leading through the sand barrens and pine woods, and we had with us cattle, hogs, children, horses, and dogs which would be split out by every grove of trees through which we would pass and then had to be rounded up again. Jacob was lost for half a day. We spent those hours wildly searching for him because Mother was sure he would be taken by wolves if we did not find him before darkness fell. She was probably right. We could hear the wolf calls all the way. Finally we found him, happy as a grig, counting his toes under a paper birch. My baby sister Elizabeth had just learned to walk and cried most of the way, surely clearing our path of wolves and any other game. She was angry because Mother would not let her walk on her own. We wandered in these pine woods, were mired in sand, got lost for days, and never on the trip saw another living soul. We kept pressing on relentlessly, however, for Father was a skilled husbandman and he knew he must get us to Sandwich and well dug in by Martilmass. Any improvident soul who had not laid by for the winter soon after that time would surely die in the Hungry Moon, as the Indians called it. Everyone came to call it that after the great dying of the colonists in the first year at Plymouth.

To let you know how remote Sandwich was then from the rest of the world, let me say that John Davis ordered hinges and hasps from a Boston merchant. The man did not deliver them and John took him before the General Court at Plymouth. Not only did John lose his case, but he was fined fifty shillings. The merchant pointed out that John had told him he would mark the entry to Sandwich from the sea with a pole and a white cloth tied firmly onto it; he did not, and the merchant sailed the length of the cape without seeing the least sign of human habitation.

It was a bright cold early November day, all of us wet and chilled to the bone when we passed the last salt marsh and broke out of a small stand of pine and found Edward Shillingham swinging an ax. He struck the ax into one of his trees and took us on through marsh and wood to Sandwich town.

It is and was the most beautiful place of all the places on earth I have seen. A great open pond always a sheet of changing light, now silver, now greenish black as old stone, and now deep blue, crowded about with ancient trees as if called there to meeting and speaking in whispers to each other with every passing wind. It is as though God had set out a playing field with a margin and the bright flat pond as its ornament. The pond watered a hollow in low hills where there would one day be a mill and burying ground. The meeting house was already there when we arrived, and three thatched cabins with wooden chimneys. The first ten families had been there less than one season. The most joyful and the hardest moments of my life were lived there on that flat field. Also the one from which I still bear scars inside and out.

Thomas Dexter, George Knott and his young wife, and all the Feake family greeted us as Edward Shillingham introduced us around. The children were shy at first, but that was quickly over and their cries echoed across the pond. You thanked God for any child your age who might come out of the woods in those days, as there were so very few playmates. The men and the boys helped us with the cattle which we put in common pasture near the pond while Father went with the older men into the meeting house and the goodies gathered my mother into one of their homes and little sister, eager for her new stories.

Edward Shillingham took me by the arm as I was leading our best sow into the pasture, and said, "You had better go with your father and see to your posterity." I gave him the rope end gladly and went into that sober assembly for the first time as a man among men.

William Wood met us in the darkness of that large cabin. He was as richly dressed as Edmund Freeman had been. We were away from Plymouth now well and truly, and sumptuary was not such an issue as it was nearer to the mother meeting. I particularly remember his breaches were tied with red silk ribbons. He would have been a scholar in any time in any place in the world, but in this tiny place he seemed the greater still, and his erudition hung about his neck as though it were the chain of the Lord Mayor of London. In fact, he had just returned from that great city across the sea where a book of his had been published, called *The New England Prospect*, designed to attract others to the colony by describing its virtues and omitting its faults. His map of the New England plantations was not only popular in the old country, but the only one ready at hand in this new one. The map had been engraved by a London house in 1634 and it may still be in use for all I know. He was also a graduate of a Cambridge college and very well-spoken, although like most who love their books more at home by a candle than in the public square. I never heard him speak above a whisper.

He said to my father, "It is fortunate you have come early, sir. Edmund Freeman speaks very well of you and tells me I must offer you the best of the western plots."

I wondered if that was what he told all the settlers, or if there were some to which he said, "You seem a scurvy sort and so I have set aside cold marsh bottom and sand specially for you." He was carefully folding out upon the table in the dim light a handsome map of his own, making and drawing a line with his fingernail across it. "Yes, Thomas Burge, yours is a fine parcel indeed. There is water I know of here," he tapped the map, "and a river bank and marsh as well." His hand swept from one side to the other as everyone watched silently. "And here an outlet to the sea. We plan to situate a trading post on this promontory of the land next to yours."

He rested his hand for a moment on the great expanse of the sea with all its possibilities for this little community, and looked up for a moment as if he was sniffing the herring on the wind. "This is salt marsh full of Indian cranberries. This is fine meadow to fatten your cattle, and this is upland where I would set in an orchard if I were you." He seemed reluctant to take his hand away from the magic of the map and we all stood for a moment in that same silent magic.

At last my father cleared his throat and said, "I must get to work on it now. I will need a larder within the next week and a shelter from the winter."

They all laughed; as farmers themselves they knew and recognized his understatement, but I did not.

There were many times when my father and I were far apart in this world, sometimes to my great peril, but we have never been as close as we were that day walking his new land. That taciturn farmer, slow to anger, unable to share his joy or grief, expanded that day, putting his workman's heavy arm around my shoulders as he had never done before or after. We walked every one of those acres of land and marsh on that crisp day, walking his future and what he dreamed would one day be mine. We laid out the cabin walls in our imagination, walked miles of fence rows yet to be, tasted the cran-

27

berries in our bog, smelled apples in an orchard not yet out of the seed, planned the arc of nets shoaling out from our beaches, and turned the first rock where the larder would be dug. I can see us now, dark figures in a sunset, our backs against the wind, looking out across that special land. It was like something experienced as a child for the first time: a gift beyond describing and never again quite so special or so sweet. We did not know that day that we had the choicest of all the plots laid out in that new land, for on it rose an ancient spring gushing with fresh water so abundantly that it made fresh water marshes of all the meadows around it, but we knew it was ours, and God's bounty filled us and overflowed in that place. The spring flowed so freely that my father could give the water away, make ponds of it for his neighbors to store their fish in, and draw up sweet beakers for our drinking until the last trump sounds. I can hear the bubbles rising and breaking from its depths even now. There is another memory of it more intimate which I will share with you in time.

The next weeks my father, my brothers, my mother, and I labored as if we had been struck mad, or were set to twirling in a witch's spell. The winter seemed just over our hill to us, we could smell it and feel its fangs at our back. We dug a pit which we lined with straw and our neighbors filled it with their surplus of vegetables and dried Indian corn.

My father and I cut the trees, planning where each would fall, sometimes falling ourselves with exhaustion on their white limbs when they finally did come down, and Joseph, Jacob, and John would strike off the small limbs and trim the logs square as best they could. I can see us all through a haze of blue wood smoke raising a barn for our animals with the bright fall leaves flying around us. We laid in great barrels of brine, slaughtered two of our older cows, and set their great cuts of muscle in those pickling barrels. We then set to work on the house, all of us putting our shoulders to the squared-off logs while father mitered them to fit with a small ax and much standing back in puzzlement, head scratching, then starting again. Mother then caulked the joints and chinked the spaces between the logs with clay. I labored, stripped to the waist, in that bitter cold, rolling field stones, with the help of boys from Sandwich, and setting them for the chimney. We did not have time to cut planks for the floor that first winter and so we pounded out an earth floor. We had no paper to wax for the windows and so we drew out the leather from our slaughtered beasts across them. We finished shutters during the winter and had them hung before the spring. We killed one hog and hung hams high in the chimney to smoke during the winter.

Henry Feake was the local thatcher and we pulled grass and reeds (until our hands bled) for him to tie and thatch down with vent staples from our new king post. We raised great flitches of bacon under the eaves and our neighbors gave us lumps of cheese against a hard winter to store away in our loft.

It was a great adventure and a wonderfully complicated endeavor to build that complex, interdependent thing which is a farmstead all by hand. Each part of it designed to hold some other secret, learned through great pain and death over the centuries, which might save a life in the blank, blind, heartless, stone hard winter to come, each part moving, growing, and changing by different laws like the hams slowly smoking in the chimney and the beef brawn coming in the barrels of brine. It was a time of joyful labor, of happy pain and dreamless sleeps.

6

I REMEMBER ONE incident around the Sandwich pond when we were frozen at last into our winter hibernation.

We were on our way to meeting this particular morning, as the law required of every family in Plymouth, and the wind was blowing a terrible storm of dry snow, the sort which cries out when you walk upon it. It was such a storm that the wind made sheets of it as if you were looking through windows on the world and on those windows were curtains between you and it flapping, stinging your face and burning your cheeks red. Even my mother, who I had never thought a pretty woman, seemed pretty with her red cheeks fiercely kissed by that white morning. It was about a two-mile walk from our land to the meeting house at the pond in the center of Sandwich. The day was such that you would get lost if you did not know a friendly tree here and there to welcome you on your way. Mother, as I say, looked quite beautiful in the wind with her clothes all blowing this way and that. Father had little Elizabeth on his shoulders and she was wearing his great floppy hat. Joseph and I, all in our best homespun, were walking soberly with the adults. What a grand show of elegance we must look, I thought to myself as we neared the village. Behind us, however, Jacob and John were doing their best to make the powdery snow into snowballs and pelting each other, taking advantage of every tree and hillock and making quite a war of it. Few of the snowballs hit their mark because they came apart on their way to their target. My mother took it as long as she could and then stopped suddenly and turned almost catching Jacob in her skirts.

"The devil is much at work this Sunday morning," she said clapping her hands, "and here are two of his incubi, I think, playing at war on the Sabbath." She grabbed Jacob by the ear. "Thomas, we have work with these two."

We all knew what that meant. Father put down Elizabeth and went to a nearby bush to select a switch, taking out his scalping knife to cut one, measuring it and testing it for suppleness. Joseph and I found convenient rocks from which to watch the show out of harm's way. There and then in the presence of God, or any goodmen or goodies who might pass by, two of the fine Burges had a good meeting-day whipping. Sobered and prepared for the sermon, we then all marched on to meeting.

The Reverend Mister Leverich started his sermon as he always did, by telling us we were the most blessed of all the peoples of the earth for we were the children of Canaan, the chosen, and this new Canaan was set here like a handmaiden of God in the antechamber of the English Israel: the only land where the sweets are not sugar in the mouth, but the comfortable words of God we carry each day on our lips. He told us again the familiar story of the dear saints who first came to Plymouth and reminded us we were indeed fortunate to have them with us as good examples. With their help we can search out the tares day by day in this heavenly garden and pull them out root and stem. I looked about me for tares, but in that red-cheeked, bundled-up, chilly lot I could see none except perhaps my own brothers. "Be watchful my children, even in your sleep, for the fiend neither sleeps nor dozes and he bides his time and watches for them in the last watches of the night. He will grasp us in secret ways and work great sin amongst us."

He took his text that day from James: "Do not err, my beloved brethren. Every good gift and every perfect gift is from above, and cometh down from the Father of Lights, with whom is no variableness, neither shadow of turning. Of His own will begat He us with the word of truth, that we should be a kind of first fruits of His creatures."

"Wherefore, my beloved brethren, let every man be swift to hear, slow to speak, slow to wrath: for the wrath of man worketh not the righteousness of God. Wherefore lay apart all filthiness and superfluity of naughtiness and receive with meekness . . ."

Just then the meeting grew much lighter and a chill wind whipped across our backs. Reverend Leverich stared behind us at the door in amazement. All of us turned, expecting the Good Shepherd in his glory. But there in the half-open doorway was a full grown hairy sow with her head up, sniffing the air. The men in the meeting leapt up and were after her at once and she lit out at the sound of them as if she well knew that she was not numbered among the "first fruits of His creation."

The women waited only a moment before they followed and the children with a great shout after them, leaving Leverich alone in mid-sentence. We came blinking out into that white open space before the frozen pond, and there was a great brown hairy boar and two of his sows running and sliding about the snow with half a dozen good husbandmen dressed in their best after them. A sow would run pell-mell this way with a goodman after her. She would then wisely turn sharp to the left, leaving a skid trail until she could get her footing again and her goodman would foolishly leap to his right, lose his footing and smash, good hat and all, feetfirst into a snowbank. It was quickly apparent the low slung hogs were better at this event than the men. We all joined in with cries and shouts and the old boar harmonizing with his mighty, gruff squeals. When someone would get ahold of his leg he would drag that child, goodie, or upright farmer sprawling across the snow until that one would let loose and another take his place.

At last the two sows had been caught, penned up, and identified, for they were Goodman Gaunt's. Then the boar took it upon himself to have no more of this, with his womenfolk so roughly handled, and so he decided to turn the tables, first charging this little group and then that one, sending us scurrying and slipping out of the way of his tusks. At last, in one of his lunges the boar snagged a tooth in the skirt of Goodie Barlow. The pig was more surprised at this than any of us and went running for the frozen pond with Goodie Barlow dragging behind him by the skirts as though she were sledding. She was not a small woman. Out they went onto the pond, and the boar, of course, lost his footing on the ice and went sailing like a dancer, sprawling, and tumbling and the good woman, flying this way and that on her rump, and then flat on her chest on the ice until there was a great ripping sound and we saw much more of that good woman than ever had, or would, be seen again. Her husband, George Barlow, cursed a great curse then and set out upon the ice himself to retrieve what he could of his wife and her dignity. He skated, lost his footing, and with a great falling and rising finally brought his poor wife back across the pond, doing his best to cover up her nakedness with his greatcoat. George Barlow, much put out, set off with his wife for their cabin. We then started back at the boar, which was soon easily caught because he was rather sailing on the pond, unable to get footing there.

When Goodman Peter Guant had them all penned again and the pen secured, he turned back searching, for his hat. No sooner did he find it and have it firmly on his head than there was Master Barlow in his way, very red in his face.

"Why, sir, do you have no rings in the noses of your hogs, sir?" he shouted at Gaunt.

"They are God's poor creatures, sir, and rings give them great pain."

"It is the law, sir," George Barlow shouted, his face close to Gaunt's. He knocked Peter's hat off and it went flying in the wind.

When he had his hat on his head again Goodman Gaunt said, "They are poor creatures with feelings even as you and I, and have you not heard them cry out when they are ringed?"

Barlow was close after him. "It is the law, sir!" and he knocked Peter's hat off again.

"We will talk about this another time, George," said Goodman Gaunt, finding his hat and putting it on his head again.

"You are right we will!" said Barlow, chasing after him and hitting at his retreating shoulders. "We will talk about it in Plymouth town, for I mean to take it to law, sir. You must ring those hogs, sir, or I shall ring them for you."

It is probably at that time that George Barlow got his taste for the law, and the darker side of it at that.

Reverend Mister Leverich drew us all together then by the pond side, all of us excited, most of us out of breath, and the wind blowing and everyone swatting off the snow and searching for the bruises they may have taken in the battle.

"There is a lesson here!" he shouted. "There is a lesson here and God has set it before us this Sabbath day for our edification and remarking. There should have been rings in the noses of those hogs. And why? For their good governance. Had there been we could have taken them meek as you please to their master. The ring in their nose is like the virtue in the heart of a good man, or the obedience in the heart of a good woman. That is, it is their virtue, and it is by that you may grasp them and bring them back to the right path. It is your virtue, my brethren, and I would grasp you by it in time and draw you to the true path of pure religion."

We all winced with pain at the thought. Still, there was a sermon and a text none in Sandwich would soon forget. None at least in that winter season, but there were other people coming and there would be another season.

7

IN THE NEXT spring the word came from Plymouth there would be an expedition against the Narragansett in the great forest and each town was called upon to contribute soldiers and horses to serve in that expedition according to their population. Sandwich was to send four and it fell my lot to be among that four. The troops would marshal at Boston, be trained, and then march against the sachem Missasoit who threatened war against several of the towns far to the west of us. My father, brothers, and I had cleared enough fields by then to start spring planting, burned the stumps, put in young apple trees, and purchased nets from Boston, trading what wampum we had with the Nauset for beaver pelts, and that with the Boston merchants for their nets.

They could now find our trading post from the bay and visited it regularly in any small coasting vessels they could lay hands on. We had a good haul of alewives from our tidal flow with which to start our new crop. In those days we planted maize in the Indian manner. Among the Indians the squaws dig holes in the ground with a stick and then drop one alewife in each and after it come some kernels of Indian corn: the yellow, the white, or the blue. "One for the cock, one for the crow, one to rot, and one to grow." When the hole is filled the corn will grow, with most of the labor being God's.

As I say, four of us were called up from Sandwich and we mustered first at Edmund Freeman's house. His was the largest house in the village, and he was our headman, if we could be said to have a headman then. He was licensed by the court as Governor of Cape Cod as Mister Leverich was too narrow a man and of too small a mind to lead us. Goodman Freeman was a tolerant and open fellow; and that to his great sorrow as time would tell. We all appeared, as the order of the General Court required, in homespun covered by a well-fitting buff leather jacket. His wife welcomed us in the main room, for they had more than one, in their house. The children had all been packed off to their beds in the loft. All except his pretty eldest daughter. She was obviously very spoiled by both parents and eager to see the young men all dressed up for battle. Her eyes were sparkling at the idea that she would sit in on Sandwich's first council of war. Presently, Master Freeman entered in his greatcoat with the gold lacing.

"Boys, I am glad you are all here tonight. We shall call the roll: Master Thomas Burge the junior, George Barlow, Richard Bourne, and my good friend William Almy. We all answered "Here" as our names were called.

"Boys, you will first go to the town of Boston to exercise upon the common there. I am told Boston is very fine these days, so do not have your heads turned there." We laughed at this, but we all had in mind more than a little head turning when we did get to that city. "You each have your own muskets. And I have other weapons I will issue to you in a moment." He sat for a time thinking. "War is . . . well, it is a necessary thing. It has been the lot and necessity of man since the time of Joshua and probably some bit before that as well. I would not like to see one of you, my brothers, for I consider you brothers, even as if we were of the same mothers, we are surely of the same blood . . . I would not like to see any of you fall. But that is the business of wars. Men die. But I beg you see to it that happens to none of you. I am no great orator to speak on the matter of war and peace, but there it is." We sat for several minutes very solemnly looking from one to the other and contemplating the consequences of human conflict.

"Well, boys, I shall now issue you weapons. From now on these weapons will be your responsibility. Bring them back to me after this expedition. Should one of you be killed by the savages, remember these are the property of the village and another should take them up and bring them back to me. Many a fine sword has been lost in flight, particularly in the woods. Do not drop them into some savage hand. Try not to get blood on them if you can. Or what I mean is do not get blood on yourselves."

With the help of his wife and daughter he opened two of his large bound trunks, fumbling with their wrought locks, and revealed a great deal of handsome silver plate. I had never seen such a treasure. I could see party gilt platters any king would have been proud to show, some with arms embossed on them.

What the three of them issued to us, however, were helmets of steel without visors, but of very simple and elegant design, and some cuirasses, each with a different fine design etched into the metal, as well as long swords and bandoleers. We had our own ball and powder, but he issued us some handsomely made small hand-guns.

"These are what remain from twenty suits of small armor I brought with me from London when I first came to Saugus," Edmund said with pride. "I was given them from the Tower of London many years ago. They will make a brave defense, my boys, against the arrows and tommy hawks of the savage." He was lost in thought for a time while he looked at them. They came from another world and time. They were messages from the lost, and he ran his hand along their metal as if touching that other time.

"I had to leave ten of them at Saugus with the governor there to secure this place for us."

There was surely no grander band of armed men in all of Plymouth as we stood that evening in Edmund Freeman's front room with our armor flashing in the firelight.

Goodie Freeman gave us all a long draft of mulled cider and a cut of her best cheese.

We all knew that Goodman Freeman would have to give us a

rousing sermon now on the virtue of our project, but none of us wanted to rush the evening.

"London is a place to see, Thomas. You are too young to remember home, I am sure, and of course, it was a place of persecution and vice in those days, as it yet may be, but I would be glad to find myself on Pudding Lane, or walking on the bermudahs overlooking the great River Thames, or doing business upon Change once more."

"Edmund, surely you have no such wish," his wife said abruptly.

"Yes I do, my dear. I love our new land, I could not live an upright man except in this New Israel, but I am now thinking of a small rum and one particular Devon cream of my acquaint in a crisp meringue. I am reminded of some of the songs we sang then."

"You will not sing, Edmund!" his wife said hastily. "Sarah, it is time for you to be in bed. Up to the loft with you."

"But, mother, I want to hear Father sing."

"There will be no singing tonight, Sarah. You gentlemen will excuse our daughter if she bids you good night now and joins the other children in the loft."

"No, I will not sing, my dear, but opening the trunks has made me think of other times on the Bankside. It should make you think of them, too, Mother. Just smell it in the air that comes from them."

"It would be better if you were to put those memories away where they belong, Master Freeman," she said, and hurried Sarah up the loft ladder.

"I have a job here and I must prepare you for the work which is ahead of you. God has given this good land for our heritage and He has given us the savages for our trial." At this, Richard Bourne looked as though he had something to say, but did not, and looked away instead into the fire. Finally Master Freeman continued, "For what is easy won is of little value and what is hard won through much travail is our chiefest joy. You are to secure that heavenly joy in mortal combat with the Narragansett nation. They are a fierce people who know no godly law, but if you are steadfast, surely trusting in God's defense you will fear no adversaries.

"We have recently selected Thomas Burge the senior as our representative in the General Court at Plymouth. You will first accompany him to Plymouth, make a good show among the Plymouth men, leave our representative there, and the rest of you ride on to Boston. There you will learn an exercise at arms. God willing, you shall go from there to the great forest to fight the sachem Missasoit who was once our good friend, but now makes war upon us. He has fallen away into the ancient ways of his kind.

"We will muster in the morning before the pond so that the people of Sandwich may see what fine warriors they will send to our defense. You will do some shooting for the amusement of your families, I will issue you some horses, and upon that moment you will depart on your adventure.

"Now, drink deeply, men, and there is also some stew with clams in the iron pot on the chimney crane which we will be eating in a moment, if my wife will bring some spoons."

The next morning we formed up in surprisingly good order. All four of us were on handsome, big-footed work horses, surely very like those the knights of England ride, and we in our buff coats with helmets and cuirasses shining and flashing in the sun. We practiced with our swords at sword play, although I doubted that any Indian we might meet would thrust and swing with us with a sword of his own, and we fired our muskets once out across the pond. It was the first gunpowder ever discharged across that body of water and it sounded, we thought, reassuringly like the crack of doom. The smell of gunpowder, like rust or blood, which blew back across us in the smoke, made the blood in our veins answer with a rush. All the children covered their ears, or hid their faces in their mother's skirts. It was a brave sound, but the echo which snapped back seemed more real than the firing itself, as though an enemy beyond the trees were answering it.

We settled my father at the General Court at Plymouth with as much fanfare as we could muster. As we left there, riding up Leiden Street, I would say there were twenty-five of us. There were still no roads to speak of, so we spread out somewhat on the land as we traveled. At one point we came upon an old farmer on the way in his leather and long beard and we gave him quite a scare. He was sure judgment was overtaking him and he ran and leapt like a fox, but every way he turned another rider was coming down upon him.

Now I will tell you what Boston looked like then, for she was a much different town when we rode up to her than she is today.

8

FIRST, THERE WERE still wolves in the land, and as it was evening when we approached the long causeway, across marshes we could hear the sounds of their sorrowful calls far off in the woods. We were on a well-traveled road raised high above the marshes on either side and the city was ahead of us on a peninsula of land with hills at either end and quite a curious prominence in the middle like a three-pronged fork sticking up, or a set of three rough old teeth. It was, by a long sight, the largest city I have ever seen. Much larger than Plymouth. It must have had more than one hundred houses and more than a dozen streets running this way and that around the hills. I am sure London must be much larger, but I cannot imagine her being any grander. As we came riding along the causeway and into its streets we began to marvel at its houses. All the chimneys were made of stone and none of wood and clay as most still were in Sandwich. They were also all roofed with wooden shakes and none were thatch. We wondered what had become of all the thatchers there. The sides of the houses where covered with pieces of wood cut thin and overlapped like the scales of a fish. This was my first sight of clapboard. Most amazing were the windows. I had never seen glass in a window and I pulled up my horse close to one, leaning over to touch it. They were particularly striking as the setting sun was on them and here and there, as we rode in that orange light, it flashed in the panes of houses as though it were striking first one and then another on fire. Everywhere, it seemed, was the smell of cooking, or of rotting food.

The greatest amazement of all, however, awaited us as we rode into the city's center. The road became broader than any must be in any Christian city, and there in our way was a building of great size, and for all its size two stories tall. The under story was an open gallery supported by posts and above it various fine rooms, one of which proved to be the armory in which we were billeted.

The next morning there was much scurrying and clanging of arms as we prepared and rode out in double file through quite a large crowd to a fortified place high in one of the hills. There was musket fire, speeches about the Narragansett nation, and at last the firing of some pieces of naval ordinance, which surely could be heard in England and gave us all a good scare.

From this fortification you could see out across a great bay with piers sticking far out into it at all angles like so many sticks dropped here and there in the game "pick-up sticks." There were more ships than you could imagine, each lying at a mooring or swinging at anchor waiting for a mooring to clear. Everywhere there were sailors in their skirts climbing on the rigging or walking on the quaysides and streets. The masts of the ships lying all about in the water seemed almost like a small forest.

In the other direction, on another hill, there was a great windmill and the triple-topped hill between us. We were told that a beacon was set on one of those teeth so that it could be lit in time of danger, the militia called, and the ships set to sea. It could be seen far out at sea, they said.

That evening George Barlow, Richard Bourne, and I had in mind a dinner better than the soldier's mess and so we went out to one of the two taverns then in business in Boston: Mr. Cole's on the High Street just opposite the handsome home of Governor Winthrop. The price of a meal, like everything else in the Bay Colony, was fixed by the General Court, and dinner at Mr. Cole's was six pence. The law said that an ale, a quart of beer, or hard cider was one more penny. I can tell you that was the best meal I have ever eaten for seven pence in my life. Master Samuel Cole, the proprietor, greeted us warmly as we entered. It was not required to knock. You simply walked in upon them. We were served by his handsome daughter soberly but fetchingly dressed in blue. After his second quart of beer, however, George Barlow began to get a bit loud and Master Cole joined us at our table.

After a few pleasantries he leaned forward as if to tell a story he didn't want everyone to hear and said quietly, "I suggest you get your friend some air. The gentleman in black by the fire is the beadle of the High Street and he sits here of an evening to keep an eye on public morals; as I know you are soldiers of the Great Court I know you need some heady sustenance, but I am sure none of you are tipplers. On the other hand, I see him casting his eye in your direction, and I can warn you, young gentlemen, from past experience it is a jaundiced eye."

"I have a right, do I not, if I have paid my penny, to drink beer in your establishment," said Barlow.

"Yes, sir, I am only giving you warning."

The beadle could be seen shifting in his seat.

"Come on, George, let it go."

"I will not," said he.

"I do not ask you gentlemen to leave. I simply give you a warning you would be wise to heed."

As we shushed him as well as we could, Barlow leaned forward and said, "Very well, I will take my business elsewhere."

Mr. Cole looked very much relieved.

Barlow gave the beadle a hard look as he went out, which left us all worrying that we would have him following us all evening, but that officer of the court obviously felt he could find some larger fish, perhaps an adulterer out with his paramour, if he stayed fast stuck by that warm fire.

It being a Saturday night, we were not yet ready for sleep, and the night was clear, so we wandered on through the many streets toward Mr. Hudson's: the other ordinary house we had heard of. It was a darker place than Cole's and not as well-appointed. We seemed to be its only customers, but for one red-faced Bostonian who soon joined us.

We ordered four ale quarts of dark beer and set to.

We wandered off at last with our new Boston friend in tow, jumping or falling down from the quayside to the shingle and sitting there. Hudson's was actually on the quay and only a few steps from the bay itself. I suspect he did a good business among the sailors.

We sat for a time talking, soothed by the sound of the sea and enjoying the fishy smell.

"Keep an eye out for portents in the sky," our Boston friend said. "In recent nights there have been lights in the sky. Two men I know were coming to this very pier in a dinghy when they saw some lights come up out of the water as though they were moons, but very near. These two lights rose near to them and then joined, forming the face and body of a man. They set to their oars with all their might and by the time they had reached the shore here, the apparition had departed."

"I would also have put a good deal of water between my boat and those lights," Richard Bourne said, and chunked a stone into the bay.

"I would have rowed to it and found out what it was,." Barlow said, still much in the spirits of the evening.

"Oh, but we did find out what it was at last. Those lights have been seen many times since then: once almost in the Governor's garden, once by the fortress, again by Noddle's Island and then again by John Gallop's Point. If we sit long enough here we may see it. At Gallop's Point a voice was heard across the water."

"I don't believe that," said Richard.

"Well, I didn't hear it, but many I know did."

"What did this voice say?"

"It cried out 'Boy, boy, come away!' and shifted its place from time to time across great distances in the bay in the wink of an eye. The voice was heard again the following night ten miles away on

Noddle's Island, and very full of anguish; it cries out in anguish again calling some boy away."

"What did they believe it was?"

"Ah, yes, one who knew about it suddenly remembered a ship sailed by a Virginian named Chaddock who admitted to a knowledge of necromancy and was said to have murdered his master back in Virginia. Now his ship was driven up in a storm and all aboard, including Chaddock, were drowned. All their bodies were found except the master of the ship: this Chaddock, and he it surely is who is crying out across the water to some boy who has sailed with him."

"Shh! No, is that his voice now?" said Richard and we all strained to hear it, but he had not been serious.

"That is the price they pay for their evil ways. Those Virginia men ridicule us, you know. I remember a ship's master who scoffed at the pure thinkers and once when he lay in port he was asked to come to meeting but he refused. He cooped his men and himself up upon their ship on the Sabbath and would not have any row in to the shore. Not an hour passed but fire took to some gunpowder below decks and he and all his men were blown to pieces, so that parts of them were found for weeks after."

We stared for some time out across the bay in silence. It was very dark but for the starlight and here and there lamplight seeming to float upon the water. There was a cool breeze full of the smell of fish and the sound of the water playing in among the stones.

"It was also remarkable that some good men of Boston were on their way to his boat that very day and would have been aboard and shared that evil master's fate if a squall of rain had not come up and blown them away from their course."

"I wonder if they put a penny in his mouth," I said.

"Did anyone ever ask if some man of Boston helped that master to his judgment?" asked Richard Bourne.

"Well, even if they had it would have been a just punishment for his scoffing at the brethren."

"Or so the sin was judged after the punishment," Richard said, and walked away to the pier, leaning against it looking out into the bay.

"He was possessed of Satan," the Bostonian said with certainty.

"How do you know that?"

"He would not have been punished in such a manner if he was not."

"Look here, Barlow has fallen asleep on the stones. Give me a hand."

We slung him between us and began to walk back to the armory with our Bostonian still close behind, eager to illustrate the works of Satan and their rewards.

"I will give you another example. Ten years ago, or there-abouts, there was a good woman: Dorothy Tallaye."

"I think I have heard of her."

"She was an upstanding woman with a family and then one day she was possessed of Satan."

"How could you tell?"

"Though at one time she would be seen every Sabbath in the meeting, and often at other times as well, she now stopped going to meeting at all. That change was very sudden, and then she attempted to kill her husband and children by refusing to give them food, saying the need for all this was revealed to her in a dream. The good people shunned her, and she got much worse; and the magistrate ordered her publicly whipped. She was better for a time after that, of course, but then the Devil found the upper hand again and she became worse. She broke her child's neck to save it from the sufferings of this world arising from her husband's evil and the evils she reputed to the town. She admitted all of this in the open court. But she would say nothing of this until she was told she would be pressed to death if she did not speak out and tell the court of the means of her sin."

Richard then stopped, saying to the Bostonian: "I think we have heard enough, sir, of this sort of thing." We left the Bostonian, another story still on his lips.

"I sometimes wonder if the savages have not more civil graces and mercy than these Bostonians. They simply kill a man."

We carried Barlow on to the armory in silence and then with much shushing and care we got him to bed without being detected.

I dreamed that night of the sea, and of that poor woman and what her life might have been like had I been a husband to her.

As the next day was the Sabbath we were roused early and stumbled to the meeting. The meeting house in Boston was the finest I have ever seen anywhere. It had a high ceiling and great leaded windows of clear glass which went from the height of the benches to the ceiling itself. The benches were finely finished and painted white, as was all the woodwork. I had also never seen so large or fine a company as assembled there. All the ladies seemed great beauties and their gowns were of colors to bring out this one's fine blue eyes and that one's bright red hair gilded in the sunlight from the windows. Not a man there was in country leather and some were in velvet. But it was the sermon which captured my heart, cleared my head, and swelled me with the pride of our New Israel.

The preacher came out all in black with many small black buttons here and there about him and handsome pure white ribbons across his chest called preaching points which he must have had cleaned in only the purest water and some goodie labored over with hot irons. He cleared his throat, looking out and about to see who was there and who was not, and then up into the rafters as if some others, invisible to us, might be there as well. When the spirit had quite filled him up and he seemed much larger to those who were watching, he began.

"Now, as our good brother John Winthrop has often said: 'a family is a little commonwealth, and a commonwealth is a great family.' As a family is not bound to entertain all comers to its door, neither is this commonwealth. In the blaze of the beauteous discipline, we are, my brothers and sisters, much like the poor thresher in the fields full of grain, who has hoist up into the crotch of some great tree, and God, like the good husbandman he is, grasps a good hold on that tree and shakes it mightily. He shakes it as though he would sunder it limb and root and send it flying through the air making a great rain of earth and little twigs. Do you not feel the great tree of our commonwealth shaking from its roots? Grasp onto your brother in this sanctified assembly and hold him fast, be wakeful that he fall not into the pit, where the fires are never quenched and the worm never dies, into the mouth of the dragon which gapes, gapes with the curling teeth of false doctrine to swallow him up. Come to the labors for which you were called. Come to it.

"Look up, my brothers and sisters, where the sun darkens in the sky and rolls no more and the moon turns to blood and the stars send out threads like the hairs of your head.

"Satan is now sitting among us, and he blazes red with his passion. He casts about him with his net like the fisherman, waist deep, casts out into the sea, and the little fishes are a multitude about him, he casts out for the innocent of heart, even for the children, as a spider casts out her web and limps out upon her stick legs for the unsuspecting, and his welcome is that old venom of heresy. Know that beast not, my dear ones, know him not.

"For Satan, you see, looks upon this land where the Gospel is manifest, where it sprouts out like green corn from every hillock and the songs of the sweet sisters are honey soft, and at that he gnashes his teeth until the gums bleed.

"He sees, writ upon our foreheads, the scriptures and knows that he must dissemble to break those joyful bonds, my brothers and sisters. He must prevaricate, our pure laws which ring like silver bells, ever now, out to his red children in the gut of the great forest. He must mist our minds like a hot morning upon a cold sea.

"Nor has he far to blow with these mists among us until he comes upon a man who has not laid him down a firm ballast of the comfortable words of God, and by screwing false doctrines into his ears pretending they are holy writ makes him a very Beelzebub to his purpose, even though he may seem as sweet and fair of face and voice as you or I. He is no more of a man than the little ape the man at the fair has which will leap across a rope at his sinister command. Idols are peeping from his mouth and his whole head is a nest of vipers.

46

"Where the wind is fresh you may sniff out the fruits which are rotten, and so it is here. So it is here.

"What should be done for the healing of these comfortless exulcerations among the religiously wise? What should be done? First, let our ensigns warn that all Familists, Antinomists, and Anabaptists should pass by these shores. Let there be no stabling and no litter here for those marked with such pitchy hands. Let every man take his brother into his Christian care, and permit no heresies chinked in to crack our state like ice crystals.

"Then let us take our pink knives and pruning hooks, some for the lesser and some for the larger, and search out the rot among the branches in the orchard—any place where the Devil may hook his little finger in, or one of his incubi push up its black tail among the golden shafts. Let us search out the proud Nebuchadnezzar among us who will lay waste to our state for his own gain if we give him but a nostril's width among us. If I had four evils I could fall to my knees and scrub from this commonwealth they would be the standing of the Apocrypha in the Bible, foreigners taking up a place in my country and driving my people into a far place, alchemized coins, and the toleration of diverse religions.

"Know Satan, know him all in this sanctified assembly, know him so you do not midwife out of your own bodies such a one. Know his green eye for it wanders, it panders after the skirts of good women. Know its mouth for the kisses of toleration it seems to give. Behind its blue lips are the blood-stained teeth of division such as our mother country now groans under for her sins. Know its breath, for it is the breath which pants for change and speaks not to the wise: it has an evil stench. Know his limbs, for they spread out upon the earth and are always moving among us, never still, always proselytizing to his iniquity, but gnarled like an old apple branch with carnal disease so you may recognize him. But most of all know his scaly tail, for should it but tap on you it would bind you round and round until you are of it and a Dagon to its service.

"If the state of England open its gates to false religions they have made the land a dancing school for the Devil, and hung the Gospel, which I now kiss, upon that old traitor's girdle.

"Amen, amen, amen!" And he kissed the Good Book passionately.

I can tell you we went out of that meeting with our hearts beating wildly, full of zeal and refreshed at a pure spring.

When we returned to the armory we were told we were disbanded, the danger had passed and we could find our own ways home. We looked at each other, however, and knew a worse danger was coming.

9

THE FOUR OF us from Sandwich set out riding together in our full armor across the causeway.

George Barlow kicked his horse until he was alongside Richard Bourne. "Richard, do you know why we were disbanded?"

"The war is over I imagine, George."

"Well yes, but how it ended."

"Obviously you know."

"Yes, I overheard it in the armory. The sachem Missasoit heard of our preparations here at Boston, and was so frightened by it he let loose the villages he had taken and came in all humility to Plymouth and asked to be let in. When they took him to the General Court he went up to Miles Standish and kissed him on the mouth."

"I don't think I would have done that. I hear he is an ugly little man."

"I am speaking seriously here, Richard."

"I know you are, George."

"He kissed him, as I say, on the mouth and swore he would from this time be a Christian and raise his son and two grandsons as good Christians, and on the spot he gave his two grandsons Christian names."

"What were the names?"

"I didn't hear that."

"Well, it is a sad thing in a way, George, they are such proud people."

"What do you mean, sad? They will become Christians and do no more damage to us."

"I wouldn't count on that, George."

"Well, the General Court counts on it, and that is enough for me. I guess I am not as intimate with the savage as those who love them."

"What do you mean by that?" William Almy said, catching up with the rest of us.

"I know what he means, William," said Richard.

"I imagine you do. There are some who love the Indians among us."

"We should love all of God's creation."

"But I expect Richard loves them a little more than we do."

"And what is that supposed to mean?" asked Richard, pulling up his horse.

"Come on. I don't have time to fight you, Richard."

William Almy pulled his horse in between the two. "What are you saying, George?"

"I will say no more."

"There is nothing secret about it," Richard said, riding on. "Master Tupper and I go once each week to the Kingdom of Mashapee, and teach the Bible to the Indians there."

"Teaching the Bible is not all you do there, Richard, the way I hear it," said George.

"Whatever you have heard, that is all we are doing there. They are much in need of instruction. You will surely agree to that."

"Since when are you such an authority on the Bible that you may teach the savages?"

"I am no authority, but Master Tupper and I are the only ones who will go to them."

"Ah, yes."

"If you would like we would be glad to have you with us, George."

"No, thank you, I have better things to do than spend my time among them. They smell."

"How about you, Thomas, will you come to the village of the Nauset when we get back to Sandwich?"

"I will think about it, Richard," I said, "but I have a stop to make on the way."

"You had better think again before you ride with Richard here. Those who love Indians may have other bad habits as well."

"Well, I don't care much for the Indians, but I do care for their lands a great deal," said William Almy, "for the lands they have in their nations. I was thinking about it all the way to Boston. I had planned to leave you when we entered the land of the Narragansett. I have very little to hold me in Sandwich. I am not a religious man. Now that there is peace in the Indian nations I think I will turn west and cut out a farm in the rich land there."

"And find yourself an Indian squaw to live with as Richard has."

"Let it be; neither Richard nor I will take Indian women. There are plenty of white women in the Connecticuts."

"Are you serious? You will not come back to Sandwich?"

"I couldn't be more serious. I will ride on to the Connecticuts, or even beyond."

"Keep a good grip on your scalp if you do," George said.

"I will be leaving you for a time as well," said I. "This is my chance to return to Duxbury side for an errand, and from there I will ride on to Plymouth and see if I can join my father there at the General Court. I would dearly love to see them at work making this nation."

Richard Bourne turned toward me. "Let me ride with you, Thomas. I have never seen Duxbury, except as we passed through. That is, if your errand is not too intimate."

"It may be. Time will tell that. But I will welcome your company."

"Am I to ride home alone, then?" said George. "I have no social engagements at Duxbury and no fine relatives in the General Court."

"Don't worry, George," William Almy said. "I have no taste, I will ride with you as far as the Cape."

"George, you are welcome to ride with us to Duxbury side and even on to Plymouth if you like."

"No, thank you, I have things to do at home. I have a wife to return to as none of you have."

We parted then: William and George to the south, and Richard and I rode on to Duxbury.

"What is the delicate business you have in Duxbury then, Thomas?"

"You know I lived there for a time after we left Saugus. While I was there we lived with a family with two daughters."

"Ah, yes, you need say no more."

"No, my father and Elizabeth's laid plans for us to marry one day, and we have set aside land for her father in Sandwich with that in mind, but much time has passed. For all I know she may already have married."

"And what do you plan to do about that in Duxbury?"

"I am not sure."

"Are you going to ask her to come home with us now?"

"What?"

"Are you going to ask her to marry you now, you simpleton!"

"I don't know, Richard."

"Well, I would make up your mind before we get there, if I were you."

"I thought I might just visit."

"I think she will have some expectations of your visit, don't you?"

"They don't know I am coming."

"Oh. Well, it will be an interesting trip for me, then."

"I do want to marry her."

"Then marry her." As we rode on our horses nuzzled each other, shook their great heads, and whinnied quietly. "Do you love her?"

"Yes, I do. I know I do. I have thought about it every day I have been at Sandwich."

"If you love her, marry her. There are few enough women in the colony, and to find you love the one who is promised to you is quite a thing. Take action! I wish I were in your spot, Thomas, I wouldn't hesitate."

"Yes, Richard, I know that, but will she marry me?"

"Well, there is only one way to find that out, Thomas, ask her!"

When we had made our way to Duxbury and I saw that familiar crossing where William Bassett had met us in a driving rain it was as if the place were drawing me on. I spurred my horse into a gallop which Richard could hardly match.

But when we came to the house itself the place seemed smaller and meaner than I had remembered and there was much which needed to be done, but William Bassett greeted us warmly, his youngest daughter in his arms. Elizabeth herself was out in the fields, and we had been talking some time when the door opened. With the sun behind her she made a figure of beauty in the doorway, her golden hair like a gloria around her. I could barely bring myself together enough to introduce her to Richard.

Her father suggested Elizabeth and I should walk out into the fields. We were silent at first, awkwardly walking side by side, intimate friends and strangers at the same time. I wondered if I could touch her hand. The idea of it grew so large in my thoughts that I could not understand what she was saying to me and I realized I must seem a great fool. We walked on down the lane and turned at the orchard which had grown greatly since I left.

It was well in leaf and far beyond its spring bloom, the orchard grasses knee-deep with little insects leaping up from the grass in clouds as we disturbed them. The sun on their wings made an intricate illuminated lace work in the air around us.

At last I took Elizabeth's hand as we walked in and out of the shadows of those trees, sensing the magic of the place.

She held me at arm's length with the hand which held mine and looked up at me. "I knew you would return, Thomas Burge."

"I had to return, Elizabeth."

"Things have changed here, Thomas."

"They are all the same to me, Elizabeth."

52

"No, time has hurt us here. Father cannot keep up the land, and we are poorer than we were. Surely you have noticed it."

"There is land for you in Sandwich. That is what I came to tell you."

"Is that what you came to tell me, Thomas?"

"No, no it isn't."

"We can't take land from the Burges. We are not some poor relations of yours. We are no relations of yours at all."

"No, that isn't what I meant, Elizabeth. I didn't come here to offer you land in Sandwich. That isn't what I came here for."

"Then why did you come?"

"All the time I was building in Sandwich, all the time I was in Boston, I was thinking about you."

"I think that unlikely."

"It is true, Elizabeth. We all wanted you with us."

"All of you did?"

"Well, no, what I mean is I did. I did, Elizabeth."

"I don't think Goodie Burge did."

"She loves you too."

"Loves?"

"Yes, loves."

"There is a word for a man of Saugus to be saying to a good girl in an orchard in Duxbury."

"Yes, Elizabeth, I do love you."

"And how many others do you love in your uniform of fine armor?"

I lifted off the cuirass and dropped it to the ground. "I love only you."

"I believe you do. Yes, I believe you do," she said, and looked as though she were more saddened than happy at the thought.

"I want to marry you."

"Oh." And she let go of my hand and walked away a little.

I followed her. "Elizabeth, I want to marry you. I love you. Will you marry me?" I can remember my overwhelming desire for her. I wanted to possess her completely. I wanted to possess her passion with my own, there in the field like the red foxes in their season, burning and turning in their passion in the grass, or meadow voles in a frenzy of desire in their lightless burrows, afraid to lose a moment of passion in their short lives. I wanted to possess her like the other things I owned, like my home, my arms, my life. I wanted her to be mine, and only mine. I could not imagine a morning again from this time on when I would not find her beside me. "I want you, Elizabeth. I want to possess you."

"I am myself, Thomas. I am not a thing to be possessed."

"I mean . . ."

"I am not one of your animals. I am not a horse. I am myself."

She turned then and looked at me. The sun made her eyes seem deep and transparent and such a blue as never was dreamed of in Delft. There was a crease of pain, however, deep down in them like the slightest hairline crack, and she looked at me with puzzlement. I should have noted that, but I was in love.

"You don't want me, Thomas."

But I did. I had never wanted anything as I wanted her that day in the dappled sunshine of the orchard, in the pulsing cloud of midges, glowing in the sun, and I would have taken her there and then and never left that place.

"What do you know about me? You don't know me, Thomas."

"I know you, Elizabeth. I know you."

"Listen to me, Thomas. I am very different than you think. I am not one of the goodies. I don't even know who I am. I don't know if I love you. I don't know if I can love at all."

"Then I will make you love me."

"Oh, will you, Thomas? No, I don't think you will."

"I will love you as you want to be loved."

"But don't you see, I don't know that."

"Let me hold you, Elizabeth," I said, and she did. We clasped together clumsily at first, and it was as if we had never touched all those times in the loft. I felt her firm breasts against my chest, the curve of her back and the swelling of her hips, and she could feel how passion had swollen me as we pressed together. She pulled away a little, grasping the side of my face in her hand, breathless, and gazed deeply into my eyes with a puzzled look. She smelled rich with the aroma of the early summer grasses in her hair as though she had been lying in the fields, and it was a mighty perfume. To this day I am fixed by that look of hers as though I were looking into the deep corners of the sea.

10

THE TIME HAD come for Thomas Burge to return to Duxbury side to claim me as our fathers had agreed he would so long ago. Since that promise was made, it had not gone well with my family. Thomas has probably not told you that. When my mother died my father also died in a way. The people at the meeting did all they could, but they had families of their own. One of the goodies who had lost a child was wet nurse to my sister. I think she had an eye for my father, and if she had not brought food to us, covering him as he sat there in the cold staring vacantly into the ashes of a dead fire, and set by what the men brought in from our field, we would simply have curled up in our misery and died right there.

I remember how there seemed no reason to comb my hair or wash my clothes, even my face. I became one of the little wild things of the field. I would look up suddenly and see there were stars in the sky and no one had called me to supper. I would eat berries and wild things. God was truly all that kept me alive in that terrible time. As if to mock us, the fields grew up in briars and little trees, and there was no one to cut them down, and in the spring there would be no one to plant the new grain. We — I mean not just our bodies, but our minds as well — grew up like those fields with briars, all tangled in knot grass and lady's bed straw.

Then when I came down from the loft one morning the sun

shone in through the paper of our windows and I thought I saw my mother in distress, standing by the fireplace and wringing her hands, looking at her beautiful pots all grimy with the dirt of that awful winter. She looked as if she had simply been away for a time and now, back again, was horrified at what I had done. I clambered down the ladder, but when I came into the room she was gone. No one was there but my father sleeping in his chair. I pulled her best brass pot from the crane and took it out into the sunlight. With my dress and the water from our stream I washed it and rubbed it wildly with earth until it began to shine as it had when she was there. And then I saw my face in it and I cried and cried, because I was as ugly as an old woman, my hair all knotted and my face dirty, my clothes little more than rags, my body as thin as the skeleton in the dance of death in our Bible. I ran naked into the bitter cold water and sent it shimmering around me, washing away forever all that evil winter of death. I ran to the cabin, and, digging through my mother's things, found her brush and comb, and fixed my hair, as she had, combing and braiding it. I took the spices from a little bag I found which smelled so much of her that I felt I was making myself into a part of her or making myself into a real woman. I rubbed those spices on my skin until I could not smell the smells of death any more, only the spring smells of many flower gardens; only the smell of my mother. When I finished I took out one of her dresses and put it on. Standing by that cold chimney as I had seen my mother stand for all those days I felt taller, I felt proud, I felt truly a woman.

I shook my father. Took him to the stream where I had found my rebirth and washed him there until his life was washed back into him. Then, I realized he was the source of my greatest sadness. He had always been such a happy man but, broken and beaten as he was that winter, it seemed to me as though the end of the world must have been just there in front of his chair. He had made the season and not God. I had lived in that black season with him, for his sake.

We cleaned the house and laughed and cried together as we

found the treasures and the sorrows she had left us. At last, we went out into that spring day to our neighbor's house and brought back my mother's last, most beautiful gift, my little sister Trial, to live with us.

All that year we healed. Each day we were stronger. I served my father as my mother had and he even learned to laugh again, to break the soil at last, and to cut down the saplings from the forest which had hoped to recapture our land when we showed our weakness to them.

I was strong again, and Father was as strong as he would ever be. My sister, Trial, was fat now, and pink and happy as I had once been in that house. She would never know the family as it was, never know Mother, but all her life would think that the way we were that year was the way it had always been. My father grew to love her, and as he did his color came back, and I knew he was living for her and that was healing him. But I would always be his best love for I had saved him. I felt the strength of God in my veins and I didn't care what they said at the meeting. I didn't care that they called us mad. I was myself. No one would ever change me again, I thought.

Then Thomas Burge came riding up our lane. Riding into that little world I had made. Riding in his uniform with his armor shining in the sun so that you could barely look at it. I saw him and Richard Bourne from the meadow. The flash of his armor had caught my eye. Before I went to him I lay down in the grasses and flowers and prayed to God as hard as I had ever prayed before. I asked Him what I should do, but He was silent. I should have known that silence was a warning, but I was lonely, and young, and yes, I was in love with that tall, thin, dark man on horseback, that man flashing in the sunlight, that man of light.

While we were walking in the fields that day I told him all that had happened and how I had been changed, but he said nothing, as if he were not listening, or wasn't interested, and why should he be, I suppose, as I am only a woman?

When we came to the orchard he took off his armor and

dropped it in the tall grass. Taking my hand, he proposed to me very sweetly. I don't know why I was not prepared for that. Perhaps because I had changed so much I expected he would have changed too. All those plans my father had made for me in front of the fire were so completely forgotten, lost in the dust and grit of that year. I had long ago presumed they were forfeit to time. But here they were again. Here was a contract entered into on my behalf before time began for me. I was now a stranger to him and to that contract. How could he know he wanted to marry me? How could I know? I wanted to warn him. I wanted him to know that I had a heart so torn that I wondered if I was like a child who had not eaten for a long time and no longer wanted, or needed, food. Did I have any love left? I knew how to survive but not how to love. There was a great vacancy there. Could I be a wife?

I was happy and safe here. I had made this land safe. I had seen the worst it could do and felt its hardest winter. I knew which trees to cling to and where God would hear my call. I knew where to cleanse myself. What waters clear and which foul. Here I knew where death lived. What horrors might another land hide in secret places for me?

What would married life be like after all? What would it be like when I had the responsibilities my mother had? Did I want a child to love me as I had loved her? What would it be like to be with this strange dark man for all my days without escape? What would happen to my father? And worst of all . . . and worst of all . . . what about the wedding night? What pain and shame lay for me there in that bed? And what if I should have a child? Could I survive the pain? Could I survive that final terrifying dance with death and pull a little breathing, crying, sucking baby out of his hands? Could I do that? God, could I do that?

But then Thomas took me in his arms and I felt the spirit move within me. I began to believe I could marry him. Then I said, "Yes." From that moment my expectations were only of joy. I could not fear him, although I should have. I could not fear our wedding night. I looked forward to it with joy, with a rising joy of expectation like the expectation of a Christmas feast, like the expectation of a gift on my birthday, with an expectation that no night of love could ever fulfill.

We could have made love there in that orchard. Perhaps we should have, there among the green leaves, the rough orchard grasses and the moths flying up to catch the sunlight in their wings. Perhaps we should have, and that would have been an end to it.

11

WHEN WE RETURNED to Sandwich Richard Bourne took me, as we had agreed on the road from Boston, to visit his Praying Indians as he had promised in the Kingdom of the Mashapee.

Although I had seen Indians all my life, and considered them part of the landscape like cattle, or dogs, or children, I had never visited an Indian village, or seen them at home in their lodges, although I had often heard stories about how they lived. Most of these stories I was sure were much exaggerated, as they were mainly cautionary tales to children who might wander far from home, as to what would become of you if a pair of red dusty hands should come unexpectedly out of some bush and snatch you away to live as a slave among them. In fact a time would come when all those stories would come true and captives would be taken and held hostage, confirming all those tales of evil; but not on this bright day and not in the Kingdom of the Mashapee.

Turning our horses down a narrow path not five miles from my father's land, we rode on several more miles. Then topping a rise and gently turning our horses through a pine wood, we saw in the distance a stockaded village, larger than Sandwich by a great deal, it seemed to me, and with such a quantity of smoke rising from it that I began urging my horse on, shouting to Richard that the whole place was surely on fire.

"No, no," he said, pulling his horse up to mine. "Rein in, Thomas. That is just the way with them, rein in, you will see." As our horses went on at an easy trot, he continued, "They are just savages, expect no more of these people. They are still living as they lived in the woodlands. All we have done is to draw them together in these palisaded places for their own protection. Master Tupper and I are laboring to learn their language, teaching them the Bible, the English law, and how to raise cattle and crops, but they are very slow to learn, shiftless, inclined to suddenly disappear into the forest after venison and to forget all they had planned to do that day. Worst of all, they seem to take very little seriously. Yes, they will never be as you and I, Thomas, they have neither the mind nor the will for that. But they do seem to take a great interest in the Bible and one day we hope some from this village may go, as some others already have, to England and be truly educated. Now do not be surprised at anything you see in the Kingdom of the Mashapee. When you feel uneasy do not let on that you have any doubts. Put up a brave front and follow my lead."

As we came closer we could hear and see the first of their many scrawny dogs. As soon as we were close enough these mutts began nipping and yapping at our horses' hooves so that the horses shied and pranced in circles, almost out of control. But no one came to our aid, or seemed to notice, or care about the dogs setting upon us.

Finally, we dismounted and approached the village on foot, kicking at the dogs and shooing them with our sticks. We tethered the horses to two trees outside the compound, setting them up in a little siege surrounded by the dogs. In that invisible pen our horses moved about uneasily under the shade of the trees with their great eyes wide and wild and their hoofs flinging now and then at the hindquarters of the nearest dog skulking around them. The Indians eat horse meat and Richard did not want to tempt fate by bringing the horses into their camp.

The large entrance gates were not bolted and no one greeted us as we entered. Richard said this was not unusual and that it did not mean that they did not know of our coming. In fact, they probably had news of that soon after we turned off the main trail. Inside the stockade was a very large village indeed. The interior was mainly of well trodden earth, but here and there large sections were fenced off as the earliest settlers had done with wattle fences and inside these were all sorts of crops growing and kitchen gardens of herbs for their cooking pots. The adults sat around on the ground, unmoved by our coming, it appeared, except for their bright black-eyed stares, but the children quickly began crowding around us, laughing, shouting to each other in their pleasing soft language, and grabbing at anything that might hang from us. One actually took my stick and ran away with it. When I chased him he mischievously jumped this way and that until he at last gave it back with an insolent grin. Many of the children were as naked as Adam and Eve and none thought that unusual. Here and there you would even see a handsome new mother with her breasts exposed, giving suck to her baby in the face of God and the world.

Amazingly, with all this mass of children there was no sound of babies crying as you would have heard in a civilized town of the same size. The air was almost solid with the smell of human excrement, dust, smoke, and filled with the babble of voices and a rhythmic clicking as if hundreds of looms were at work there all at once. The village gave a feeling of great distance with row on row of wigwams and everywhere brown bodies as far as the eye could see.

Their wigwams were little more than huts made casually from saplings bent over and tied to make half hoops, then tied together along their length to make long low half-cylinder buildings which seemed almost an extension of the ground rather than a building set upon it. These were completely thatched over with an assortment of reeds and topped with large slabs of tree bark. Each had an opening about the center to let the smoke out and they belched forth such quantities that you would swear they must be furnaces and all fire within. The thick smoke burned my eyes and by the time Richard had led me to the central wigwam, my eyes were tearing so much I could see nothing of it. As we went, Richard put his hands on the heads of the little Indian children as he gently moved them out of the way, and now and then he would bend down and whisper something to them in their language and the child would embrace him, or just put an arm around his leg. The men stood unmoved and silent like statues, watching us, only their eyes moving, but many of the young women were very beautiful, with their dark eyes sparkling, and they would look me up and down without shame as no white woman ever would have.

Richard had his Bible under his arm and now and then one of the children would kiss it, which brought a lump into my throat. These poor little savage creatures had been brought to such a love of God by Richard's hand alone.

Richard led the way into the low wigwam and I followed him, stooping into the darkness. The inside was as close as a ship's hold and we were crowded into it, though it was quite large, all of us sitting on the beaten earth floor. With the smell of naked Indians (and who knew what strange roots rotting there) plus the thick smoke, I could hardly breath. I felt a cold sweat breaking out on my chest and back and braced myself with my hands on the earth to keep from falling. My head began spinning, but by concentrating on the light on a smoky beam near the smoke hole I controlled myself.

After a time, when greetings had been exchanged in their language, Richard leaned back to me and said, "This is the great sagamore of the nation of the Nausets. We are fortunate to come when he is in residence. He has a great domain here and in the islands south of the Cape in the middle of the ocean. The sagamore is a good Christian and speaks English very well. He has taken the Christian name George."

This sagamore was dressed in breaches, a jerkin of fine leather tied at the waist with a sash, and a broad-brimmed hat, although he was barefoot. He carried a sort of scepter, or it may have been a fan in one hand. This seemed to be carved out of one wonderfully thin piece of wood: round at the top like a paddle and with a handle in the form of some squatting beast.

"I know you do not take tobacco, Richard, my dear friend," said the sagamore in flawless English as though we were all sitting about the front room of the governor's house, "but perhaps your friend will share some of this fine tobacco with us. It is brought from far away to the south, and the best I have tasted." With this he pulled a long-stemmed white clay pipe from the fire of the sort used by the Dutch and carefully wiped the end on the lapel of his coat.

"No, thank you," I said, imagining for a moment the reeling nausea a puff of their tobacco would surely bring. Even if I had felt I could stomach it, the use of tobacco was still officially forbidden in Plymouth and I had only once tried it. The Indians were so addicted to it they would have kept up the habit should it mean perdition. The first Indian to greet the new settlers in this land was in search of tobacco from them. There were also those now in the Bay Colony who smoked every day and considered it a great curative. I looked away and swallowed hard to keep my gorge from rising as the sagamore lit the pipe from an ember.

Five other Indians sat close around the sagamore, some naked, but for a loincloth of deerskin, and many eagle feathers in their hair and around their necks. Some were fully dressed in deerskin neatly tricked out with black and white wampum and mantles of porcupine quills. They solemnly passed the pipe of tobacco among them, each taking a deep drag on it and releasing the smoke with a sigh. I remembered that I had heard that the tobacco will make a third nostril in those who regularly take it for the venting of the smoke. When the sagamore let out his puff it hung for a time under his broad hat, trickling up around the brim into the sunlight in the dark room as if there were a fire of hell within him, or he some Greek sibyl comically dressed as an ordinary man.

"What will you read us from the white man's dear book of wisdom today, Richard?" asked the sagamore.

"Today I had planned to continue to read to your people about that man much tried by God. Do you remember him?"

"Ah, yes: the sachem Job. You started that story when I was last here. It is a particular favorite of mine. We are good Christians, you see, young man, even as you are," the sagamore said, leaning forward and touching my knee with the stem of his pipe. He looked me in the eye for a moment with a smile. "We had our own gods once. One lived in the ocean's waves. Sometimes when the sun was just right on the water you could see her moving there like a dark shadow in the cupping of a wave before it crashed on the sand. She was a favorite of my mother and she would sit for hours, looking for her in the undersides of the waves where they are green. Some lived inside old trees where a child could slip his fingers into a crack and just barely feel their soft flesh with the tips of his fingers. Some slept under the earth and now and then you could feel them moving and turning in their sleep at night. One of the strongest ones lived deep in the depths of the spring your father now owns. There was also one god, like the bark of a white birch all shredded away, whom you would meet in the night; she was the spirit of suicide. Some moonless nights they would surface in that spring and take deep breaths, then slowly and silently sink again. From time to time if you squat very quietly beside that spring and watch and listen, you would see the bubbles when they exhale ever so stealthily and secretly; and then if your senses were very sharp you could smell the breath of those gods in the night air. They could bring you a loved one if you had none, but it was dangerous because they might also grasp you by the foot and pull you in, but then, love is like that, too, isn't it? Also, the lover it might bring you might not be the best. Who knows?"

I was amazed to realize that this Indian knew who I was and where my father's land lay.

He continued, his face and voice as placid as if he were reciting. "Then one day there came a great wind from the south and when it came I knew that this wind was your God. He tumbled the gods of the waves shivering onto the beaches, He broke the trees, tumbling the old gods out among the dead leaves, and I myself heard those old gods screaming and groaning in their agony as your God tossed them out of their hiding places and blew them out across the lands of the Wampanoag, the Narragansett, and the

Pequot and straggling out at last into the lands of the Mohawk: an evil people who are always painted black as though they were in mourning and who cut their hair in a scalp lock across their heads to make their scalps easier to take and have a war cry like wild laughter. They live on the other side of the mountains. Those gods will not be missed, my brother Thomas. They were evil, some of them, indeed as full of mischief and evil ways as men are, very like men, in fact. They did only what pleased or amused them and frightened their people. But your God is so sweet and kisses us when he comes upon us in the dark so that we love him now and have forgotten all those cold evil old gods we once thought so powerful. We have even forgotten the spirit in the beavers and the foxes. We say nothing to them when we meet them in the forest now. Brother Richard Bourne helps us to know the great God, Jehovah, and his blessed son the shaman Christ who gave his life for us." And George, the sagamore of the Nauset, sat back with a great smile of contentment thinking about his new God and drawing a long draw of smoke from his white pipe.

"Today I will read from the Book of Job," said Richard as he searched for his place in the old Bible. "You remember how proud Job was and how God discoursed on his punishment. Now, here Job begins to understand that punishment and understand the power of his God. As Richard started to read, the sagamore raised his scepter to cover his face as though it were a mask.

'Oh that I were as in months past, as in the days when God preserved me; when his candle shined upon my head, and when by his light I walked through darkness; as I was in the days of my youth, when the secret of God was upon my tabernacle; when the Almighty was yet with me, when my children were about me; when I washed my steps with butter.'

The sagamore stopped Richard by raising his hand and translated this to his men who did not know the language; they seemed to think it very amusing. One touched the soles of his feet and showed them to the rest.

'. . . and the rock poured me out rivers of oil; when I went out to the gate through the city, when I prepared my seat in the street!

The young men saw me, and hid themselves: and the aged arose, and stood up. The princes refrained talking, and laid their hand on their mouth. The nobles held their peace, and their tongue cleaved to the roof of their mouth.'

The sagamore had to stop him here again and illustrate the passage with his own tongue. The others drew their breath in fear and amazement.

'When the ear heard me, then it blessed me and when the eye saw me, it gave witness to me: because I delivered the poor that cried, and the fatherless, and him that had none to help him. The blessing of him that was ready to perish came upon me.'

The Indians thought about this for a time, arguing among themselves, and then one of them indicated a bite on his arm. Neither of us could imagine what this gesture might mean and the sagamore seemed unable to translate.

'. . . and I caused the widow's heart to sing for joy.'

This the Indians seemed to understand and found quite funny.

'I put on righteousness, and it clothed me: my judgment was as a robe and diadem. I was eyes to the blind, and feet was I to the lame. I was a father to the poor: and the cause which I knew not I searched out. And I brake the jaw of the wicked, and plucked the spoil out of his teeth . . . But now they that are younger than I have me in derision, whose fathers I would have disdained to have set with the dogs of my flock. Yea, whereto might the strength of their hands profit me in which old age was perished?'

Several of the Indians had questions here and Richard answered them directly in the Wampanoag language. Richard said to me: "They are marveling at the great age to which the men of the Bible lived."

At length they fell to laughing and pointed at the oldest Indian there: a mangy looking fellow in a worn jacket, almost toothless, and with long strings of white hair. "He claims that he is two hundred years old, but the others don't believe him." This fellow finally began to laugh too, waving his hand as though he were fending off their teasing.

'For want and famine they were solitary, fleeing into the wilderness in former time desolate and wastes who cut up mallows by the bushes and juniper roots for their meat.'

Richard tried to describe what these things might be, but he was not all that sure himself. At last they settled on ground nuts and the root of a wild flower we call artichoke root that the Indians love and plant in every village.

'They were driven forth from among men (they cried after them as after a thief), to dwell in the cliffs of the valleys, in caves of the earth, and in rocks. Among the bushes they brayed under the nettles they were gathered together. They were children of fools, yea, children of base men: they were viler than the earth.'

"You see, Master Thomas, they did not live in wigwams as we do, but lived wild on the land. There are still Indians who live like this and you should be careful of them for they are indeed, as this book says, viler than the earth."

'And now am I their song, yea. I am their byword. They abhor me, they flee far from me, and spare not to spit in my face.'

At this passage the company grew very quiet, much more solemn than they had been. There seemed to be no word in the Wampanoag language for spitting in someone's face and it apparently was not a custom among them. The sagamore illustrated what it meant by spitting in his hand.

'Because he has loosed my cord, and afflicted me, they have also let loose the bridle before me. Upon my right hand rise the youth; they push away my feet, and they raise up against me the ways of their destruction. They mar my path, they set forward my calamity, they have no helper. They come upon me as a wide breaking in the water: in the desolation they rolled themselves upon me. Terrors are turned upon me: they pursue my soul as wind: and my welfare passeth away like a cloud.'

After a long silence George asked, "But tell me again, why did our God do this to the sachem Job who was such a good man and cared so for the welfare of his people?"

"Because he was proud and rejoiced so much in his riches and power."

The sagamore thought about this for a long moment with his head resting sideways, his cheek in his hand. Then he raised the wooden paddle to cover his face and his countenance suddenly brightened. "Ah, yes, he should not have cared so much for the things of this life."

Richard looked at him in amazement. "Yes, that's right."

The sagamore gave a shy smile, and returned the paddle to his lap. "But your people lay up cloth you cannot use and food you will not eat in your lofts and outbuildings and you say it is good stewardship. If we then take what you do not need you beat us. You put away our wampum in your wooden chests rather than wearing it as we do."

"Yes, George, we can be as proud as Job was. This is a message of hard words not just for the Indians, but for us as well. When we are as proud as Job we will also be punished."

"Ah, yes. Now, your book says that God can be cruel, surely that cannot be. Our old gods were cruel and might have done these things, but our God loves all his children, doesn't He?"

"A father who loves his children does punish them sometime for their own good?"

The sagamore debated this with the Indians for a while and then raised the paddle again to cover his face; finally he lowered it and said, "Ah, yes, I see it now. He is not evil, as our old gods were, just out of mischief, but he is cruel only now and then for our own good."

Richard turned to me and said in a low voice, "It gives me such pleasure to feel I am bringing this wisdom to these people for the first time."

"Now, what we have been learning here today about our God reminds me of a question many of my people have wanted me to ask you. I have thought about this question and cannot find an answer for them."

"I'll do my best to answer, George," said Richard, "but remember I am just a simple farmer and neither a learned man, nor a minister."

"Ah, yes, I know that, Richard, but you have always given us good answers. There is an island of the Nauset south of here in the great sea, as you know, and when those people come to this land looking for their brothers, the beavers, which they believe in their ignorance are little men living by every river, in families as men do in little tight lodges as men make for themselves, except that the beaver's lodges are under the water, they do not find their brothers the beavers as they did before. They are gone and all their lodges are empty. These ignorant people then come to me and ask, 'Where is our brother the beaver?' and I have no answer for them. Now, I have killed these little brothers myself, in great quantities, and sold their pelts to the white men in your villages; they seem to love them very much, finger the fur, and run it through their hands and say this one is better than that one for some reasons we cannot see, but then the pelts are gone. You do not wear the fur to keep you warm in the wintertime as the beaver does when he is alive. What do you do with it? Do you eat it? If you do I should like to know how it is prepared so that I may try some myself."

Richard laughed. "No, no, we don't eat them. We send them over the sea to the people who live in England and they wear them just as you do. We send them there just as they send us gunpowder and all the things we need to live here."

"And you keep none for yourself? That is very generous of you." And the sagamore shared this with the others, who were amazed.

"Well, no, we sell them."

"Why don't you wear these warm skins?"

"We are simple and godly people and that would be an unseemly luxury for us."

The sagamore hid his face again behind his mask and thought about this. "Ah, yes, I see; our brothers the beavers are no longer in the rivers and their lodges are empty, but their skins make the great sachems across the sea warm in the bitter cold of their lands where they have no beavers. The little spirits of our brothers the beavers also add to the great spirits of those great sachems in England and make them the greatest people in creation. That is why you send all their pelts to England."

"Yes, well, in a way, but we have been paid for them just as you have."

"Yes, yes! I would like to see this land and the pelts of our little brothers the beavers. From those we have already sent, every man, woman, and child must have several fine coats of beaver skin. I would like to see that."

"A good Christian, though, should not covet rich clothing, you remember."

"Ah, yes, yes, brother Richard Bourne, I remember that. It is a commandment, isn't it?"

"Well, yes, it is in a way, and a law too."

"Ah, yes, and a law too." George crossed his arms and leaned forward, "Could we not help those who live across the sea to find Christ by not sending them any more of our little brother's pelts?"

"Well, no, most of them are beyond saving."

"Oh," said George and, deep in thought, covered his face again.

We sat this way for a long time waiting for the sagamore to start speaking. I had to shift my feet because my left foot had gone numb. George put his scepter down and, giving me a hard look, continued.

"On another matter, your people seem to be taking more and more of the land on this cape and they are not buying it as I was told they would."

"Well, you must be sure it is your land they are taking and not just the land which is lying fallow without an owner."

"All the land on this cape is ours, is it not? You have explained this to me before, but I never seem to understand what you are telling me."

"Yes, well, you do not own land unless you have done something to improve it. Built a house on it."

"My wigwam sits on this land, doesn't it?"

"Well, yes, of course it does, but who is to say where the land around your wigwam ends and where the land of another wigwam begins?"

"I do not know."

"Well, you build a fence around the land on which your house stands, you see. That fence marks where your land ends and another person's land begins. Then it is written down in a book in Plymouth saying where it begins and ends."

"Ah, yes," George said, touching the end of his nose with the wooden paddle, "but if I built a fence of wattle all the way across the land side of the Cape could I not then say that all the land around my wigwam on this cape inside that fence was mine, except those small places where your villagers have built fences around their land before I built mine?"

"Well, no, let me see, your land would then have a fence on only one side and not all around it."

"But the other sides of the Cape are the sea, and no one builds fences in the sea, do they? The fishes are free there. The sea belongs to the fishes and so I can say that my land begins where the land of the fishes ends."

"Well, let me think. No. The land that is encompassed by a man's fence must be the land he can work and plant, run his cattle, or plant his trees."

"My squaws plant corn wherever they wish all over this cape, the deer in the forest are our cattle, and all of these trees are my trees. No white man planted them. How do you not know that my ancestors did not plant these trees in a far time?"

"But it cannot be a land beyond what you could walk and work in a day. You cannot rule the world. If you could a man could say all the land in the world is mine because in a lifetime my wife and I could plant plants on it, or I could build a fence anywhere on it."

"But does not the sachem king of England do just that? Does he not say he owns all of his land and all of my land as well?"

"Well, not exactly. He rules all that land, but other men own all the little parts of it. Each of us has our own little farm, and he rules it, but it is still ours."

"That is very sad for him. Then he owns no land."

"No, he does own land."

"But only the land he can work in one day?"

"Well, he and his servants. He does own land."

The sagamore raised the scepter to his face; after a long time he lowered it. "Ah yes, of course you are right, and now I understand this thing. But I may ask you about this again one day."

"Shall we sing a hymn now?"

"No, I think this is not a good time to sing a hymn. When I am singing I fear I am in danger of losing myself. The world shimmers and the old gods try to snatch at my people as they do when we drink your liquor. We are still children of the forest, remember, brother Richard, and it is best not to tempt us." He then began an animated discussion with two of the older Indians among them.

"What are they saying?" I asked Richard.

"I'm sorry, Thomas, I can't make it out, they are too fast for me."

At length the sagamore said "I am sorry. They are asking me if anywhere in your book it says where fire came from? I am telling them, this is a trivial thing your God would not talk to them about in the great Bible book. But now that they have asked can you tell me if it does?"

"No, no, I don't think it does."

When the sagamore told this to the others they were quite excited, all talking at once.

"They say, since your book does not say how fire came into the world, that they will tell you how it happened and you can add it to the book."

"Well, nothing has been added to the book in a very long time."

"Yes, well now we shall add this story."

"No, you cannot add anything to it."

"Ah, yes, but since it does not say that we cannot believe this it is all right that we do, isn't it?"

"Well, I suppose it is," Richard said reluctantly.

"I will tell you about it and then you too can know how fire came into the world. Long ago in far off times some of our ancestors were sitting about on the beach of the island which you call Nantucket. It was at night and they were eating shellfish and singing songs and looking up into the night sky naming the stars and following the course of the great white snake which runs all across the sky. They were very cold too, because, of course, there was no fire yet in the world to warm them. Far to the north in the northern sky they saw a star they did not know the name of. They watched it very closely and noticed that it was wandering around as though it needed to find a place to hide, but it could find none. And then they realized its problem, because as they watched, it suddenly shit a great ball of fire out behind it and that ball of fire spiraled around in the sky and began to fall. It fell right down on the beach of the island where they were sitting.

"They all ran up to it and once they had discovered how to stand near enough to keep warm and not get burned they liked it very much, and so they decided to take it home to their village. They all went searching for bits of driftwood to use to push it to their village. When they had found enough they all got on one side and their sagamore told everyone to push, but their sticks went straight through and some of them got burned. They then noticed, to their great amazement, that the sticks they had used to push it all had a little of it stuck to the end. They rejoiced at this and each one carried his fire stick to some other village in his canoe and built fires in that village, and the people of that village took sticks and carried it to other villages until every village in the world had fire. Now go back to your people and tell them how fire came. Tell the great sachem king in England and I am sure he will put it in your book."

As we rode back to Sandwich we were both deep in thought. Richard finally said, "I sometimes despair of ever teaching them anything, and then another time they seem perfectly reasonable and you might expect them to quite easily build a cabin in Sandwich itself and no one take note of it. I wonder if I am doing any good for them at all."

"I am sure you are, Richard," I said to him, and we rode on.

Very soon word came from Duxbury that Elizabeth would marry me here in Sandwich and that her father and little Trial would accept the land my father had set out for them and settle here when a suitable cabin had been completed. In those days there were mainly old married people and little children in the land, but very few people of marriageable age and so marriages were much less common, and all the goodies were eager to prepare a great wedding feast and make our marriage and the coming of the Bassetts a sort of festival.

11

THE REVEREND MISTER Leverich decided, after some meditation on the solemnity of the thing, that it was proper and so preparations began.

I would bring Elizabeth to my own cabin that I had finished on my father's land. My father, brothers, and I set to work on a new cabin for the Bassetts on their land.

It was one of the happiest times in my life: a time of expectation which can often be better than the realization. Edmund Freeman brought me a gift of a fine moss green velvet which I sent off to Boston to be made into a waistcoat and William Wood agreed to use one of his valuable pieces of parchment to draw up a proclamation to commemorate the event.

Elizabeth, her father, and her little sister Trial had been settled in their new cabin in Sandwich now for some time, and I had been to visit her there every day. William Bassett had brought both cattle and seed with him from Duxbury and with my family's help they would survive the winter and be ready for a good spring planting. His winter root crops were already in the ground. Elizabeth and I were to marry late in the summer: in September, just before the leaves begin to fly.

On the day Elizabeth and I were to marry I walked to the new cabin my brothers and I had built on my father's land. As was the custom, all the land belonged to my father during his life and his sons lived only in the expectation of their inheritance. Until that time we were tenants without rent on the land. The cabin smelled of new logs as though the adz had just finished its work on it, and the caulking, not yet dry, smelt like Indian clay pots, or brick drowned in rain after a drought. The house was green and new, but each unevenness was already a memory for me. As I walked in its door I realized that I would be a father and a grandfather here, and with God's grace die an old man within its walls. Yet, the whole was such a new thing to me, and seen with eyes on which no scales had hung as they did on Esdras in the Apocrypha. My eyes had seen no pain, they were the eyes of a fresh heart, and it was more than I had ever dreamed. I had never owned anything of any real consequence before this time. But this house was mine. The size of it amazed and delighted me. I could almost hear the sound of Elizabeth singing her own favorite songs into this place.

The land around it was all for my use and one day would be mine. I was at once, on that sunny morning, a wealthy man and not the child I had been the day before. The land was full of bright sunlight, but the wind was up in the trees, thrashing around as if there was an unseen rain whipping them, and as I stood long and quiet in that bright interior there was a great sound of struggling outside one of the windows, as if some creatures were fighting for their territory they had lost to me without their knowing. Then some large animal seemed to leap into the window. At first, I thought it must be a wolf and cursed myself for coming out unarmed.

I was as startled as it was when it finally struggled its way into my sight. I saw then that it was only a great brown turkey looking ruffled: dislodged from its roost by the wind. It looked at me out of its red eyes in its naked head, shaking its wattle uneasily and staring at me in utter stupefaction. But I recognized it at once as our first wedding gift and I moved so quickly to secure it that it barely had time to struggle. I grabbed it and safely tucked it under my arm pinning its wings, when it began to make a terrible raucous noise and kick its legs.

The two of us, the turkey and I, made one more inspection of the cabin and as we stared into the chimney place I pointed out where my gun would soon hang and said to him, "What a pity you came so early, Master Turkey, for one day I will have a weapon here to give you a proper salute and more courteously welcome you into our cooking pot. But there is still time for your chicks to find that better welcome here another day. As it is, you will add to our wedding dinner and welcome us to this new place. I will make fans of your wings for the hot summer days on the door stoop, I will trim your feathers for quills to write about this day, and your bones shall make needles for Elizabeth to sew up our lives as we fatten in them." We went on our way rejoicing, or at least I rejoiced, to the center of Sandwich where I might find someone to add my poor fat companion to the wedding feast.

When I got there the place was alive with activity. The Bassetts had been seen earlier leaving their cabin and would have been there already if they had not stopped at so many new neighbors on the way.

My father and mother had gone home to look for me and they had a good laugh as I came casually strolling along the path in my muddy boots and country leather with my turkey under my arm. "I'll take that one and get him into the pot," said goodie Feake. "I trust you will be more gentle with your next catch, Thomas. I hear she is almost here. And you out hunting. What will she think? Get home and get yourself cleaned up."

The dinner had begun all around me and I could smell the wonders the goodies had contrived. It would truly be a harvest home.

As I turned, about to retrace my steps to home, Edmund Freeman stopped me. "Thomas, I have something for you."

And he led me back to his house where, inside, his family was all gathered around for a great presentation. His wife was there beaming and Sarah, their proud and pretty daughter with her eyes full of wonder, and all the little ones. There laid out on their table was my moss green velvet waistcoat with fine brass buttons on it. Sarah touched it gently, smiling shyly at me.

"Try it on now, Thomas," Edmund said.

"No, no, what are you thinking of Edmund," said Goodie Freeman. "Look at him caked with mud and who knows what all filth. You men have as little sense as the turkey Thomas just brought in — strutting here and there, but not even aware of where your breeches are."

Sarah giggled, "How will he know it fits him unless he tries it on?"

"It fits, or it will not fit, and that is that. He will try it on at home after Goodie Burge has a good scrub. That is that, Edmund."

"But mother," said Sarah,"I would like to see the groom in his finery. You promised."

"You will see him soon enough, Sarah. Be still!"

"Thank you, Edmund," said I. "I will look like the King of England in this. I only hope Elizabeth will like it."

"Oh, she will," said Sarah.

I knew my mother had made me a suit of her own homespun, laboring on it for months, and I wondered what she would say or think now that I had gotten such a green foppery from Boston to contrast with her decent, careful hand-work. So I took it into the house surreptitiously and smuggled it away so she would not see it until the last minute. Then it would be too late. Even if she told me not to wear it, then it would be too late to take it off. She would have to accept the thing, godly or not.

Bundling it up in the homespun, I went quickly out, saying I would see them when I came back from bathing. Jacob and Joseph made fun of me for this and chased me half way down the path. I had taken the soap my mother forced on me, however, and when I came to the lane leading to my father's spring I looked both ways and dodged into it. I laid my new wedding clothes neatly across the stile with my old work clothes beside them and stood there naked as Adam.

12

I RAN ACROSS the dry field and the water field to the spring and leaped into it all at once; the coldness took my breath away. It seemed to chill me to the heart and set every corner of me tingling and shivering. I was so complete in the scourging of the month's accumulated mischief that I made an unusually liberal use of my mother's soap and even went so far as to wash my hair. I went under water until it set my eye sockets aching, then leapt out like some dog fresh from a swim, flinging my hair out and sending a ransom in water jewels flashing around me in the sunlight.

At last I staggered into the water field, my flesh blue and numb. I rubbed away at it vigorously, my teeth chattering and every muscle taut. The sun, however, was as warm as on midsummer day, and so I lay myself out in the warmth on grass of the dry field with my hands behind my head. Tiny dots of sun exploded in my sun-dazzled eyes; I was half awake and half dozing. The sun slowly reclaimed my flesh from the cold. It is said to be the poor man's fire. As I lay there I thought of something which had never come to me before: whether Elizabeth would find my body pleasing. Or was it seemly for a woman to even think of the body of a man? She would surely have no thought of it. What was the body after all, but a passing thing? If the soul was lovely the body was nothing and had no meaning. The soul could be loved. The body was little more than a tree which would one day rot away. Is a tree pleasing? It is just a tree. She surely would think nothing of my body one way or the other, and I nothing of hers. On the other hand, the body is the first thing one sees about a person,

How happy I would make her, I thought. Of all my treasure she would be the foremost. She would soon be mine and I would own her. That strange blonde creature standing almost to my shoulder, her intense blue eyes full of thoughts I would never understand. She was such a treasure of beauty I would close her up in our cabin like Edmund Freeman keeps his plate and she would always be there for me when I wanted to enfold her in my arms. If I needed someone to talk to she would be there. When I needed my cider mulled she would be eager to put the hot poker in it at my command. She would prepare all my food for the rest of my life, make my clothes, and so encompass my existence that it might be said that she had made me, but I would own her.

But owning a woman like that was not just the reward I had for being a man, it was also a grave responsibility. I knew that. I should have to find her food, keep her warm, in shelter, in fine clothes, and happy. To do all that is the labor of a man's life and his calling. Then, there was that other thing: begetting children, and, of course, making love. I tried to imagine her eagerly begging me for my love or if she would be shy and take it coyly, lying patiently for my caress to come. What might it feel like to enter her and become a part of her for a moment? Would I hold her down with her wild hair flying? Would I take her in the morning, or whenever and wherever I could?

There I lay stark naked in the field and very greatly excited by the thought of her and what we might do tonight. I lay in my father's field, under the watchful eye of God, but fully erect like some satyr ready to make love at any moment to any heathen spirit which might come out of the woods, or slowly surface in the bubbles of the spring, also quite naked and ready for the game.

Just then I heard a rustling in the leaves and I sat up, covering myself as best I could. After a moment's silence there was the soft sound of a female giggle, ever so quiet. I leapt up and ran for my clothes, and as I turned I saw the skirts of a little girl disappearing into the underbrush. Should I call to her, or chase her? I thought not. She had certainly seen all there was to see. From the way she was running I certainly need not worry about her being a spirit of the woods. She was just some little girl from the village. Why, I wondered, had she stopped so long, watched so quietly and then giggled, revealing her presence. No proper lady would have stayed once she saw me there at rest in the clearing.

I climbed into my homespun suit, trying to scratch away the

itchiness of it so I would not embarrass myself. I also had on a linen shirt my mother had made from our own flax, my best boots and, of course, the moss green waistcoat which wrapped me up tight as a parcel, making me feel taller, straighter, master of all I surveyed. I could not wait for the others to see this fine luxury. I left the old suit on the stile so it would not smudge my new clothes, or soil the fine effect. Let the rain wash it. There was no one but Indians to steal things from us in those days, and so I had no fear leaving them there. The worst I might find on my return was that some family of field mice might have moved into my pants leg. I combed my hair out to a fine point and ran for a way to let the wind dry it. At home I had a broad-brimmed hat and I walked along the path, eager to get it and set it on top of my present splendor, finishing the effect.

As I approached I saw my mother loading a pot on the old wagon. She did not see me and I thought I might just get past her into the cabin without her noticing my waistcoat. When she turned she looked at me sharply and I knew she had seen it. Then a strange look came over her face; perhaps of sadness, perhaps of joy, but surely of quizzical amazement.

"Well," she said after a moment, smoothing out her apron. "Well, Thomas, so your mother's simple honest handwork is not good enough for you. Many a man has married quite satisfactorily in the homely things his mother made for him."

We stood there for a time simply looking at each other as though we were newly created.

"Thomas, it is all right. It doesn't matter to me how you will look. It matters to Mistress Bassett. I am sorry you felt you had to sneak around me, but it doesn't matter to me. You certainly look fine in your green velvet, but under it, Thomas, you are the same old stick still." And she hugged me very hard, then looked away, crying, I think. "Mistress Bassett has a fine thing coming to her in you, my son, for all your green velvet, better perhaps than she deserves."

That was the only criticism I ever heard my mother say about Elizabeth. I had no idea what the meaning was. There are few enough men who can say that about their mothers. Mother was a great talker, very proud, but she let Elizabeth alone and made her the only thing in the world about which she held her tongue. If she judged her, and she must have, she never let me know. Isn't it strange how people can talk among themselves about the most trivial things, but not about what may shake the world one day?

I put on my new hat. For all I turned it this way and that it always seemed bigger than the fellow it was set upon. At last I settled it at a rakish angle just shading one dark and sinister eye and hinting that there might be some dark mischief hidden there, but when I came into the cabin's great room my mother was there and she set it at a perfect parallel with the floor planking again, checking its level with a practiced eye any geometer would have envied.

My father was sitting by the chimney, much drawn into himself as if he were cold, although the day was fine and there was no fire on the hearthstones. "Come sit by me, Thomas."

My mother and father exchanged a glance and she said, "I will leave you men alone to talk about those things men talk about which are unseemly for women to hear." She gave my father another long look which I knew very well, the look she gave when she meant her instructions are to be carried out, and left the cabin.

"Thomas, you have come a man now."

We sat for a long time in silence thinking over this revelation.

"That's true, father."

"You have come a man."

After a long time in which it became increasingly apparent he was not going to elaborate on this theme I began to grow impatient. "I know that, Father."

"There are some things in the world . . . ." he began, but then after some thought he realized this was not the way to go, and so he started again as if searching out the wind for a favorable tack. "Women . . ."

We looked at each other for a time and then away.

"Women are a different thing."

"I am not a child, Father."

This stopped him fully and, labor as he could, he could find no starting place again.

"Of course, you know your mother, your sister, and some of the girls you have met at the meeting, and then Elizabeth too when we were there with her family, years ago . . ."

With this profound thought it seemed for a time that the conversation might end, to my great relief and his. But, at last, he pressed on. "They are women, of course."

"Yes, they are. I know they are women, Father. I have known many women."

"But not as wives."

"Of course not, Father. I know what happens between husbands and wives. I am not blind, or a simpleton. I have lived in this world for twenty-five years. I am not coming to this marriage as a green child."

"Yes, yes, there is no need for us to fight about this here, Thomas."

"Well, then, say what you have to say and let's be through with it."

"Now, I have a place to say these things, you know."

"Say them then, and be done with it. Mister Leverich and the company will be gone before you say what you have to say. But I have told you I have no need of a lecture on men and women, or anything else, for that matter."

"Well, I am not eager to give you a lecture on that subject either, and so we can stop right here."

"No, no, I know you promised Mother. Go on then."

"No, that's all there is to say."

"Mother will ask you if you have. She thinks I am a little child still and need to be told where to piss."

"That's enough of that. Your mother is not at issue here. I am speaking to you. Sit down!"

"All right, all right."

We sat for another long silence while our tempers began to cool.

"When I first saw your mother it was in her church at St. Stephen in Brannel, in Cornwall, I expect. It was a little town west of St. Austel and the church with a high tower, a barrel vaulting and a font I remember supported by four kings and two lions fighting on it. She was a distant cousin of your grandmother — one of the Pyes."

"I know that, father, do you think I have been around this family deaf as a post all these years?"

"Your mother was a virgin then, of course."

At this shocking revelation a great silence fell. I grew increasingly uneasy, for I knew he was about to tell me what I, for some reason, did not want to hear. I kept from scuffing my best boots together only by a great act of will.

"In time we would come to love each other, your mother and I, and in the course of time . . ."

"Well I know that I love Elizabeth."

"Love is not so easy, Thomas. Yours was a planned marriage, ours was also planned."

"We love each other, father, and would have married had our marriage been planned or not. You did not make this marriage. You may think you did, but you did not. We made it."

"What I am trying to tell you is that no matter how a marriage was made, love comes when it comes. You work . . . Love is not just there one morning. Your mother and . . ."

"You don't understand at all, father. How can you understand another man's marriage?"

"Your mother and I.. . ."

"Is this to be a history of your marriage, or may I get on with my own?"

He looked down, thinking this out in his quiet way, but slightly flushed with either anger, which came easily to him, or embarrassment. Which of these I could not tell. It was always a struggle when we tried to talk. For me it was as though I was trying to see into a stone, and for him as though he were trying to discover forms in a fire.

"All right, father, I will listen to you. Thank you for being interested."

"I say your mother came to me a virgin."

"Yes."

"And I had no experience of women then, you know, but what I had read in the Bible, of course. I was one of many children, and my father never spoke to me as I am to you."

I could sense his anguish at talking about such intimate things, but my impatience was growing every minute we sat there in the half dark, so that I had little sympathy with this tongue-tied old man. He seemed smaller to me sitting there drawn up near the chimney place. He would surely drive me mad.

"And there came a time . . ." he gave me a wild painful look and I now decided I would just hear the old fellow out, but now he seemed unable to find another word and looked as though he had something stuck in his throat.

"Then, there came a time when your mother and I were alone. It was our wedding night as it will be yours. Do you know what I am saying?"

"Yes, father, of course I know what you are saying."

"Well, that time is coming for you."

"If this conversation ever ends. Yes it will."

"It is not what you think. . . . Women have their own desires."

We sat in silence.

"You will see it is not what you think. Be prepared. God will help you both. He has ordained that a woman shall cleave to a man. He will manifest that to her in time."

"Yes, thank you, father."

And that was the end of it. After a long moment of silence we both stood up, and shook hands, and my mother met us at the door and kissed me sweetly on the cheek. I fancied she gave my father a sly look over my shoulder, but I no longer cared about that. She had obviously been crying. They now watched me, as I went out, armed with my father's sage council, into a cool sunlit world and down the old familiar path to Sandwich to meet my fate.

13

Naomi said to Ruth, "And now is Boaz not of our kindred? Behold he winnoweth barley tonight in the threshing floor. Wash thyself therefore, and anoint thee, and put thy raiment upon thee, and get thee down to the floor . . . And it shall be, when he lieth down, that thou shalt mark the place where he shall lie, and thou shall go in, and uncover his feet, and lay thee down; and he will tell thee what thou shalt do."

That is the way it must be with me and Thomas. That is the way it will be, and we will one day be the lineage of some new Jesse and of some new David. I thought this in my childishness.

Here is a list of the things I brought with me from Duxbury side and will bring to the home of Thomas Burge: a small copper pot which was my mother's, which has some special memories, as you have heard; a hitchel with which I will be able to work flax; an old spinning wheel and some thread of my own making; a great many bedclothes, some of fine linen and some which I have ornamented with my own handwork in a pattern of sheaves of barley for Ruth and Boaz; a small piece of work which Trial did for me, not well done because she is still young and had no mother to show her the stitches, but very much loved by me; and all my clothes and caps. That is all the dowry I could bring him. It seems a very small list of things now, doesn't it, but at the time it seemed a great wealth of things to me.

My sister, Trial, was thrilled with the idea of marriage and her singing in and out of the house, and through the day, cheered me. She helped me with my bath and brought me flowers all the day long from the marshes to put in my hair. I had blue vervain, and some gentian bluer than any late fall sky. These were to bring out the color of my eyes. We then added white flowers, because it was a wedding, and I did come to it a virgin. Trial found some white nodding lady's tresses and late-blooming fringed orchids: white flowers to make a crown for a bright wedding day. I also rubbed myself all over with some mignonette I had saved in a little box from my mother's garden. I rubbed my cheeks until they were red. And dressed in linen my father had bought me and lawn, and good homespun until, with my crown of flowers, I felt as fine a bride as ever there was here in the New Israel, or over the sea in England. Trial and father laughed as I paced around the little cottage like some great princess in a fairytale, or ancient beauty about to start a war among the Greeks. My father thought me a great beauty, I know, and Trial knew no better than I did of beauties, but in truth, I am a plain, good girl, if perhaps too well-endowed to keep all of me properly tucked up in the virtues proper to a maiden and a sister of the sweet, homely, and pure religion.

For all that, I had a great eagerness to be with my new husband, that strange, dark, tall man with a straight nose and troubling eyes. I had little fear and worry that it could be anything but full of the joy it always had been in my dreams. I even had no fear of that first night, as I often had in the past, but I awaited it with enthusiasm. I was eager now to be no longer a maid.

I knew what my future would be and I was ready to go rushing into it with the joy of this fresh, sunny day.

But I was sorry to leave my father too, and his new home as yet not made a home by the hand of a woman, and I cried all the night before thinking of him so frail and yet so beautiful with only little Trial to see that his boots were clean and his fine clothes brushed and that he ate properly and did not go out into our fields alone and cold. I had saved him you see, as I had saved some fledglings in the cup of my hands at home and as I had saved little Trial and they were more than father and sister to me. They were creatures of my making. They were still in this world now because I had put them there as if I had born them on that morning I had looked at myself in the copper pot. And in that way they had also made me. There were hidden, secret things we knew, when we looked into each other's eyes, which no one else knew. There was a woman who lived only inside my head. There was a place and a time only we garnered up. Yes, I wept all the night before Thomas and I married, but not for fear, don't let him tell you that, as most brides do, but for loss.

As we went into the town that day it was like some May procession in the heathen times with neighbors we did not know at every fence post to welcome us and invite us in. We did visit the cottages of George Knot and his family, as neat and clean as if there had never been dust in the world and all their little children's hands fresh cleaned every hour; the home of Richard Chadwell where, as it is to this day, everything was topsy-turvy and every little shirttail was out as if they had set out each morning to be as different from their neighbors as ever they could; finally, at the house of the Newlands, the place and the parents were all as somber and serious as if it were a meeting house, but their many boys would just stand down by the barn laughing and marveling and telling jokes and pointing at Trial and me until we were quite embarrassed and went on with many apologies from the elders and harsh looks at the bad boys by the barn.

When we came into Sandwich it was as if it were all some sort of great cook shop with boards and tables set out everywhere and the good women of the village at such a hurry and scurry with dishes and pots that they had not a moment to gossip with a friend and barely a moment to take notice of the grand progress of the bride with her little family.

There were meats such as I had never seen in Duxbury: corned beef, pickled pork, country ham, and great slabs of bacon from which pieces were cut and dropped into the pot, or turned on a stick over the fire. There was Indian bread of the yellow, the red, and the blue and standing dishes like loblolly, sampe, hasty pudding of hominy with milk, and hominy loaves turned out of molds. There were more dishes of pumpkin than I can tell, but particularly, my favorite where you dice the pumpkins and simmer them on the crane just off the fire for at least a full day until they are the consistency of good baked apples. You then add butter, vinegar, and ginger root, if you have it, until it has a tartness much like that of apple, and this is served with fresh fish. The people of Duxbury always spoke of fish as Cape Cod turkey since they were in such abundance there and came mostly to us from the nets of this new land, but for this feast there was real turkey among the small fowl, geese, and duck. I was told this was because Thomas had hunted it for the table, but he was gone now again back to his father's house to prepare himself. There were good brown breads of corn and rye (but more of the former because the rye was scarce), Indian puddings, clam chowder, and lobsters, although they were considered poor food and fit only to fill the odd corner not filled with better fare. About the brains, liver, and kidneys in their pie crusts was a grand salmagundi of cellared and fresh vegetables. Of the fruits there were fresh and those preserved as jams and such a quantity of apple pies and hard cider enough to have made tipplers of the whole town. Here and there plates of fresh cream were set out with spoons in them and the children would help themselves, leaving grave grandfather mustaches on them until one of the goodies could get at them and wipe them off with her apron.

The greatest show of all, however, was a deer which some Indians had brought in with them. These Indians were a particularly filthy and greasy lot and I was amazed and horrified at the way they were let stand about as though they were freemen of the place and eat with the rest of us, as though there were no distinction between them and the civilized people. I was told that they were Praying Indians, but I did not see they were any less wild than the others I had known, and one particularly ugly one with matted hair they said was the sagamore. They treated him as though he were some sort of nobility. Manners are less precise as you get farther from the mother meeting, I had been told, but I did not expect this, even this far from Plymouth. I worried for my life and that of my family if this was to be the way the savages were allowed to walk among us from now on here. But Mistress Feake, whom I mentioned it to, agreed and said they have a town of their own to the west and rarely come into Sandwich except on special occasions.

"Is this one of those special occasions? And will they think it special enough to scalp us all?" I said, just close enough so that this sagamore might hear me.

Mistress Feake laughed at that and we walked on together toward the meeting house.

There we walked through a gathering like a fair full of folk with the sun dappling through the trees onto the feast and a town in its best with a wild Indian under every spreading tree and the pond shimmering, the paddles of the water mill flashing sunlight.

Near the pond there were several boys playing at stool ball and some others pitching the bar. As we approached, the minister of the place came out of the meeting house with some others to meet me and as he saw the boys at play his face reddened and he began to chase one until he had caught up the ball and put it under his coat skirts. "You will not play ball here, John," he said to one of the boys.

Another older man whom I had seen before when he came to Duxbury to offer the Burge family a place at Sandwich stepped forward. He had been very handsomely dressed then, I remember, so you might think he was the headman of the place. He hurried up behind the minister and said, "What harm can it do, Mister Leverich? This is not the Sabbath. I take no exception when you stop the boys from playing on the Sabbath, as you know. But this is a celebration and here is the bride. Let the boys play. Have done, Mister Leverich for once!"

"One day, Master Freeman, you and all this town will regret your tolerance of the joys of the flesh. One day you will pay a price for your permissiveness. And I shall be here, Mister Freeman, to remind you."

"I will take that chance, Mister Leverich. Give the boys back their ball."

"God knows, and you shall know in time," the minister said, and threw the ball so far the boys had to run for it, stopping it just before it went into the pond.

14

ELIZABETH AND I married on that warm sunlit day in September in a homely town in what was still the wilderness, with the families of good yeomen and many Indians as witness. I remember it with crystal clarity, but I wonder now if the eye of God was really there, as it seemed so surely at the time, or if He was still in Somerset watching in among the hay wains in that county and not looking among His new people.

We tarried for a time in the village finishing the feast, and I remember looking around and being very fond of those simple people, all a part of the same dangerous adventure: still people who had set out in a fragile boat on a tormented sea; still cupped in the hand of a storm; still huddled in a sort of hold with all of a wild land crashing about them.

Now pumpkin is a very windy fruit, as you surely know, and in that happy assembly all wrapped up in their wool and homespun, if you listened very closely you might hear a sort of music coming from dozens of hidden wind instruments ranging in tone from soprano to baso profundo: This was surely the symphony of the new people, eating new things, in this new forest.

At last Elizabeth and I broke away and started in silence with her cold hand in mine down the path which led westward out of Sandwich. Some little boys followed us a way until their mothers caught them, and then we were alone, tremendously alone in the woods, and there seemed nothing to say.

"Is it a good house, Thomas?"

"It is sound."

"I mean, is it a house in which we will be happy?"

I could think of no answer to that. What a strange question.

"We have not brought my bedding with us, Thomas, we will freeze. Turn back."

"No, no, my mother has given us some bedding."

The sun was in the southwest and shone in our eyes, blinding us now and then as it flashed through the branches; we had to shield our eyes with our free hand. Now and then the silence was broken by the restless sounds of birds searching for a nesting place and flights of swallows wheeling above us in the deep blue sky, catching the last insects of the night and the last warming rays of the sun before it set.

Her cold hand was now warm and moist and she withdrew it from mine as we walked on, side by side, looking around us in silence and not looking at each other.

When we came at last to the turning and looked across the stile at the cabin it startled me. It suddenly seemed smaller than I remembered it to be. I looked at Elizabeth, wondering if she was disappointed, and there were tears in her eyes. I thought of her in the bastinados, so vulnerable, and I touched her. She started a little. As she looked at me in the dark twilight I could not make out what the expression on her face meant, but we kissed then and I held her. For just a moment we were very alone, but there was pleasure in that, not fear.

"Do you love me, Thomas?" she said with that same earnest look I had seen in the orchard at Duxbury.

"Yes, Elizabeth, I have always loved you."

"I cannot tell it, Thomas, how can I know?"

"Why, you can know because I have married you, Elizabeth."

"That means nothing."

"It does to me."

"Why would you want to marry me, Thomas?"

"I have always wanted to since the first night I came in out of the rain and you hugged me by your father's fire."

"I am not pretty, Thomas, I am a plain girl."

"You are the most beautiful girl I have known."

"And have you known many, Thomas Burge?"

"No, not many, Goodie Burge."

She gave me a strange look then and we walked on in the half darkness.

In the cabin I searched for the kindling and logs I had set out to make a fire, fumbling around in the darkness, dropping and kicking things. Elizabeth stood in the faint light of the doorway, for we had no candles. When I had blown the sparks into a flame and had the flue drawing I turned to her. She had taken two steps into the room and taken off her cap in that unconscious gesture of a person who has come into her own home. That made me happy.

I agonized within myself that the room seemed small and mean in the firelight. The light of it seemed only as large as the hearth, and all that part in shadow was not there at all. "I wish you had seen it first in daylight."

"I will see it in the daylight tomorrow, Thomas. It is best I see it in the firelight as that is the way I will see it every night for the rest of my life."

"It seems such a small place in the firelight."

"We need no more than this, Thomas."

"Oh, I have forgotten," I said, and searched out the candlewood and bayberry dip I had set aside for this night. We each took one and put it into the fire and looked at each other, kneeling there on the hearth as the bayberry twinkled as if we were lit by a storm of small stars.

We were there a long time on the hearth, talking, perhaps aware of the maplewood bed and what would happen in it tonight and not eager to start.

I had made the bed myself and strung the rope springs and my mother had stuffed the mattress with goose down and laid the comforters and pillows on it.

At last the night was totally black and the fire began to falter. I poked up a flash of sparks from it, put some more bayberry candlewood in it, and blew up another little flame full of sparkling lights.

Elizabeth stood up at last, turning away from me and stepping into the shadows. She was undoing her white collar and loosening her bodice. She looked down, then over her shoulder at me like a wild thing in a moment of fear at the sight of the hunter.

"I must see you, Elizabeth. We are married now. There is no shame in a husband seeing his wife."

She turned slowly and deliberately, but still with the look of fear in her eyes. They sparkled now with the reflection of the bayberry. She let her dress fall. Beneath it she had only petticoats. I could see she had worked them finely with embroidered passages from the Scriptures in each fold. It was the custom for a bride to embroider her favorite verses on her underthings for her wedding night. She stepped out of them one at a time and then was naked and glowing in the firelight. Her skin was so fair that it was white as linen, but wonderfully smooth; her breasts were very full and sent a thrill of excitement through me. It seemed to me I had never seen anything so beautiful. Her breasts were so very white that I could not see where the nipples were, but for the delicate shape of them like some exquisite ornaments she had kept hidden from the world and only I would ever see. She was slimmer than I had imagined and might have been a girl, but for the subtle flare of her hips. I was fully dressed, but took her in my arms. She resisted for a moment, looking at me with those startled bright blue eyes, now almost purple in the darkness, and then she kissed me. She needed my warmth as the dark night was becoming chill, then she slipped under the comforter, naked and beautiful. I still could see her body in my mind's eye and I yearned for her so that I could barely get my trousers off. The green velvet flew with the homespun to the floor and there I was naked and filled with passion, but still wearing my boots, and I heard her faint laugh under the coverlet.

As I slipped into the bed Elizabeth held up the coverlet to make a cave and we kissed there in that secret place. It was a cave of flesh and love with laughing human walls. I touched her hip and felt her firm body under my hand, her breast which fit so perfectly in my hand with the little hackles of excitement rising on them.

"Is this proper, Thomas? Is this the way it is? Should we be doing this?" she whispered, and I felt her warm breath on my face.

We were as close as people ever are in this life and about to become for a moment a single creature. A creature of joy, I thought, apart from time and place.

"I am afraid, Thomas, I am afraid. It will hurt me, Thomas."

I rolled above her, supporting myself on my arms and looking down at her body below me.

"No, Thomas, not now. It will hurt me, Thomas. There is plenty of time."

I rested my weight ever so slightly on her. I could feel her trembling, but I could also feel her breasts pressed against me. I knew her fear, but I could not stop myself.

"Thomas, wait. Just a moment." She closed her eyes very tightly and put her arms around me. I realized how small they were and was all the more excited by the feel of them. We were together in an adventure which she and I would have only once. We were pressed together in a moist bond that marked the beginning of a journey. We were both moving together in a new rhythm: pressing on into that journey. Breaking the gentle bonds of custom to touch at last as only husbands touch their wives, bonding us as no ceremony had, as no contract might, bonding us beneath those modest bedclothes, forever in the wild passion of animals quite apart from the philosophies of thinking men, their beliefs, or even the conscious mind. It was primitive and wild as I had never dreamed it would be.

I felt myself start to fit smoothly into her and then stop, striking something quite unyielding, not soft and easily passed as I had expected. I pushed harder and felt her body tense beneath me. I opened my eyes and looked at her face contorted with pain. Her fingers dug into my flesh and I knew she wanted me to stop, but I could not now and I struck once again against that hidden wall and once again until it gave way suddenly and she cried out in pain. She clung to me and I wondered if I should stop, and if her pain would turn to pleasure if I relented, if I waited just a moment. I raised my body up again and saw that pale, soft body glistening with sweat beneath me, glowing, her pale hair flung out across the pillow, her blue eyes open now and bright as firelight, but with an undertone of pain somewhere beneath the sparkling surface and the slight smell of blood. I could almost see her thoughts, but I could not stop myself and went on until I released and released again the pent-up passion of all those years into her, making her my own, marking her my own and ignoring her small cries of pain.

"I am sorry, Elizabeth," I said as she turned away from me and I withdrew, but somewhere in my secret soul I was not sorry, I exulted in a primitive joy.

"It's all right, Thomas. It is all right. I didn't know what to expect. I didn't know. The pain will quickly pass. You are satisfied, that is what counts." And she drew herself up and away from me under the comforter.

I put my body around her and pressed it against her, hoping that the feel of me might kindle a passion in her, but it did not. I could feel small shudders through her body as though she were crying. "I am sorry, Elizabeth, we will try again later and you may not find it so hard to do. You will see."

"I will never like it, Thomas, if it hurts like that. But it is enough that you will. It is hard, Thomas, because it is supposed to be. God has punished me. Never mind, Thomas." She touched me. "Never mind. It is not your problem. It is a woman's problem. Why did no one tell me? It is my problem. I had no mother to tell me." And she began to cry.

I tried to comfort her by holding her tightly in my arms, that was all I could think to do, but she turned away into the pillow and would not be comforted.

I slept soon, but my dreams were troubled by Elizabeth's face in pain. Every corner I turned, there it was: sometimes near and sometimes at a distance. Sometimes I would rise up into the sky like a bird, then suddenly forget how to fly and fall, tumbling, seeing her face at every turning. And now and then the face of some good woman I did not know reproving me. Then there was a long path through a summer wood, but troubled with little birds, blue-birds flying into my face in great flocks and picking at my collar points, striking at my eyes. There was some nameless small animal with its sharp teeth hiding in the grasses of the fields ahead of me through which I must pass, I knew, and no defense against it. Its face was a proud mask with a defiant smile.

I woke up in the middle of the night suddenly, in a cold sweat, my heart pounding. I was lying on my back. Was this still a part of the dream? No, there was Elizabeth lying beside me, her breathing soft and steady deep in her sleep as I would surely see her day in and day out for scores of years to come, as long as I might live, or she might live.

The moon had risen with a vengeance and the cabin was as bright with the moonlight as if it had snowed upon us in the night. I could see every detail in the white light, but I was somehow afraid, unable to move, my mind frantically alive, but my body paralyzed with fear.

15

I FELT A stickiness on my leg which must be Elizabeth's blood, I thought. I lay there for a moment with the thoughts rushing through my head, none resting there long enough to be recognized, unable to decide what I should do. At last I moved my hand on the bedstead to make sure I was no longer dreaming. I must get some water from the spring to cleanse us both. I eased my body off the bed gently, so as not to wake Elizabeth, who moved in her sleep and said some parts of words in that unknown tongue of sleep, but did not wake.

I thought again that I might still be sleeping myself as I stood there naked in the white moonlight of that room with the bed and the sleeping figure behind me. At last I dressed and found a pail for the water — picking it up gingerly so that it would make no sound. Quietly, I raised the latch and stepped out into a world that looked like a drawing, in black and white, with shadows in the thickets so black they might be made of black velvet or deep holes cut out of nothingness, leading out of this life. The moonlight was white and bright as day and the moon herself hung like a face in a pitch black sky with a graveling of stars, like sand scattered to dry the black ink and the slightest wisp of a cloud backlit by the moon as if it were some fine cloth hung on the night. I could see the path very clearly and it drew me to it, although I knew I was on a fool's errand out in the pit of this night, where only Indians and spirits moved: a child fetching water. But the errands you wake to in half sleep, no matter how mad they are, seem more compelling and drive you on, as I was driven on across the stile and down the path, noting every stone and stick, tingling with fear at each stealthy sound in the dark wood chilling me through as no night wind could.

When I came at last to the dry field near my father's spring I marveled at the beauty of it with the moonlight lying on it like a rime of fresh frost. I hesitated before stepping from the dry meadow into the wet meadow, and some instinct made me look down. The hair on my neck rose as I did, for the earth all around me seemed to be moving and shimmering with tiny wet backs. Thousands upon thousands of frogs carpeted the ground. They were in constant damp movement in the moonlight, piled three and four deep upon each other, but silent in their dance as if I had been struck deaf. And when I looked up, that carpet of moving fleshy creatures stretched out as far as I could see.

I edged a foot into them and felt their slimy sides as they fell this way and that, oblivious of the giant walking among them. There were hundreds and hundreds crawling on their bellies, climbing on each other, riding each other, pressed to each other like succubi and demons in the grass.

When I came to the spring I had to hunker down among them, clearing a space with my hands for the pail. I sat there on my haunches, Indian style, as if in a trance for at least a quarter of an hour, aware of the movement of life around me, wondering if it would engulf me. The spring was so smooth I could see the reflections of the moonlit trees in it like a drawing in white chalk on the face of the water. As my ears became more accustomed to the silence I began to hear the faint sound of the movements of the frogs around me and then my body tensed as I became aware that I was also hearing the sound of bubbles in the spring, and I smelled a strange sweet smell in the still night air.

At last I dipped the pail into the spring and felt it fill, watching the ripples spread out, causing the reflections of the trees to dance. The water seemed colder than I had ever felt it.

I carefully made my way back through the meadow of frogs watching every step. As I came into the dry field I looked up and was struck with horror. A black figure stood before me silhouetted against the moonlight, the brim of his hat casting a shadow which made him seem to have no face at all.

"God save me, who is there?"

But he gave no answer.

"Why are you out at this time of night?"

"I might ask you the same, Thomas Burge."

I thought I knew the voice, but I was so startled I could not place it.

"Don't you know me, Thomas? Are you walking in your sleep?"

"I don't know. I may be."

"I am your neighbor Peter Gaunt."

"Oh, yes, Peter, thank God it is you. I could not imagine what I would meet out here." I was able to take a breath again and stood a minute to stop the pounding of my heart. "What are you doing out here so late at night, Peter?"

"I often walk in the night and pray here by your father's spring."

"And pray?"

"Yes."

"Don't you get enough prayer on the Sabbath at meeting?"

"I do not pray there, Thomas."

"You do not pray at meeting? Why not? It is true you are often not at meeting in defiance of the law. My father has mentioned that."

"I am not surprised he has. Yes, I do not go to meeting except to please my wife."

"Are you a heathen then, Peter?"

"Well, not exactly that."

We walked on for a time. I could think of no reason why a man would not go to meeting unless he was a heathen and servant to the Devil. I looked at Peter, but still could not clearly see his face.

"Can I trust you, Thomas?"

"Of course you can."

"I have never been of your faith. My family was not, and I was not when I came here. I came here in fear of persecution for my religion, though, just as you did, or as your father did."

"But what religion is persecuted in England other than ours?"

"Many are. When I came here for the freedom to worship I found it was not here and so I must hide my faith out in the night. I have a family to worry about. They do not need the shame of it. They do not need to see their father in the stocks or worse. It is that important, Thomas, that you do not tell anyone what I tell you tonight."

We walked on in silence while he wrestled with himself as to whether he could now turn back, or if he must tell me.

"I am an Anabaptist, Thomas; you have heard of that, have you not?"

"I have only heard the ministers rail against Anabaptists."

"It is better that that is all you know. God has protected me and my children, but He may not be so kind to you. God walks with us here. This is His temple."

"Tell me about your faith then if I am now in its temple."

"No. Thomas, I will not proselytize and endanger my life. But I am sure that I am to this land like John the Baptist was to Israel and another will follow me who will be greater than I could ever be in the cause. In time another will follow me. Remember what I tell you. But, now I remember, this is your wedding night. What are you doing out walking in the company of a sinner like me in the middle of the night when you should be at home with your bride? Shame on you, Thomas, get home."

"Yes, sir, this is my turning now. God keep you safe tonight, Peter."

"And you, Thomas. You are more in need of his care tonight than I."

Although ten years passed I held the memory of that night with me and nothing would wash it away, as though it were a claret birth mark, marking me forever in some hidden place and with some meaning unknown to me. I changed, my body changed, my life changed, my relationship with Elizabeth changed, but the memory of that night, its disappointment, its mystery, and its strange dream was unchanged. Whether it was an augury or a memory only I could not say.

16

THE EARLY YEARS of strife with Elizabeth gave way at last in a slow collapse of resignation. Elizabeth had a sternness and a metal in her I had never known was there. I had thought she was just a woman. Just a creature of pleasure, delight, and beauty to hold and to protect. But under the softness was sinew and it did not give to my touch. We quarreled at times in those years so fiercely that it might seem we would come to blows. Once I remember a terrible quarrel across an old stump and me with my sickle in hand and she daring me to strike her with it. The image of that blade and her flesh still causes me to shiver. I remember the heat of it. I remember some of the words. I remember the sweat on my hands so that the haft almost fell. I can see Elizabeth's face through my own sweat and tears. I cannot remember, however, what it was we argued about. Somehow, I cannot remember any of the things we seemed to argue about. Of course, none of them were really what we were saying to each other.

There was no formal truce. There was no time when we held each other in our arms and said, "We cannot live like this." There was no point when love ruled anger. There was simply a point when familiarity and routine smothered all the rest and we subsided into the everyday, the heat of the past wasting away like the sparks deep in a log on the fire as the night comes. But it was not just the heat of anger which passed away. Her golden hair was cut short decently, and as it had no curl in it to peak out from beneath her cap it was pure without a whisper of naughtiness, her white caps tight around her head, her old blue dress, her quizzical looks with something hidden and still wild behind them, the tilt of her chin at the window as she watched the birds come to the crumbs she had put out for them, her head down stirring something at the fire, how she moved at night and I did in some slow ancient dance in our bones through time, kneading, planting, winnowing in season, the sound of her footsteps on the planking like the pendulum of a clock, her blue eye sighting the world through a needle's eye, her busy hands sewing a straight seam with a measured rhythm; all of this, once penny bright, now darkened.

We lay together through all those nights and no children came. We labored, but there was no spring.

Season in and season out we waited in that enclosed space, brushing past each other, restlessly listening for some whisper of life quickening which might signal the true beginning of our life together: a quickening which might transform our mutual solitude into a family. But that season did not come, only another tedium of expectation and the forms of cooking, planting, washing, mending, eating, and sleeping. The children who did not come were the ghosts of that house, and like ghosts, always just on the periphery of vision, around a corner, under a chair, beyond the lip of the opening to the loft.

Our neighbors looked at us in wonder and spoke behind their hands. We were fellow prisoners to the thing: she less the woman and I less the man. But like prisoners in a deep dungeon we did not speak of our crime, whatever that might be, or of our imprisonment, but of the days when it would be over and of the day to day.

Elizabeth was barren. God withheld his hand from her womb. And even that, in time, became a commonplace.

Finally, we stopped making plans and sorting names. The girl

Delight, or the boy Thomas, would not come from that other place. We knew they would never come. At last we were silent altogether and would sit for hours in the firelight thinking our own thoughts like storekeepers in an empty shop.

Elizabeth was often at her father's house. In the first year the Quakers came to Sandwich her father was ill and she was there every day to see to him. He had been sick since the spring planting. Trial was busy in her process of becoming a woman and in that process she had her meetings and her moods and could not properly care for him, or so Elizabeth thought. She would often say, "How can Trial leave him alone as he is? She is out raising the Devil's eyes among the men of Sandwich while her poor father lies sick and may die. I was never such a child as she is." And other bitter talk, for all that she loved Trial. Trial was very pretty in a wispy way, with fine blond hair and the same wild look behind her eyes I had loved in Elizabeth. Sandwich was her home. She had more laughter and fun in her than Elizabeth ever had and would run with the boys in the field and not be afraid of them. She needed the hand of a mother and Elizabeth needed a child to mother and there was none in my house. So Elizabeth took her ailing father and that bright, wanton, happy girl as her charge. The neighbors thought her a saint for that. Who could not love such a daughter and sister? Who could not? No one but her husband. No one but me.

She would set out in the morning for her father's house singing to herself with a basket for them under her arm as I would make the first footprints of the day in the dew of my father's fields. And those who saw us would say, "What a fine pair they are! How well they care for those who cared for them." But there would be no meal for me when I came in at midday and I would simply fall on the bench with the noon sun coming in through the shutters onto my face as though it might nourish me. Every muscle would cry out and I could feel the great weight of my body upon the bench as though I would never be able to lift it again and I would sleep a dreamless sleep until I would start to fall and wake with a start. I would lift myself and swing round on the bench, and rest my head in my hands until the pain in my back subsided. Then I would rub the raw places where I had torn up weeds all day and brush away all the dirt I could. At last I would begin a frantic search for some crust on the shelf or morsel from last night's supper left in the pot which Elizabeth had not taken to her father. Then out again into the blinding still afternoon, wondering if silence could strike a man dumb at last. I would sit in the sunlight, struggling on my boots, caked as they always were with mud, wondering if I was anything more than a horse in mindless labors stretching my muscles to the breaking point in the same endless round. I would trudge down the lane alone until my brothers joined me, but there was little to say to them. I knew now why my father had been so silent all these years: mind and tongue silenced by brute labors, silenced by the blows of life. When the darkness grew so deep you could no longer see the leaves on the trees, I would stand a moment, look back at what a small amount had been done in that day, and begin searching my bleary way home. But Elizabeth would not be there to salve my labors with a word or offer me the touch of another human hand.

When she did come swinging a lantern into the cabin, with her basket empty, ready to begin another meal, I might ask her how her father was or not ask. Either way she would say, "He is as good as could be expected," all the time not looking at me. We would eat our fill, but I would go to bed hungry for something, though what I could not say. She would busy herself at the hearth and come to me later as I slept. There was neither joy nor sadness. Time passed and the sun turned above me, but I was unmoved: still and alone like a stone in the bottom of a pond. God's ordinance to Adam to punish him for daring filled my days, and blackness and Elizabeth's turn-ings in her sleep filled my nights.

One damp morning I stood looking out at the lane with the palms of my hands pressed against the door frame and I said to Elizabeth, who was finishing her preparations behind me: "Stay here today, Elizabeth, stay here, and I will stay home from the fields."

"What?"

"Stay here with me."

"What mischief are you planning now, Thomas? I cannot do that."

"Please. It is important."

"My father is ill, Thomas, I will stay another time."

"Will your father ever be better?"

"What are you saying, Thomas? What do you mean by that?"

"I don't mean anything. I know he is ill. I know as much about his illness as if I were his physician."

"Stop that, Thomas!"

"I am sorry he is ill."

"Then you understand, don't you?"

"I understand my wife would rather sit by her father than be with her husband. I understand that!"

"He is ill, Thomas."

"I know that! I know that! Don't say that again!"

"Why are you making such a quarrel of this? You don't expect I will leave my father, who has loved me, alone to die so that you may have some company?" With this she picked up the basket and tried to pass me. "Why are you doing this?"

"Because I have asked you to stay, Elizabeth. Because it is important to me."

"It is a small matter."

"To you it is. To me it is not."

"I am going, Thomas. Will you get out of my way?"

"Do not go. Do you hear me Elizabeth? I warn you: do not go today!"

"You warn me?"

"Yes, I warn you!"

"Will you beat me, as Feake does his wife, will you do that?"

"No, Elizabeth, you know I can't do that."

"What will you do, then?"

"I wouldn't hit you, no matter what might happen."

"How do I know that, Thomas? All I can see is a man standing here threatening me with force. This man is not my husband. This is some stranger come here in his form to torment me."

"Elizabeth, please stay."

"I am going now, Thomas!" she said, and pushed me out of the way. But I ran after her and caught her by the arm at the stile. She turned to me with her eyes dark and full of anger. Anger I had rarely seen in them before.

"Elizabeth, please, we have become strangers."

"You are the stranger, Thomas. Not a man but a boy. Let me go! You are jealous of my poor father lying sick in his bed, an old man who may soon die, and you are jealous of him."

"Yes, Elizabeth, I won't deny it, I am jealous of him."

"Jealous of a sick old man and a child without a mother to keep her. God forgive you, Thomas."

"What they are, they are, but you are my wife. You must stay if I ask. You must."

"And what sort of daughter or sister would I be then? I am that, too, you know. I will tell you. I would be as good a daughter and sister as you are now a husband if I should not go."

"That's not what we are talking about. We are now talking about your duty as a wife."

"My duty! My duty! Have I not carried out that duty dry and wet, hot and cold. I have labored in that duty for you, Thomas Burge, as if I were your slave. And have I not lain with you should I wish or no? My duty! What do you know of duty?"

"There is some duty there, or do you think there is none?"

"I know a great deal more about duty than you ever will. It is you who turn away from me."

I cried and struck out as if I would hit her, but at the last moment I could not and struck the blow into the fencepost. She stepped back in fear nevertheless.

"You are a child, Thomas, now let me cross the stile."

"And what if I do not?"

"Then I will go another way. Now let me pass."

"Let me go with you then, Elizabeth."

"As you are now?"

"Yes."

"No, I have things to do and so do you. You cannot come a puppy dogging after me. What would people say?"

"They would say, there is a loving couple. That is what they would say."

"They would say, there is the village idiot and his dame. No, I will have none of that!"

"Then you should have none of me if I am such an idiot: the village idiot. Why do you live with me at all if you think I am the village idiot and you would not be seen with me? Stay at your father's house! Be a wife to him, then, if you can be no wife to me."

"You fool!" she said, pushing her way across the stile. "Get out of my way!"

As I watched her down the lane I felt the anguish of what I might have said to her, of how I might have stood resolute in indignation, of how I might have made her see me as I stood so alone, and see the contrast with those wives who hold their husbands dear. The flush of anger and frustration flooded through my body with such a rush that it made me limp and I gave in to it at last falling down against the stile. I sat there neither feeling nor seeing the world around me until the sun found me at last and I pulled myself up and began a weary walk into the field. I labored there, but there was no heart in it and as I grew tired I would fall down in the furrow and let the horse walk on ahead until it would halt in surprise, looking back at me in dumb amazement.

If I could only tell her how I felt. But there would be another quarrel and again it would all get lost in inarticulate anger and misunderstanding. I should have told her that my life was empty. That I was crying to her from the bottom of a well, and she my last chance. She would have cradled my head in her arms and touched my hair and said she was sorry and she would stay, knowing that my joy was truly her proper labor. She had not known what pain I felt. We would, at last, be together, we would be husband, wife, and lovers all at once from then on.

I realized then to my surprise that I was speaking out loud, and I was embarrassed, although there was no one there to hear me but the old dumb horse flicking its ears. "You will see!" I had said. "This is not the way God planned the world to be. This is not the way my world will be. I am my own master."

I felt as though all the drab world about me might come apart and beyond it would be some revolution which would change the world and change my life. I dreamed of it, and I dreamed about another woman than Elizabeth, not so morose, but with a joy which would refresh me rather than draw me down. Some dreams are futile, but some are not.

"Freedom," I said out loud, as if all those trees were prison bars and I on a chain's length yearning for a redemptive vision just outside my reach. Elizabeth must be that tether, I thought. It is she who holds me in bondage. If I were free all of my problems would fade away with her. Joy would replace sorrow, that smiling, happy, supportive woman would replace her sour looks and make my hard life a purpose.

But that evening when she came home she said, "He is as well as can be expected" and set about her chores. I said none of the things I had planned to say. It was somehow as if I had said them already. They were now as resolved for me as if she had been walking by me all day long as I plowed and me telling them to her. It was as if she had listened to me and had heard all I had said. The mind in its distress plays such tricks upon us for our own good and to set our hearts at ease. Meanwhile, she in her white cap and old blue dress was as busy as a weaver in his loom, and as distant. I did not cry out to her. We scarcely spoke, but sat by the fire waiting as we always did at night: waiting for life to quicken where there was none. Healing today's wounds for another day. But I was ready for change.

I first heard of Mary Dyer from Edward Shillingham when we met him on the road to meeting on a Sabbath. He was eager to tell us about this stranger he had met at this very spot the day before, and he gave us the whole story of it as we walked.

17

"WELL, SHE IS a handsome woman," Edward said, "and came up to me quite boldly."

His wife cocked an eyebrow and put a hand on him, saying to Elizabeth, "Are you sure you didn't come up to her, William?" And the two women laughed. "She was a young woman and quite pretty."

"You have told us that once already, Edward."

"Well, she was. I must tell the story as I saw it, my dear. She was not dressed as the country women dress around here. She had a fine cloak of gray with a hood: of some soft material from England, I would guess. And she walked up to me as if I were one of her particular friends, put her arm in mine, and asked me where she might find lodging and if I knew of a village called Sandwich. I said, 'You are in that village now,' and she seemed very happy at that and inquired where she might find the meeting house. I said I could show her."

"That surprises me, Edward," said his wife. "It's hard enough to get you there myself on a Sabbath, but then you have told us this woman was pretty, did you not, and that she put her arm in yours. That was why the directions came into your mind so quickly, I would guess."

"Who was with her?" Elizabeth asked.

"Why, no one was. She was quite alone."

"Alone on a strange road! That cannot be. What sort of woman would walk alone on a public path in a strange village?"

"She was quite alone, and as we walked she asked me about Mister Leverich and Edmund Freeman as though she knew them, or knew of them, and asked if I ever wondered by what authority they might govern my life, and I said they governed because they had been sent here to do that by the General Court in Plymouth and she laughed at that. She also asked me if there were any dissenters hereabout, and I said I thought only perhaps Goodman Gaunt."

"The Devil can take many disguises you know, Edward."

"If this sweet woman was the Devil he is wily indeed. She seemed an innocent and gentle thing and she talked to me all the way to the pond and up the hill to the meetinghouse."

"If I were the Devil here to lead men astray that is the very guise I would take," said Elizabeth. She said it lightly, but I felt there was more to her remark.

"What did she speak to you about?" asked Goodie Shillingham as though she were now taking the matter more seriously.

"Now that you mention it, she did speak much about my soul," he said, giving his wife a wink.

"Maybe she hungered after it, Edward," his wife said, and we all laughed. "But if that is how the Devil comes to Sandwich I suppose I should be glad it is only your soul he is interested in."

"You are a wicked woman," Elizabeth said, and we all laughed.

It was a bright blue day, with the smell of the sea on the wind, not brimstone, and who could have guessed what an adventure we were all starting on? Others joined us, waving and shading their eyes from the sun, wanting to see which neighbors were there on time.

We gathered in the meeting, swatting flies and fanning ourselves. Sure enough, there among us was a stranger dressed as William had said and sitting with the Gaunts. She sat in front of us and so I could not see what she looked like, but she did seem slim and young. The interior was dark, filled with dust like grains in the sun from the window, and packed, with the people of the village filling every bench. Mister Leverich came in at last and we proceeded as we always did on a sleepy Sabbath, with the children restless and babies cooing in their mother's arms and speaking in tongues. Little boys were pulling at anything about the bodies of the little girls that they could get a good grip on, squirming as if they were made of jelly and could not be set up straight on the bench. The girls squealed with imagined injuries and chastised their offending neighbors until they were themselves quieted. The elderly would now and then begin breathing heavily and nodding off until abruptly tapped by the warden's wand, when they would sit up with a start, to the amusement of the children who had watched for that very moment, and the children would need quieting again.

It came at last time for the sermon, always ponderous and often so familiar as to have been heard just the week before. Mister Leverich put on his little black preaching cap and a fine Geneva gown he had had sent from England over his black doublet, as he always did to signal that the message was coming. He fussed with his wrinkled preaching points and began to address the matters which lay before him, setting the proper tension on his rope to take him through an hour and more. I cannot remember his text; although it was, as usual, an admonition against some sort of evil behavior he felt was just then endangering his always wayward flock, and a stern description of what God's retribution would surely be upon those of us who were the secret sinners in our town. We were quite used to this sermon and could recite parts of it, for he gave it even at Christmas time. In fact, more especially at Christmas because he felt that was not a celebration of Christ's birth, but a pagan feast the Romans had kept alive with the excuse of our Savior, so unholy worldliness might have an excuse to revel in the streets. We could all tell from his start that this would be a long one, and we pressed down among our neighbors like the bears do in their burrows when they feel in their fat sides there will be a long winter.

He had barely gotten beyond his prologue, however, when, to the amazement of the congregation, our young stranger stood up in her place.

Everyone looked at her, sure that she had been suddenly taken with some illness and would push her way to the meetinghouse door to find some air. Mister Leverich hesitated in his explication of his text for only the blinking of an eye, and then like a dragonfly on a smooth pool, he darted on.

"What makes you think you can vilify these good people in that manner, sir?" the stranger said in a clear, loud voice, high, but with timbre as if she were used to speaking in public. "Think for a moment, sir, before you cast stones among these good people. They are the people of our Lord Christ and they bear His mark. Remember what He said to those who stoned the prostitutes."

The word was unknown to the children, except that it had some dark meaning, and the business it might describe was beyond the experience of every one of us. No one ever spoke in the meeting unless called upon, and certainly not during the sermon, and so we sat there dumbfounded, with our mouths hanging open. Even the children were silent and the elderly attentive. Some of the goodies near her involuntarily raised their hands toward her as if they would hush her, but she was a creature of such wonder that they did not dare to touch her.

"I am speaking to you, Leverich. Am I speaking clearly enough for you?"

Mister Leverich stood in the small pulpit with one hand slightly raised, caught in the middle of a gesture he had started to illustrate a point before the world fell apart around him in broken shards, and now he could not complete it. So it might be for all of us at the Judgement Day, and this was surely something of the sort for Mister Leverich. His mouth stood open, but at first no words came forth. How could there be words for the end of the world? When he did start to speak his voice was hoarse and uncertain. "Madam, sit down. I do not know where you have come to us from, or where you are going, but we are conducting the worship of our Lord here."

"Is this some god with which the rest of us are familiar, or is this some god of your own making and not our Lord, Jesus Christ? Christ said that we should forgive our neighbors for their sins."

Edmund Freeman came to his senses, at last, and stood up as if he would speak to the woman, or restrain her.

"No, Edmund, leave her alone," Mister Leverich said, pulling himself together, aware that in this place the spiritual authority should take precedence over the temporal. "I am in control here," he said, his voice cracking.

Edmund sat down, but with obvious reluctance.

"We are in a Christian house, young woman, as you well know, and you are a visitor among us. I will thank you to sit down, hold your tongue among your betters, and take some sound instruction with us."

"The scriptures are here for us to read, sir, and for those who cannot read I will read them aloud now if they wish." With this she turned to the congregation. I could see now that she was a pretty woman, indeed, with a long intelligent face, quite serious, but vibrantly alert with the most compelling dark eyes. She was dressed in a style uncommon in the Bay Colony, or Plymouth Plantation. Although she must have traveled a long way across hard paths to come to Sandwich there was a pleasing neatness about her and a modesty. Her gray hood was made of silk, or some other fine fabric and worn with a tippet trimmed in a fine line of fur. You could just see the edges of a delicately worked lace cap with her dark curls coming out of it as though she had carefully set them there for us to see. She had a moss green stomacher tight laced. Surely, she was the most elegant and strangest revolutionary any field of battle has seen.

"I see here in this book," she said, tapping the Bible as she held it up open to a text and pointing at it with a long delicate finger, "there is mention of priests, but Christ rejects what they have to say about the evils of man and preaches the good news. But I see there is mention of Pharisees."

Edmund stood up again, but Mister Leverich signaled him to sit.

"Who is this?" Mister Leverich said after a pause in which he realized her remark had been pointedly directed at him. "Sit down, woman, and be instructed!"

"By what authority do you instruct me, sir?"

"I am put in this pulpit by the General Court at Plymouth, madam," he responded after a pause, "but I have no need to answer to you for my charge."

"And I am put on this bench, as these others are, by the power of Christ!" And she struck the Bible, making a loud crack. "Which is the more valid license, sir? Which is it? We are all here ordained by this book and so let us share what we know, and not listen to your ranting, sir. Let others stand up as I have and affirm our faith."

Some automatically began to rise, but Mister Leverich said, "No, no, keep your seats! And you, young woman, leave this meeting at once, or I will have you removed."

"Is this your meeting house, Leverich? Do you have some lease from the General Court on this property? Have they set you up here like some tradesman at the fair with this place as your stall?"

"Of course not, madam, and I will hear no more from you about that."

"Does not God set this house up among His people for the use of His people, and would you deny me and these good people the use of it?"

"The use, but not the abuse, madam."

"I have broken no windows. I have simply let wind out of one of its inhabitants."

"That is enough! I will not have this meeting blasphemed!"

"I have said no blasphemies, unless you think you are the god here."

"You have gone too far!" George Barlow said, rising with an angry scowl, but Mister Leverich silenced him with a look.

"I mean that I am His representative here in this place."

"Are you that? Then you are a priest to these good people like the papist priests. I was not aware that I had entered one of those churches. You are some sort of intermediary, then, between these people and their God?"

"No, of course I do not mean that. I abhor those papists. You are a stranger here. These people know what sort of man I am. They know that." His face began to redden as he took a tighter grip on the lectern. "I was educated to preach as I do at the university at Cambridge."

"Of course you were. I could tell you were a man of learning. You are a decent good man trying to do your duty, I am sure, but where in this book," and she held the Bible high over her head, "is there mention of any of the colleges at Cambridge? Where does Christ say that such and such a school, no matter how fine, and I have no quarrel with Cambridge, makes a man more likely to see his way, or to lead others? 'Follow me' is all he tells us. He does not set out some syllabus."

"I know who you are, you know! You have not fooled me! You are one of those heretics whom they call Quakers."

"That is true. You have found me out, Leverich. I am not ashamed to admit that I am one of the Society of Friends, whom the world calls Quakers because we have been so struck with the inner light of Christ that we seem to quake. Here, feel my hand," she said, and put her hand into Goodie Gaunt's. "Don't you feel it shaking?"

Goodie Gaunt looked up at her with amazement, which told the whole congregation that the woman was indeed vibrating with some inner power.

"There is a quaking, is it not, my beloved?"

"If you have some quarrel with the religion which is taught here, tell me what it is, then. If not you have made a long journey in vain," said Mister Leverich.

"I have no quarrel with what these good people believe. My quarrel is only with how it shall be taught. I come here to teach the word of Jesus Christ as it was taught to His prophets and apostles."

"I know how it is with the Quakers. No one can say what you believe. It is all contradictions, puzzles, for any one of you thinks and says whatever he wishes. Unless you believe what George Fox tells you to believe. Is that the way it is with you? Are you just one of those who follows this George Fox?"

"I have heard him preach in England when I was young, and there is a great fire in him, but what I teach is what Christ has taught me, not George Fox, or any other man."

"The heresies of Fox are beyond counting, but let me tell you just a few: that the soul of man is without beginning and infinite; that it is contrary to the scriptures that God took it upon himself to have a human nature; and that nowhere in the scriptures is there proof of the trinity."

"I will not dispute the texts with you. I have not come all the way from Providence Plantation to argue some doctrines with you, Mister Leverich. All those are small change to the fire of Christ within these people. The rest is for some old graybeards at Cambridge to argue on a rainy day. The sun is shining brightly today. I am here to spread the news of Christ."

To my great surprise Elizabeth stood up then. I thought at first she would start to dispute with Mister Leverich as well, but instead she turned to the Quaker lady and said, "You are a woman. Know your place. You have no right to stand up in this assembly. It is not the custom of this congregation that a woman should speak in it unbidden. It may be otherwise in Rhode Island, but that is the way it is here. I have held my tongue as long as I can out of respect for the men here. It is not seemly and proper that a woman should speak as you have and in this place and to these good men set for your governance. Will not one of you be man enough to show her her place?" Elizabeth looked around at all of us. "Thomas!" she said, and I looked down at my boots.

"You are right, Goodie Burge," said Mister Leverich, and he left the pulpit and sat down and looked away as if the matter was now closed, to his great satisfaction.

After a moment of silence Goodman Freeman stood up, signaled to George Barlow who joined him, and they went to the Quaker woman. She stood her ground, her hands on her hips, staring at them, as if to challenge them to lay a hand on her.

"As a lesson to you, mistress, so that you will not do this again, I must sentence you to a day in the stocks," Edmund said.

"For being a woman? Is that, after all, why you will put me in the stocks?" she looked at Elizabeth who had now sat down again beside me. "To Christ there is neither man nor woman. We are all one in His eyes, and each as dear."

"I will take you now, mistress, before you bring a worse punishment upon yourself. I would have no hesitation to whip a woman for what you have done." George took her firmly by the arm.

"It is for being a woman then that I am being punished. I do not think there is a law, even in Plymouth, about what sex a person is born."

"No, of course not," Edmund said in a tired voice. "You are charged with breach of the peace."

"Breach of the peace!" she laughed. "It is that man in the black cap who has broken the peace." Mister Leverich realized then that he still had his preaching cap on and snatched it from his head, putting it in his sleeve.

George Barlow grabbed Mary Dyer roughly at that and took her out of the meeting.

Surely there is no soul in Sandwich who will ever forget that meeting and Sabbath day. We sat for a long time in stunned silence. Mister Leverich said nothing more, but just looked away, distracted.

Finally we all stood up and trooped out of the meeting in silence to see the Quaker lady in the stocks.

If it had been the intention to punish her it was a failure, for she sat in the stocks like some warrior, or martyr: a stunning picture. Few of the men in the village did not also notice she had a handsome ankle set up on view in the stocks, and the furbelows bordering her petticoats were not lost on us either.

Worse than her appearance in the stocks, soon she began to sing hymns. We tried to ignore this, continuing the visiting we usually did in town on the Sabbath, but she sang the hymns with gusto in a high sweet, clear voice and the children soon began to gather around her and sing along when she sang one familiar to them. She would then stop at times and look at them with such infectious love as they sang to her in the stocks, that quite a crowd began to form.

18

GEORGE BARLOW TOOK this about as long as he could and then came out to her in great anger.

"You are being punished here, woman. If this punishment is not sufficient to your crime I have others."

"I have been beaten by better men than you, sir," she replied, "and I no longer fear the whip."

"What sort of woman are you?"

"I am a soldier in the Lamb's War. In that army there are neither men nor women."

"What you need is a husband to put you straight and give you occupation."

"I have a husband, sir, in Rhode Island."

"And he lets you travel out in this way! What sort of man would do that?"

"A good man and a good friend. He makes the money so that I may continue my work. He has no aptitude for it, you see. And . . ."

"And what?"

"And he fears the fire. He is afraid he will be burned to death. He cannot abide that fear."

"Here, get away from her, you little longcoats," George shouted and started to drive the children away.

"No, please, they are a pleasure to me."

"Get away. This woman is being punished for her blasphemies. Get away! Take good instruction from her. This is what you will come to if you live as she does. You girls be governed by your husbands and you will not end up like this."

The area around the stocks was now full of people, and Mister Leverich and Edmund Freeman joined us from the meeting house. The Quaker began singing brightly again as though she were a traveling player, or some bird caught in a cage.

Edmund went up to her and said, "You must stop this singing."

"You may hold my foot fast so I cannot dance, but you would

have to pull my tongue out before you could stop my singing. It is the way the spirit of Jesus manifests itself in me."

"Whatever it is I cannot have you singing here."

He stood for a long time thinking and looking at the Quaker, who looked back at him with a fixed stare. "I will not have you whipped. I would not whip a woman, and I think you would rejoice under the lash."

"We have come to a problem we cannot solve then, haven't we?" she said sweetly.

Edmund continued to think. He was by nature a gentle man, but he had from the General Court a strong admonition not to suffer those who were not of the church and to keep order. At last he put his arm on the stocks, not looking at her, and said "You have done what you hoped to do here. There is not a person in this village who has not now seen a Quaker. There are surely quite a few who admire you, but I cannot tolerate you here. Do you understand that?"

"More of it than you would think."

"Yes, well, that is your calling. But I must keep the peace here, and I cannot with you here singing in the stocks."

"What shall we do then?"

"What indeed?"

They looked at each other for a time and an understanding seemed to be growing between them.

"Well, I have a suggestion which might serve both of our purposes."

"And what could that be?"

"You will give me leave to gather together all of these good people I can for a meeting tonight. You must not interfere with their coming, or punish them for it. If I fail to recruit them in the Lamb's War, then that will be that and I will go my way and you will have your village as it was before I came."

Mister Leverich broke in angrily, "You cannot do that!"

Edmund turned to him, "I can do whatever I want."

"Then I will take this to the General Court in Plymouth. The law is clear."

"I will have no martyrs butchered in my town, no armed uprisings. If Plymouth can come here and deal with this, fine. But it is not here and I am. I will do what I must." Turning back to her, he said "And if you should proselytize some to the Quaker faith here in Sandwich?"

"You will tolerate them here."

"I cannot protect them from the law."

"I know that. Christ will do that."

Mister Leverich broke in again angrily. "Surely you are not planning to engage your soul and the souls of all these in your charge and in mine in a contract drawn up with this witch?"

"If you do not hold your tongue I will hold it for you. This poor woman is no more a witch than you or I. If you have in mind burning witches you will not do it in this town." He turned back to the woman in the stocks. "What is your name?"

"My name is Mary Dyer."

"God be with you, Mary Dyer."

"And you are?"

"Edmund Freeman: I am headman of this town and Governor of Cape Cod."

"I am impressed."

"I am not, Mary Dyer. If I make a contract with you what will I gain?"

"I will have the meeting and then leave the town and not return unless I am invited by a Quaker meeting here."

"That's not much of a bargain, Mary."

"It is the best I can offer you."

"If you want my advice," said George Barlow, "I would send her to the General Court at Plymouth."

"Thank you, George, but I do not need your advice. Now Mary, you know there are no Quakers here. I suppose you would not consider going to another town?"

"No, thank you, Edmund. I have set my heart on Sandwich."

"I thought you might have. And you will not go back to Rhode Island for fear of our laws here in Plymouth?"

"I did not come all this way, Edmund, to give up because you have stocks or a prison for me. A prison is a palace to me, bread and water is cake and sweet cream, and the locks of these stocks are the finest jewelry I have ever worn."

Mister Leverich put his hand on Mary Dyer's shoulder. "Have some respect for the governor, girl, and do not call him by his given name. I will punish you myself if you don't learn some manners!"

"I will call him as I wish. No man is my better. We are all children in the eye of Christ, or do you study some gospel other than the one given to us by Christ? Are you getting familiar with me with your hand there upon my shoulder, old man?"

Mister Leverich removed his hand as if her shoulder had been a hot coal. "I was giving you good council, wench. I will show you my fondness to you by scourging your body with my whip."

"Control your temper, sir," Edmund said, standing between him and the woman. "Now, Mary Dyer, I am more inclined to have this town remembered as a place which once had a Quaker preach here than as a place of pilgrimage where a Quaker was burned. I have no need of a Joan of Arc and holy relics for sale on Cape Cod, as you surely know."

"I felt there might be some man of good sense in Sandwich, yes."

"Good sense!" Edmund laughed. "All right, all right, but do not be fooled by the fact that I will now choose to suffer a lesser evil. I am not a man of such small courage that I will not punish you if you break your bargain. You have leave to preach one night here and you will be gone in the morning. This is not a country fair either. It is dependent on you finding some person in the town who will, as a private citizen, give you lodging and allow you to speak to those he has invited to his home. I will go home to bed now, so will Mister Leverich, and so will my constable George Barlow. You hear me George! You will go to bed. And if some persons will go to some house, Mary Dyer, and you are there I will not know it."

"Will you unlock my leg?"

"Do you agree? Will you be gone by the morning?"

"I agree."

"Let her loose. She has obviously learned from this grave and just punishment the error of her ways."

"Is there some man here who dares to be my host this evening?"

Peter Gaunt stepped forward at once. "I would be honored to have you in my house."

"Thank you, friend."

Edmund started to walk away, but stopped at last and turned back. "I am off to my bed now. Fare well, madam, it is too bad you must leave in such haste, and there will not be another time for us to become better acquainted." He turned and walked slowly and deliberately to his house.

Mister Leverich started after him angrily. "You will regret this, Edmund. You will pay a dear price for this day's work."

George Barlow stood by the stocks defiantly, but it soon became clear there would be no victories here and he reluctantly followed Edmund Freeman.

The Quaker watched them in silence, one quiet tidal pool on a turbulent beach, and at last turned to us. "Thank you, my friends. If you love the Lord Christ and dare to put on His breastplate come to this good man's house tonight and we shall share the Lamb's War. Do not come for me. Come for yourself. Come for the love of Him."

We left the village that evening without a word among us, as though we were all secret conspirators and held some longing for sin closed up inside our hearts. We dared not look into each other's eyes as we passed for fear we might see temptation there. Mary Dyer had put out a scent of freedom among us and each of us would struggle with it in our own way before the night came. We left like pirates on the dock before a voyage, afraid to say a word about our destination for fear the beadle might hear us.

We walked quietly in the lanes, but when we came to our cottages every husband, wife, and their children had out this quarrel among themselves. In its way, it was the first flavor of the freedom Mary Dyer was bringing us. Some of us welcomed it and some feared it. If one spoke for all in a family, then that was decided without debate, and they would come to the Gaunt cabin like ducks with their ducklings, or stay safe from this infection in their own cabin that night. If a family could face an open discourse then, they sat down seriously and quietly by their fires that evening and resolved who would go and who would stay. If they lived life in the heat of their own tempers, there would be loud and bitter quarrels as though this was the matter which would divide them forever, and those who would go would stamp out at last into the night with their ears ringing, their minds thrown rudely from turmoil into unshakable resolution. If it was a family full of secrets and afraid to speak with each other for fear their true relationships might surface they would sit in a tense silence which none dared to break, and those who wished to hear the message of Mary Dyer would quietly creep away when night came.

Elizabeth and I were silent for a time, for there was a secret between us we did not want to touch. But at last she said to me at dinner: "You are going to hear her, aren't you?"

"I had planned to. Yes."

"I am not surprised," she said, looking down at her plate. "She is a pretty girl, isn't she, and you were obviously attracted to her at the meeting. If you were not you would have spoken up when I did. You would have stood up on my behalf. Do not deny it! Everyone in the meeting could see that, Thomas."

"I am not going there for that reason."

"Of course you are, do you think I am a fool? What other reason, then? Are you in need of sermons from women half your age? Or is the sermon in her kiss curls and not in her head?"

"I am going because I want to hear what she may have to say. That can make no injury."

"Oh yes, has listening to heresy now become a fashion in Sandwich, like the falbalas in Mary Dyer's petticoats?"

"Come with me then, Elizabeth, and you will see if I am lusting after her, or interested only in what she might have to say."

"Go to her? Never!"

"Why not?"

"I have more of a care for my immortal soul than to go and listen to heresies."

"How do you know they are heresies until you have heard them?"

"They are, Thomas. Please listen to me. I care for what becomes of you, although you may not believe it. Listen to me. She is a witch."

"Why do you say that?"

"Thomas, look how she has bewitched the hearts of the most steadfast men in the village. Look what she has done to Master Freeman."

"She is no more a witch than you are."

"Now you call me a witch. See what she has worked on you!"

"No."

"You never have any regard for my opinion. That's no surprise to me. You never have. She is a witch. Didn't you see her eyes: the eye that captures? That is the hallmark of a witch. Didn't you look at them? Are you blind? Are the men here blinded by her curls so they did not see what is hidden behind them? Didn't you see her casting a spell on Goodman Freeman at the stocks?"

"He had pity on her. That is all. There is no harm in hearing her. Hearing her does not make you a Quaker."

"Yes it does, Thomas. I warn you. Yes it does."

"Elizabeth, talk sense!"

"I know, I know, you think I am a fool. But you will see. She is here to bewitch us. She has the mask of sin. Look into her eyes!"

"I am going. You can come with me or not. But I am going."

Elizabeth took hold of my arm and dug her nails in. There was a wildness about her. "You must not go, Thomas! I will not let you go!"

"I will."

She looked deep into my eyes. The intensity of her look disturbed me, as though she were about to do me some violence, or as though she were trying to see into my soul. It frightened me. And always there, but clearer now behind the china blue, a coldness, a message, and a secret which I could not read. "If you go, Thomas you will not find me here when you return."

"How would that be different? You are never here. You are always at your father's house. You are married to him."

"I am in earnest. If you go to that witch woman tonight I will never come to you again."

"You cannot force me to your will, Elizabeth, by threats."

"This is not some quarrel between us you can put right with some light words later. This is a matter of sin and your soul. I will not live with a man bewitched. Do not go to that witch woman tonight!"

"I want to hear her. I am not alone. Others also will come to hear her."

"Do you want to hear her more than you want me here in this house with you? More than you want me in your bed?"

"That isn't fair. I am only going to hear a woman speak, after all."

"I will not be here when you come back. Know that. This is not an idle threat."

"I must go, Elizabeth. I am my own man and have a right to do what I wish to do."

"Then go," she said coldly, and looked down so I could no longer see her eyes, but I knew from the set of her body that she was resolute.

Could I give in and prove myself a slave to her before the world? Was I so small a man that she could abuse me into anything she wished against my will? If I were a slave now would I not be a slave forever? Am I such a coward that my wife may rule who I may visit and who I may not? I am invited as a guest to Peter Gaunt's, after all.

I stood up and started for the door at last. At the latch I stopped and turned back, "It is not too late for you to change your mind and come with me. I would like your company, Elizabeth." But she sat silent as a stone, looking down at her hands, her body tense and motionless.

I turned away from her out of the firelight.

19

MY STEP WAS light on the path. I felt a freedom in my stride as if a string tying me to a cliff had broken and I was swinging free into the unknown. I felt more the man, a free man, as I walked with a brisk step toward the Gaunt's cottage. I could have sung a song into that night, but there was also some fire in my inner self, a little child crying, a fearful child reluctant to go out into the storm, a child chilled through in the rain, a child full of loss and alone.

But when I came within sight of the Gaunt's cottage the excitement rose in me again. I was my own man for once, neither husband nor son, but my own. The light from the cabin windows was candlelight and warm, and the place was full of my neighbors, busy and talking all at once. There was a feeling of celebration and expectation. Everyone greeted me. There was such a crowd in the small front room that we had to sit on the floor and in each others' laps. Children sat on the ladder treads with their legs dangling, or clung to their mothers. Those who could not get in huddled around the doors and windows, looking in and hearing what they could. The Gaunts and the Feakes were the only couples from the older generation of the founders of the village who were there. Some men and women from my generation were there, but most, like me, came alone. Of the younger couples, however, almost all were there. My brothers were there and my sister Elizabeth with the man she was espoused to: Ezra Perry. Ezra always seemed a little stiff to me for a man of twenty, but he was devoted to Elizabeth and would go wherever she would go. I wondered what a struggle there had been at that house before those children were allowed by my mother to come here. Elizabeth and Ezra would surely marry soon. Their time was come like the time of the salmon in the streams, and some children surely waited that moment to pop into the world. Richard Bourne was there, also without his wife as I was, and we shook hands warmly and exchanged the Indian greeting.

The Gaunts were gathered in the centre of the room. Peter is a gentle, long man with heavy gray eyebrows and a ruddy, cheerful face. You might set him down in any English village at some sheep auction on a market day and you could not have told him from any other yeoman there. His wife, on the other hand, is a prim lady, only just turning gray, so fastidious and careful in her every action you would think her a deacon's wife at least. Their oldest, Mehitable, was nineteen, not a pretty girl, tall and lean with a sharp bone here and there about her, but with great energy and seriousness. Her brother, Zachariah, was a year younger and very influenced by her. The two youngest sons, who were then fifteen and thirteen, are Israel and Hannaniah. The youngest daughter, Lydia, was then seventeen. She has her father's heavy eyebrows, but beneath them large light brown eyes sparkling with mischief. Her frequent smile masters her face fully, starting just at her mouth's corner and then by sly degrees spreading to a dimple, and then to her cheeks. She is a dear warm girl who could make you a friend and inspire your confidence. You always wished you might know what bit of a prank or joke she was thinking about that made her smile so. I had known her all these years and seen her playing roughhouse with her brothers, as serious Mehitable never did, but never marked her as a woman before that night. She was surely that now and her bright look took my breath away when she turned it upon me. As Goodman Gaunt instructed, I sat down beside Lydia on the floor. She laughed when our bodies touched so that I was sure the company had seen me blush. I held my breath and hoped my eyes would not give me away to her. I felt a great urge to put my arm around this small, dark, happy girl and share her warmth, but, of course, I did not. As it was, I hoped they realized I was only a family friend, as I surely was no more than that to her, I thought, and not being forward to this young girl by sitting so close to her.

Sitting on the hearth with her skirts spread out about her was Mary Dyer. She seemed much warmer and gentler in the light of the fire than she had at the meeting. She was as neat and well turned out there on the hearth as if she had never seen the stocks that day or exchanged the slightest hard word with a governor, a minister, or a village constable.

"Now the light of Christ burns in us all," she said, "but in some it burns brighter than in others for they have let it shine through and in others the less for they shade it over. So it is the custom of the Society of Friends to sit for a time in absolute silence. As still as mice now, you children. And in that silence to let the light begin to shine. Let all that you have done today and all your life and every sound and sight and thing pass away. Then like magic, or like standing long in the darkest night, in a few moments, or in a half hour, you will begin to be aware of a warmth and a light deep inside you, or you may hear a dear soft voice within you. Do not be afraid. Do not fight it. Let it come out. For that is Jesus Christ in all of you. He may council with you on what has happened in the day, or what you have heard on the road, or on the secret things in your soul. It may seem too large to speak about, or too trivial, but open your mouth and tell us, we are your friends and no matter is too trivial to interest us and no matter so large that you may not trust us with it. Tell us what Christ has made you think. Say anything, or ask anything, and all of us who are now in touch with Christ will answer it. Not all of our answers will be the same, not because Christ changes, but because there are many answers, and friends may share their many answers to find those which are best. Christ is alive within us, I am no minister, He will answer you, and when I am gone He will still answer you as well as when I am here. He has no ministers. You are His ministers, every one of you, and you must minister to each other and to all the world as friends: as friends to all mankind.

"Now close your eyes, dear friends, and clear your minds and wait in silence for him. Some days will come in which there is nothing but the silence, but he is within it still. He is waiting for you to hear him."

There was then a stillness such as I have never experienced before, not even alone in the marsh: a silence to lie in, to float in, a silence of infinite peace and contentment. It was a stillness so real you felt you could touch it. At first, I had to labor to drive out a flood of worldly ideas and pains which tried to rush in like a swarm of bees to fill and choke out the silence. But as it went on for a quarter of an hour or more the distractions turned away one at a time as if they gave up the struggle, and as each did I became more alone and also more a part of the friends around me, my mind purer and cleaner.

As the silence became clear as spring water I could feel a stirring. I could feel a warm spirit deep within me and I recognized it as my own and yet not my own. I felt the others beside me as more of a community than I had ever known and I knew they had also found their spirits. I could feel them shiver as they made contact and I shivered too. I knew what was meant then by "trembling at the word of God."

At last Mary Dyer said, "You are truly the people of primitive Christianity revived. The friends Christ called for in his preaching when He walked on the earth. The people who need no priests because they are always with the real and personal Christ. Tell me what Christ tells you. Ask us all the questions Christ puts in your mind."

"I was thinking of my mother near Cornhill where I shall never see her again," said Peter Gaunt.

"She may hear you now, Peter."

One of the little children said, "I am frightened."

"Come to me then," said Mary Dyer, and took the little girl into her lap at the fireside. "There is nothing to be afraid of. There are no devils here. There are no punishments here. We are all friends. No one is evil here. Everyone is good and loves you. You have a family you love and trust. Now all of these people here are your brothers and sisters too. None are fathers and mothers here, all are brothers and sisters. No one tells you what to do, or how to act. No one needs to cry here." She held the little girl's head to her breast for a moment. "Feel the warmth. Now let me look deep into your eyes." Mary then held the child's head gently between her hands. "I see a little flame deep within you. That little flame is Christ's candle. He is waiting in there by His candle waiting for you to find him. Look deeply. Do you see that little fire in my eyes too?"

"I see the firelight reflected in them."

Mary laughed with a relaxed, sweet laugh and kissed her. We all laughed with her, and looked into each other's eyes, seeing the firelight in them.

"Yes, that is the fire of Christ," Mary said, "and I pass it to you as you will pass it to another friend, and that will be a joyful friend you never knew you had before."

"I see it now," the child said, and put her arms around Mary's neck. She sat there happily in Mary Dyer's lap all that long night with her head on Mary's breast.

"You are now one of the children of light," Mary said to her. "I am not telling you about a religion as you have known religions, my friends. I am telling you about a way of life whose message is responsibility for the rest of mankind, release from fear, release from all authority, release from all guilt, and feeling true love. Every man and woman is a priest and as you are shaken shake others." She began to sing softly "Holy, holy, holy, Lord God of Israel . . ." and we joined in.

"I am afraid of the Devil. Every morning when I get up I look into every corner of the house where he might hide," said Abigail Knot. "I have feared him ever since I was little. My mother told me he never sleeps. Every night before I go to bed I look under it to see if he is crouching there — waiting for me to sleep."

"Even when you are asleep Christ is in you and he is awake. Have no fear of devils or men. They can never touch that little flame for all they may try to do to your body. You have a helmet of hope and salvation and a breastplate of love in the Lamb's War. We may be in an ocean of darkness, but through it runs a sea of light. I tell you through the friends you make here today, you need never again fear or flee evil in this world. Love the world. Its darkness will wash over you and be gone because you are a part of the sea of light. Tonight as you lie in bed search out the watchman Christ in you and fear no devils."

"Oh, what a happy day!" said Sarah Freeman. It was not until that moment that I realized the headman's favorite daughter was also there and I wondered how uneasily he lay in his bed tonight.

"But what if your life is too much to bear? What if every evening you live in fear?" said Mistress Feake, and her eyes grew wide and startled as though she had not meant to say that, and now was sorry she had.

"What are you afraid of?"

"Be still," said her husband, and she looked down and would say no more.

"We all will take it from you. Share it no matter how secret. We are all friends here. No one here will criticize you. There is no punishment here. We are all your dearest friends this night."

"No, I cannot say."

"Say it!"

"I should not have spoken. Please listen to someone else."

We sat in silence for a long time until at last Henry Feake stood up. "I can say."

"Please! No, Henry. Please."

"It is all right, my dear. Everyone here knows it anyway, although no one ever talks about it to us. They see how you look and pretend they see nothing. But now I will say it. I will face it myself now. Sometimes I have a demon who comes into me." He stopped for a time and everyone in the room was dead still, knowing what he would say. "This demon blinds me to the beauty and love of my dear wife, and I see her as though she were someone else, or not a person at all, and I strike her. The demon in me then rejoices and tells me she is to blame I hit this woman I love very dearly. I hit her, my friends. Not just once, but frequently. So frequently it is a part of our life like going to bed at night. As simple as that. Like going to bed at night."

"Oh, Henry!" said his wife, and she began to cry, her head down in her arms.

"Now judge me, punish me now!"

Mary Dyer smiled at him. "Now, you are truly a friend of all of us. We will help you if we can. We are not here to judge, but to help each other find Christ within us. He is within you. We love you. Your wife loves you. Christ will find a way."

"I know my wife loves me, but that makes no difference when the demon enters me. I cannot stop myself."

"As one of us, delight to do no evil. Come to one of us when you feel your anger rising. Now we know we can help you. Now, as a friend, hope to outlive wrath and contention. Put all evil out of yourself and look for none in others. If any man betrays you bear it. Let your crown be meekness. When you feel wrath growing think of all of us, be silent, put all your thoughts away, find the candle's flame of Christ, search out a friend, and embrace him. You will see. And good woman, do not let yourself be beaten. Call on a friend."

"But I must be governed by my husband."

"Why? Who has told you that? I am not governed by my husband. I am a true friend and companion to my husband. I owe him the care he owes to me. I am not his chattel, or a bond servant to him. A woman is worth the same as a man."

We sat for a time in stunned silence. No one had ever suggested such a thing to any of us and the idea seemed mad.

"Am I not a woman?" Mary said. "And look at me. There is nothing any man has done I have not done."

Then Joseph Holway stood up abruptly so we thought he would take up the argument, but he had been struck with another thought entirely. He was a gangly, clumsy youth of perhaps eighteen. "We love each other: Deborah and I. But Mister Leverich will not let us marry because he thinks I am too young and our parents do not agree to it."

"If you are in love, then marry her."

"We cannot without Mister Leverich's permission."

"Why not? He is just a man as you are and has no more of a light than you do. Consult Christ within you. Then guide your own life. Christ will guide you, not Mister Leverich."

"But he must conduct our marriage."

"Why? When you marry you are agreeing between yourselves to love each other. It is no one else's business. You do not need to blaspheme by taking some oath. You are not agreeing to love Mister Leverich, I hope. You are not selling corn to Deborah or setting yourselves up in business. You need no ceremony to promise your love, do you? Take yourselves into the fields, or by the seashore as my husband and I did, or into a meeting of these good friends and tell each other of your love and promise whatever you will promise to each other. Promise to love each other always and keep that promise. You don't need Mister Leverich's made up words to tell her about your love, do you? Your own are much better."

We all sat quiet again.

To my surprise Richard Bourne then stood up. "I must not kill my friends the Indians."

"The commandments say thou shalt not kill anyone. That is true," said Mary Dyer, touching the hair of the child who was now asleep in her lap. "No cause is so great that you should break that commandment."

"But the General Court will punish me if I do not muster to a call to arms."

"Yes, but how much worse the punishment for breaking that commandment. I would not kill any person no matter what they might do."

"They say: 'These are only Indians;' but I know they have souls just as we do."

"Yes, yes, oh yes, my dear friend. Yes, the little light of Christ is in them too, although they have never heard his name."

"What should I do then when I am told to bear arms?"

"I cannot tell you that. But if I were a man I would tell them I will not serve."

"Tell that to the servants of the Court?"

"Nothing gives them the right to speak to you and you not speak back to them. If all of us refuse for the sake of our souls what the colony asks us to do in peril of them then we will make this Plymouth colony a blessed place as Rhode Island is."

"I can't do what you say," said Richard slowly. "There are laws to govern us. I cannot say those are someone else's laws. I should wonder if Christ would really be with me then."

"In Revelations Christ says: 'Behold I stand at the door and knock. If any man hear my voice and open the door I will come in to him.'"

After another silence Mehitable Gaunt stood up and her eyes were bright. "I want to be like you and carry the word."

Mary Dyer did not answer for a long while and when she did she seemed very grave. "If you do, Mehitable, remember there is always a safe place for you in Rhode Island. In this colony there is a state church and the church is the state. There is no state church on Rhode Island or in the Providence Plantation. You will be safe there. Here you will never be safe. Let me tell you the story of what it was like for me and for a dear friend when we first came to this colony.

"We came on a little ship called *the Swallow*. We sailed into Boston harbor in 1656. The colony feared us as if we had been some army coming to their shores to capture them, but we were only two poor women seasick from our crossing and eager for some rest. Governor Endicott was away and his deputy Richard Bellingham would not let us leave the ship, sick as we were, and would not even let the ship tie up properly so that the captain felt we were in some danger should a wind rise. You see, Bellingham hoped we would give up and go to some other port, but we had not come all that way to give up. We had in our boxes more than one hundred books our dear friends in Leicestershire had gathered for us to use in this new land. At last, the Deputy Governor's curiosity got the better of him and he allowed the ship to tie up, but he searched all of our baggage, sorting out the books which he then gave to the common hangman, and made us watch while that man burned them all on the Boston Common. What harm had those little books done? What sins were bound into them that they should be burned?

"They then took us very roughly under guard and through jeering crowds to jail, and there they locked us up without food for

133

several days so that I thought they might starve us. Finally, one morning they came into our cell where we were praying, called us witches, and took us out into a courtyard. All the prison cells looked out into this courtyard and they must have told the prisoners that there would be a show that day because they were all at their windows with their hairy arms hanging out through the bars. Two prison keepers slowly stripped us naked in sight of the Deputy Governor and officers of the court and all the prisoners saying all the foul things they could think to say about us. When we were naked they let us stand that way for a time and then the judges came to us and began to search our bodies with their dirty hands. I can remember their eager hands on my breasts. They searched every part of our body for pentagrams or other signs of the devil on our skin. Thanks be to God, they could find no set of marks upon us they could imagine to be Satan's, though they tried. Thank God, for if they had they would have burned us, as they had burned our books. I was so frightened I could not speak. They even put their fingers into our private places searching, they said, for alchemized coins or other amulets of the devil.

"I have put that out of my mind, but it is one of many humiliations I have had at the hands of this colony because I am a member of the Friends. I hate to think of it and do not ask for your pity. I deliberately put myself in their hands. I knew them. I tell it only so that you, Mehitable, may know what this particular ministry can be like. Women are the most vulnerable, because they can humiliate us with their desires, and we have little defense against that. God save you, Mehitable Gaunt, if you try it. Only Christ can tell you if that is for you as it was for me."

We then sat a long time in a perfect and cleansing silence.

Lydia then said quietly, "I too have a secret love as Joseph does, but I have never told it. I love an older man who is married. I have never told him."

"Look into yourself and ask Christ if that is right and he will answer you."

We talked on through the whole night and never felt tired. But

134

morning did come at last and Mary Dyer reminded us of her promise to Edmund Freeman. She gathered up her things and loaded them onto a horse which Peter had given her. She walked beside it and others came with her to show her the road.

It was a morning as yellow as butter just turned in the churn: a clean, clear morning, a morning of the faith of light in a land of darkness, as we all thought then. Mary Dyer promised us that if Christ had not set some other business for her she would try to come back to Sandwich in the following year. We promised her a welcome, but as it turned out Christ did have another plan for her, a very special plan of his own, and we were not to see her in Sandwich again.

20

WHEN I REACHED home Elizabeth was gone as she had said she would be. She was always a woman of her word; although I had somehow thought this time she might not have meant it. It was such a small thing I had asked. Why could she not have granted it to me? No matter, I was more than glad I had been at the Gaunt's that night. No price would have been too high, I thought. She will return. She did not return, however.

I was too exhausted to go to her father's for her as I had been up all night and the sun was now just touching our door. On a normal day I would have been out in the field by now and Elizabeth on her way to her father's. My head was aching, but I was at the same time excited by all the new and wonderful ideas of redemption and release I had heard that night and with anger at Elizabeth for leaving, for her closed mind. At once I felt a freedom I had never before even known could exist and at the same time a slavery to my wife which only now became apparent to me. I wanted to shuck off the memory of her, sing a new song and find a new world, and at the same time I felt bonds which tied me to her. I had promised her my love. She had fearfully fashioned her life all on my promise of love. Only an icy and distant watcher could dash that young girl's daring commitment based only on my word. My word: what would my word be worth if I should break it in this most essential thing?

As I looked out the window of our cabin I could see her sitting by me in the bastinados and again in the apple orchard. There was a commitment of memories in common. There was also love, both physical and emotional. I did love her. What she did, what petty hurts, was not a measure full against the love I had for her. But she had left me. She had broken the bond and the contract and I had not. She said by that gesture of defiance that she held the contract vacant. I had no commitment to that little blonde head beside me in the loft, because she felt no commitment to me. If I went to her what would I say? The very sight of my abject figure slouching onto her father's land like some runaway dog returning would make me a mark for anything she cared to do. It would be a surrender and a defeat. She had never been gentle to the vanquished before. What might she say to cut into me then? What price would there be? And in the end what she said might drive me away and then I would have fought a battle with no hope of resolution. Or would she, seeing me humbled, take me in her arms in forgiveness and return to our home, to our life together? I could not picture that. There would be a price from her no matter what. What if I should join the Quaker meeting? That would surely be forbidden. Would she still live with her father in all the daylight hours and only give me those silent times by the fire, and stand a patient object of my guilty passions in the night? Did I want that relationship again? Could I pay that price? Or would I be happier here on my own?

Perhaps she would come back on her own in time: humbled by missing me. Then, what price might I exact of her? Would I forgive her and take her in my arms again? Or would I demand of her a new contract of love? Would I demand that she show her love to me, participate in our mutual love, and serve the duties of a wife cheerfully and not churlishly? That she would not set her father above me in her love? If I could I would ask a child of her. I almost cried at this thought. That is a price for our reunion neither of us could ask, but both of us would if we could. If she returned, what would I do with my anger? Would I be forced to hold it tight in my chest until it choked me? Would I be able to air all the complaints this ten years had built up in my head as I lay awake at night?

In fact, I knew what our reunion would be if it came. Yes, I knew that very well; it would be a silent reunion: a reunion without resolution. We would simply come together again out of habit and duty as we always had, our love, if it is there at all, hidden beneath our silence and deep within our bodies, while our hatred was every day under our fingernails. One day she would come back in as though she had never been gone. She would put her basket away. She would hang a pot on the crane. She would put a new sheet on the bed. She would busy herself in the sunlight in her old blue dress, and we would sit again at night tongue-tied beside the fire. That would be our reunion.

I found she had taken the bedding as a last little bitter barb in parting and that night I lay on the ropes, but could not sleep.

Planting was done at last and high summer was upon us before I had time for my own thoughts. They always turned, however, to Elizabeth. No matter how I would push the thought of her away it would come back unexpectedly at each familiar place on the land, or in the house where she would have been doing this or that had she only been there to do it. These thoughts would sometimes startle me as if someone had come upon me around a corner. Some days I even started out to her father's house with the thought in my mind that I would go to her and ask her to come home with me. Not a word came to me all those long months from her. Not a word! I was a lonely prisoner at the plow, a solitary watcher in the night. She could be dead for all I knew of her, and I could be dead for all she knew of me.

I could have gone to her, but pride is a brawny wrestler. Each time I went along that road east of Sandwich I would come to a stop as if I had come to a turnpike and had no penny for the man who turns the pike. I would stand there for a long time like an old horse asked to go an unfamiliar way when his time has come to return to the barn, and then I would slowly turn back, my pace quickening as I returned to Sandwich and set that path behind me. I saw her at meeting, but we did not speak. Trial almost spoke to me one afternoon on the road, but I hurried on as if I had not seen her.

One day I felt certain I would give in and take the road to her father's, hoping to meet her somewhere before I reached his house. I actually walked to where I could see it, then started back and forth several times, giving it up at last. I walked on feeling burned and sweating, for it was a hot day, to a beach I knew where I could cool off in the sea breeze. I could see a woman sitting there in her long dress and little cap on an old log and I walked clumsily toward her in the sand. She was very silent, looking intently out into the offing where the sea and sky were the palest blue. The two of us seemed incongruous and overdressed for such a meeting, but I was curious to know what woman would come here to my beach.

21

As I came closer I saw that it was Lydia Gaunt. I knew the log she was sitting on very well. I had often sat there thinking what a journey it must have had in the sea up from the southern colonies. It was broad and as smooth as if a carpenter had worked at it for years, and in a way the sand in the sea rolling it over and over in the breakers had been that carpenter.

She looked up at me as I approached and her face lit up with that sly smile which had so captured me at her father's house. "Thomas Burge, God has put you here on this beach just as I was most in need of your comfort. Sit here with me."

"Hello Lydia," I said, but I did not sit down for fear of the attraction she had for me and that someone else might see us there, not knowing our meeting was innocent. "I am not much of a comfort I am afraid, Lydia. I am not very good at talking."

"Don't be silly. You are the most interesting man in Sandwich and I always love to hear you talk."

I sat down.

"I need someone to talk to," she said, and she tucked her dress under her to make room for me with such a delicate feminine gesture and a bright look of confidence that I am sure I blushed. "Mary Dyer kept her bargain with Edmund Freeman and left, but George Barlow has not kept Edmund Freeman's bargain with her. He has posted a warrant at Sandwich for my father's arrest, and he has taken him to the sitting of the General Court at Plymouth for trial."

"What are the charges?"

"Tumultuous carriage at a meeting of Quakers at Sandwich."

"But we met quietly, and at a private house, and with permission of the head man of the village: Edmund Freeman."

"You and I know that, Thomas, but Mister Alden does not."

"I will go to Plymouth, Lydia, and tell him."

"No, dear Thomas," she said taking my hand in hers, "It is too late. They left yesterday. I need you now, here, Thomas; if my father is to be imprisoned or worse, I want your council and your protection."

"You know you can count on that."

"I am especially afraid for my father because this is not the first time he has been taken to the court at Plymouth."

"I didn't know that. When was he taken?"

"Five years ago. Long before Mary Dyer came. He is an Anabaptist."

"I knew that."

"You did? I thought no one knew that."

"He told me one night when we met at my father's spring."

"We often gather at that spring. It is a sort of church to my father, who is almost alone in his faith here, and has no meeting-house."

"It is a strange and yet a good place. The Indians say a spirit lives in the spring."

"I am very afraid, Thomas," she said and shivered. I put my arm around her as if it were a winter day, but it was very warm.

"Five years ago he was called before the court with the Allens, who are notorious Anabaptists. Richard Kerby, Rose Newland, Goodwife Turner, and the widow Knott were also called under the charge of not frequenting public worship as the law requires. The others were fined or released, but then John Alden came to father. Mister Alden issued a severe warning that if father should ever be called before that court again he would see to it that father paid a high price."

"Why did he single your father out?"

"Father refused to take off his hat in the court, and when Mister Alden questioned him about why he would not go to the meeting he said he 'knew no public worship now in the world' and that made Mister Alden very angry."

I laughed. "I am not surprised that made the old fellow angry. I like your father."

"I am very frightened for him, Thomas."

"Of course you are. I am sorry. It was a foolish thing for him to say but a brave one too. And now we know he is right."

"Thomas, I don't care about the rightness of it, or the religion of it. I only care about my father. I love him and I wish he were not so brave." And when she looked at me she had tears in her eyes. I held her very close. We were silent and I no longer cared who might see us there.

"Now here he is called before the court again, Thomas."

"It is not a serious crime he is charged with. Surely Mister Alden will have forgotten what he said if he is there at all."

"I have heard they are doing terrible things to Quakers."

"It is only another way of worshiping God. They surely cannot punish a person for being a Christian."

140

"Even if they fine him as they did last time there is no money to pay a fine."

"Money can always be found, or the fine forgiven."

"Don't let go. Please keep holding me. I feel much better when I am with you."

We sat there looking out at the sea, watching one little boat, dipping first to the port, then righting itself to stand as tall as a minister in his pulpit, then bending again to starboard as it tacked against a warm summer wind. She put her head on my shoulder and pressed her body into mine as if we would become one with the old log and each other.

At last I brushed her hair back and said softly to her, "I must walk you home now, Lydia. Your mother will wonder where you have gone, and she will need you at this time. Perhaps your father is already home from Plymouth." She seemed reluctant, but at last we did both get up and start to walk down the beach, hand in hand. The dune grass was motionless and we might be walking into a drawing, but for the slight movement of the waves where they broke and the turning of a gull in the cloudless sky. Another gull walked with us for a way on the beach, circling around us in great arcs in the sand, then flying ahead and arcing around us again, looking at us with her hard eyes outlined in black. I told Lydia that gull was surely one of God's goodies looking at us disapprovingly, and she laughed and put her arm around my waist.

As we walked I spotted a shell and bent down to scoop it up. I knocked the sand off it and found it was perfect. The first of its kind I had ever found without some part missing. I put it in Lydia's hand. It was just big enough to fit into her palm, a fine wentletrap with four turnings, tall and pointed sharply with its ridges clear and sharp as if it had been made by a tiny carpenter, as if it were a tiny white steeple from the sea. "The spirit of the sea has sent you this little church tower, Lydia, as a sign your father will be safe."

I closed her hand around it, raised the little fist to my lips, and kissed it. "Now it is sealed, and his safety is assured."

Her eyes sparkled as she opened her hand and held the little perfect shell up. "I will always keep it, Thomas."

We walked on up the beach with our arms around each other and her head on my shoulder as if I had truly been free. The sound of the waves set a rhythm with our walking which made the beach seem endless and the heat was an aphrodisiac which made me feel that this walk might go on forever and there be no price to pay for the innocent affection we felt sharing our problems and our small joys. My shirt was unbuttoned now in the heat and she had unlaced her front; we both had our shoes off and we laughed as we walked and talked. What a picture we must have made! What a story would pass around the village if we were ever seen, but there was a freedom palpable in the salt air. It was the freedom which makes the gulls whirl around in the sky as the wind carries them from Virginia to Labrador, climbing up the winds rising from the warm currents flowing always to the north.

Finally, we came to a rising dune with a copse of pitch pine on it and we climbed up it, laughing and sliding back until, almost on our hands and knees, we were in the fragrant nest of fallen needles, hidden among the branches.

Lydia picked a salt spray rose. The trees hid us as though we had for a moment crawled into a private place and Lydia grasped my hand more firmly to stop me before I stood up.

I looked at her in surprise, but her look was clear, and sure, her eyes full of laughter. Her hair was wild and windblown and her dress open so that I could see a hint of her small breasts. She put her free hand on my chest, let go the other, and drew me to her. She pulled me down and kissed me on the mouth. I had only a moment's hesitation, but then with the summer heat, the smell of the salt air, the pine needles, and the feel of her body so close to mine I could not resist and all reason flew away with the cry of the gulls. Her body as I held it close was balm for many empty nights. Her hand slipped up into the hair at the back of my neck and I kissed her with all the pentup passion of a decade of longing for love without guilt. Her voice, full of laughter and joy, tore away any last vestige of guilt in my mind.

We kissed again and I marveled at how her body fit so firmly into my embrace, as though God had designed just this one small woman to fit into my arms without a space between us: like some wonderfully crafted key elegantly designed to fit its lock. It was a moment of afternoon alchemy in that stand of pines. Then, with genuine amazement I realized where I was and who I was, how young the girl was I held in my arms and that I had a wife: estranged but still my wife.

"Lydia, Oh, Lydia, I am sorry."

"I am not, Thomas. I brought you here for this."

"I have a wife, Lydia."

"You have no wife. Where is she? You have no wife."

"I do."

"Do you love her, Thomas?"

"Lydia, that is between us."

"No. It is between us. I love you, Thomas. I have asked Christ if it is sinful for me to love you and he has told me it is not. He sent you to me on this beach, on this day."

"Lydia, this is madness."

"Yes, Thomas. Because love is madness. Kiss me. You know you want to."

"Yes, of course I do. But I am married to another woman."

"Not in the eyes of God. In His eyes you love me. Why shouldn't we enjoy our love? No one can tell us we cannot love."

"Lydia, I am much older than you are. You are a young girl with a life ahead of you. I have already lived most of my life. There is some young man waiting for you. I am too old."

"I know how old you are, Thomas. You are not old, and what has age to do with anything? Look at me, Thomas. Look into my eyes and tell me you don't love me too."

"We have to go now, Lydia. Your mother will be worried. You may be needed."

"I won't go until you answer me." She sat there looking up at me with wide serious eyes of a soft brown which matched the brown of the fallen pine needles, but I could still see the hint of laughter in them like a touch of gold and I wondered if she could be serious, if this could be happening at all and, what I should do?

"I cannot tell you, Lydia. What am I to do with you?"

"Kiss me, Thomas. Kiss me now and I will go."

I did kiss her, held her close, and felt her heart beating. I had thought to kiss her as an uncle might kiss his niece, but there was no hope of that. I was no uncle to her and she no niece to me.

We dusted ourselves off, picked the burrs and the pine needles off each other. I buttoned my shirt and she laced her bodice with a provocative look at me as we put on our shoes and began to make it out onto the path to Sandwich soberly, as though we had no secret between us. But we did have a secret and would from that time on.

22

As we approached the Gaunt's house we could hear voices raised and when we turned the corner and came out of the trees we saw the scene spread out on the porch. There was George Barlow with his long gun as though he were threatening Goodie Gaunt, and she with her son Israel tucked in her skirts and holding her hand on Mehitable as though she were holding her back.

"Oh, no!" Lydia whispered, "There is George Barlow, but where is father and my brothers?"

I hurried on and caught George by the arm.

"Thomas, this is none of your business, and you had better stay out of it!" George said looking at me in anger.

"Let the women and children alone, George."

"I am here on business of the law, Thomas, and you had better not interfere with that business or I will have you before the General Court as well."

"Come away, George, and tell me what your business is."

"My business is with this family of Quakers, not with you. Get out of the way."

"Calm down, George. Get control of yourself!"

"I will not be instructed by you, Thomas Burge! I have business here and you do not."

"You are frightening them."

"I have reason to frighten them. I have business here. What are you doing here?"

"That is not the matter."

"Are you a Quaker too? Do you need a lesson too, as this family has?"

"What are you talking about? What lesson have they had?"

"Master Barlow has come here to take our cattle," said Goodie Gaunt.

"Is that correct, George? Are you here stealing their cattle?"

"This is no business of yours, Thomas!"

"If you are stealing cattle, it is everyone's business. That you are sheriff does not give you license to persecute these women. You have a problem with your temper, George."

"My problem is with you now. You are obstructing the carriage of justice here. Very well, Thomas Burge, you butt in where you have no business, where you do not know the facts, but I will mark you for another time for this obstruction. I have just returned, as this woman knows, from the General Court at Plymouth where her husband stands accused of entertaining Quakers."

"There is no law against that, is there, George?"

"If there is not now there soon will be. The court issued me this judgement against the property of Peter Gaunt on behalf of the village to take seven cows and heifers, two steers, and seven and one-half bushels of peas. Here you can see it written down. If you do not know the hand of John Alden your father does."

"Let me look at the paper, George."

"Here it is. You should be helping a servant of the court, not obstructing him."

"Where is Goodman Gaunt now?"

"He is still at the court. I came on ahead."

I read the paper and it was as he had said. "Perhaps Peter is pleading now for relief from this judgement. You should wait, George, until that appeal is finished."

"I will not wait. I have a warrant here and I plan to serve it and take home what is now mine."

"This judgement does not make the property yours."

"Yes it does. For my service to the village. You know nothing of the law."

"George, just wait to serve this until Peter returns. These women cannot drive cattle for you. If you will wait I will promise that I will drive the cattle to you. I will promise for Peter. He is a good man; he will not cheat you."

"Why should I believe your promise? You may be a lying Quaker too for all I know."

"You should trust me because you have known me since we were both no older than Lydia here. You should trust me because my father has often been representative of this village to the General Court. Come to your senses, George. Behave like a reasonable man."

"I will see you in the courts, too, one day, Thomas, for this. Don't think I won't."

"I am sure you will, but go home now and I will promise you your cows."

"On your honor, Thomas Burge."

"On my honor." I was truly not a Quaker; I had sworn an oath. Quakers, as everyone knew, would not swear oaths.

"And you, Lydia Gaunt and your children, remember this and do not make your house a Quaker meeting place. They are evil people trying to destroy our state. You will pay dearly if you continue. Do you understand me?" George said, as he was backing away from the cottage.

When George was gone I agreed to spend the night with them in case he might return. Over dinner there was much good conversation about the Quaker cause.

Lydia's mother, who was also named Lydia, said she was sure God had set a special mission for her husband when she married him and had lived in dread of what might happen when that prophesy should come true, but now that it had she felt calm in the face of it. She had felt she would hate being an outcast in some cause, but now that it was come she found she felt great love for the Friends and great communion with them as she never had with the Anabaptists. She felt she was truly a Friend. Perhaps more of a member than her husband would be, and she hoped to die a member of that dear fellowship. As we sat and talked both daughters were animated and active in the discussion, as though they had always taken full part in the family's life and not been shy daughters busy in the kitchen while the men talked. Young Lydia gave me such looks that they would melt the heart of any man and I wondered if her family suspected, or if there had been some tattletale remnant of pine needles which might have given us away to some keen eye. I slept in Peter's great chair by the fire that night and woke slowly in the morning to the rustle of petticoats and the smell of roasting apples. It was not the custom of people to eat morning meals then. There would be a meal at midday and then another at sunset, but none in the morning. The Gaunts were different in this, however, as they were in everything else.

When Mehitable and her mother had gone into the dooryard and little Israel was out for water, Lydia came quietly up to me and kissed me mischievously. I gave her my hardest look, but she just put her finger to her lips to signal silence, and then a finger to the side of her nose to signal conspiracy and went on about her work. What would the world think if they knew?

I was back again in the afternoon, however, when I heard that Peter and his sons had returned. There was quite a crowd from the village. We sat on the porch and Peter told us what had happened in Plymouth.

We had shared several stories of George Barlow's actions against families suspected of being Quakers. He had not limited his persecution to the Gaunts.

Peter said: "What you have heard is true, and there is worse than that. When we reached the General Court they would hear

147

Master Barlow on what had taken place at Sandwich, but they would not hear our testimony unless we would swear an oath and most of us would not do that. Those who would not remove their hats had them removed forcibly and the court called each of us and gave out sentences, each harsher than the one before. When all the cases from Sandwich had been heard John Alden himself called Edmund Freeman to the bar. Edmund had also been called for not frequenting the house of worship although he denied that, and they found him innocent of the charge. John Alden warned him that Sandwich was a disappointment and disgrace to the colony and that he should expel those who were not fit to visit in Mister Leverich's meeting, and that Leverich would now be called regularly to report on the governor's actions. Edmund should also bring into the village those who were better suited to the church and see to the suppression of the people called Quakers. When they had finished with Sandwich they also called those from other towns and the message was the same. This is a time to have courage in the face of extremity. This is the time when saints are discovered. This is our time of trouble.

"I myself have a sorrier story to tell you. While I was there I heard that Mary Dyer had been taken prisoner in Boston with some other Quakers before she came to us in Sandwich and when she was called before the court she presented herself very bravely. They found her guilty, however, of acts against the state and exiled her, saying if she ever returned to Boston she would be executed. This was just before she came to us here at Sandwich. I also heard that they executed a Quaker already as proof they meant to carry out their threats. That Quaker was a William Leddra. Then, just before I left Plymouth I heard even worse news: Mary had returned to Boston and was preaching there."

"God save her."

With this Hannaniah Gaunt, who was sitting by his father looked up and said with some surprise, "There he is."

We all looked around to see who he meant, and there standing at the gate, was George Barlow with his gun resting on the gate post. He shouted to Peter, "Is this another of your meetings, Master Gaunt? Are these your Quaker friends? I see the widow Knott there and Thomas Burge. I am noting you. You have no business at a meeting here."

"These are just my friends come to greet me home from Plymouth, George."

"You should take a care who you select as friends," he said.

"What can I do for you, George?" They were still shouting back and forth to each other across the yard because George wisely decided not to enter the gate. "Haven't you done the worst you could do to me, George?"

"No, I have not!" George shouted. "I have come for the cattle you owe me and the peas."

"Come in then, George, and select those cows you will and I will have my sons deliver them."

George slowly entered the gate with his gun ready. He then began a sidling, dancing step, keeping the crowd in front of him as he and Peter went to the pen where Peter kept his cows. Peter was calm and businesslike as he entered the field, but George hardly noticed the cattle as he selected them and spent his time watching us as we gathered at the rail fence. When he had made his selections George went back to us and said "Make a way! I am going home now. And none of you should obstruct my progress. As sheriff here I am a servant of the court. Make way!"

"No one is going to hurt you here, George." Peter said. "We are all your friends. You are just carrying out the orders of the court. Give him some room."

"I do not need your help, thank you, Master Gaunt. Just see to it that you deliver the cattle I have selected before the Sabbath, and don't be short on your measures of peas. Make way."

At the gate he turned his horse so that he could watch us as he mounted and, setting the gun across his lap he shouted, "Let this be a lesson to all of you as to how the court intends to deal with Quakers. There will be no Quaker meetings in my jurisdiction." He turned his horse and started off at a brisk trot.

"He did not expect to find so many of us here," said Peter as he returned to his porch.

On the next Sabbath the meeting was only half attended. Those who did go said that Mister Leverich was so angry at that that he could barely speak until it came time for the sermon and then he preached a blistering sermon against all Quakers, ordering that those who were known by the parishioners should be turned in by their brethren for the good of their souls and for the good of the Quakers' souls. He said that the Quaker meetings now being called regularly in Sandwich were little more than witches' covens and that there would be whippings, there would be elders sitting in the stocks (by which we all expected he meant Edmund Freeman), and if he had management of the matters there would be hangings as well, or even burnings. He told everyone about the warnings Governor Freeman had been given by John Alden and said that a new day would now be dawning.

His prophesies were to come true. In August word came to us on the Cape that two Quakers had been taken captive at Boston and tried before the court. They were taken from there in a cart to a hill in the Boston Common and hanged. These Quakers were Marmaduke Stephenson and Mary Dyer.

We then had a meeting of the Quakers at Sandwich and I attended, although I was not yet certain I was one of them, or ready to take the chance of being one. We sat for a long time in silence and tears. Mehitable Gaunt said then that she committed herself that night to the Lamb's War. Her mother began to cry.

The following day George Barlow announced that he would follow the example of Boston, and the Friends were forced to go into hiding. From then on the Friends' meetings would be unannounced and held during daylight on weekdays when George's whereabouts were known, or in the woods where sentries could be set. The greatest fear was that the children would let slip the news of meetings and so they were rarely told. If a stranger was seen passing nearby, a sign would be given and the meeting would break up, each Friend going swiftly and quietly to his or her home as though the business of the day had taken them out.

Friends traveling through were still put up at the Gaunts to their great peril, but when a strange Friend was in residence the rest of us would watch the road and carry warnings to the Gaunts.

A finger at the lips was as common a greeting between Friends in Sandwich as a handshake had previously been. But there was not a young person in the village who was not a Friend, and many of the older couples were either Friends or helpers of the Friends as I was.

Mehitable Gaunt was more moved by the loss of Mary Dyer than any of the rest of us and it seemed she could think of nothing else. She cried at night and in the daytime swore she would follow in Mary's footsteps. She walked alone, passed her old friends by, and talked wildly about revenge in the meetings.

One sunny Sabbath Mehitable came to the meetinghouse. As the Gaunts no longer attended public meetings, in defiance of the law, her presence was noticed as we stood around waiting for Mister Leverich to open the meetinghouse door. I had just decided to make my way to her and ask her what she was doing there when she stepped into the open place before the doors and called Mister Leverich's name in a loud voice.

23

HE DID OPEN the door after she had called him several times, but he stood in the shadows looking out at her in the sunlight, his face invisible to us and his body only a movement in the darkness.

"Are you so eager to come to meeting then, Mehitable Gaunt? Why is that? You have refused to join us in lawful public worship since that unnatural Quaker woman came among us who was recently justly hanged at Boston. Why was she not with her husband? Why do you come now to my door? If you come to blaspheme our faith, leave now with your unnatural lies. If you come now, however, to recant those lies and sit among the blessed again in fear of the law, then we welcome you with open arms as a sinner redeemed and a sheep of our own fold returned. I will welcome you like the father welcomed the prodigal son with the sacrifice of the fatted calf. I will kiss you."

"I have not come here for your kiss, but to speak out for a dear saint martyred."

"Get away from this door!"

"I come to protest her murder and honor her in the only way I can. I come to remind everyone here about her."

"I will have no public demonstrations here. Get away from the door! I will shut you out of this meeting and call brother Barlow to punish you if your father will not."

"I will welcome George's punishment."

"Get away from this door!"

"I do not want to enter your dark little building. I can protest here as I can worship here. I can protest her treatment where I stand. Mary Dyer was imprisoned when she first came to Boston and stripped naked for the rude hands and eyes of your kind to look on and feel. But her body was pure and innocent for all that."

"Get away from the door!"

"I will now sacrifice my body in the Lamb's War. It is all I have. I will now give it to that cause." She opened her cloak.

Mister Leverich made a gurgling sound so then we all stopped to look, but all we could see was the back of Mehitable's cloak. She then started to turn as if in a dance and the cloak flew out around her like dark wings, revealing that she was naked in the sunlight. She let loose the cloak and it flew away in a graceful arc, falling by the jamb of the meetinghouse door. She stood before us naked in the sunlight: innocent, untouched, and beautiful. A dead silence fell on the group struck for a moment with her pure beauty.

"My body is free. It is my own. There is no sin in it. There is no sin in me. Christ has cleansed me and I am his. He lives within me. No matter what anyone does they cannot defile this body. I give it to you here as a token of remembrance of our dear friend and sister Mary Dyer, murdered for her love of Christ, murdered in the name of this man's faith and its sickness which sees sin in the innocent and cannot see Christ swelling in its children, making their bodies clean. Burn this body, but you cannot take away its cleanness and its beauty because God made it as His tabernacle."

Suddenly Mister Leverich appeared in the meetinghouse doorway behind her. His face was a twisting mask of wrath. His face and neck were flushed and he was unable to speak. I thought he would fall down dead, or faint from his anger. I could clearly see that he was trembling. Then I realized he had something in his hands and it was moving out like a snake. In a shocking moment of realization we knew it was the cat-o-nine-tails which hung on the meetinghouse wall as a reminder to us all of the authority of the state, and he was lashing it out at Mehitable with all the strength he could muster. As it coiled around her waist it jerked her roughly to the left and the whip quickly slithered up her body and angrily around it twice. Then calmly, almost gently, the cat's tails danced above her in the air and closed like a hand over her shoulder. One barb neatly cut into her small, very white breast and she cried out in surprise and anguish. Mister Leverich pulled abruptly on the whip, sending her twirling and staggering away from him as the whip unwrapped itself from the red mark all around her where it had embraced her skin in its searing grasp and sending a droplet of blood from her breast flashing out in the sun.

His face was still a wooden mask of rage and red as that droplet of blood. He swung the whip again as Mehitable said "No" quietly and cringed away from it, hugging her breasts. The whip grabbed her and threw her wildly with her arms and legs flying away, and as he withdrew it for the next lash she fell unconscious to the ground.

"Stop it!" Edmund Freeman shouted, stepping out between the priest and the fallen girl. Mister Leverich held the whip as though he were about to swing it again at her. "Stop it, Leverich! Come to your senses!"

Mister Leverich gazed at him as though blinded by the sunlight, or as if he had suddenly been awakened from a deep sleep. We thought for a moment he would strike Edmund with the whip, but instead Mister Leverich fell to his knees before him, let the whip handle fall from his hand, and covered his face with his hands. "My God! My God!" he said wildly, the words muffled. "What have I done?"

He began to cry uncontrollably and hysterically, at last falling on all fours.

He wiped his face, smearing dirt on it, got up without another word, and went back into the darkness of the meetinghouse with the whip in his hand, closing the door behind him.

Some women gathered Mehitable up. She was still unconscious. They wrapped her in her cloak and carried her home.

Edmund Freeman stared for a time at the closed meetinghouse door, then turned slowly to us and said: "Go home. There will be no meeting today."

We turned away in silence; there was nothing to say.

That evening Mister Leverich loaded his wagon and left Sandwich. I heard of him once years later on Long Island, but he never returned to Sandwich.

George Barlow the next morning swore at the meetinghouse door that he would punish Mehitable Gaunt for what she had done; and when that message reached the Gaunts, Mehitable and her two brothers Hannaniah and Zachariah fled to Rhode Island as Mary Dyer had told them they should.

24

THE OLD COUPLES who had pioneered Sandwich still went to the meeting with their youngest children, or if the father held sway as master of his house, as many did in those times, he might bring his older children grudgingly to that sad dark place on a Sabbath. They came in their dark cloaks, white caps, and broad-brimmed hats like dark, silent birds coming out of habit to the tree where one year there had been many berries, sitting on its dead branches remembering the past. Captain Tupper would preside though he was no priest. Each in turn would read the scriptures and say the familiar words as they could remember and recite them. Now and then a sweet hymn would rise as though life might again quicken there and then die with the counterpoint of untimely amens. They were a poor remnant, a little minion of old men keeping the last candle end lit; holding together a last frayed thread of what had been a fine fabric in a cold winter wind, hoping that their steadfast faith might make it lead to a firmer warp and weft in a later day and cover their want with its familiar warmth again.

Plymouth sent no more ministers to replace Mister Leverich. Perhaps there were none to send. Perhaps they hoped the issue of the Quakers, which had come upon them like a violent storm, would blow away into the offing and trouble them no more if given time to run its course. Perhaps they thought they were punishing the village elders for welcoming Quakers. Perhaps Plymouth knew the power of their adversary and was garnering its power, planning to come out against us in force on a brighter day when the Quakers might falter. Whatever the reason, there was no full-time meeting at Sandwich and in its absence the Quaker meeting flourished.

When life absolutely required the ministrations of the mother church, the state church, to celebrate a birth in one of the leading families, a birth which could not go from the field to the cradle without God's and the Protector's seal upon it, or a wedding requiring the sanctification of its holy hand, a relief minister would grudgingly be sent, but he would never sleep under one of our roofs, but fly back to Plymouth, shaking the AntiChrist out of the folds of his robes on the way home and brushing the dust of its streets from his sandals.

My father, with his long service in the General Court and his close friendship with Mister Alden, could demand such a visitation when my sister Elizabeth married Ezra Perry. When I came in to gather with the family in this time of joy at the meeting, the place seemed sad and small and many eyes turned away from me. Elizabeth and her father brushed past me as though I were some unseen evil spirit, but Trial looked back and I smiled at her for that little gesture of courtesy.

Almost all the young people were Quakers. All those who were about the age to marry were Friends and would stand up in the Quaker meeting to declare their love and announce their bonds and make their marriage pledges without the blessing of clergy.

Sarah Freeman did that, but chose to make her marriage in the cathedral of the woods before an old chestnut as an altar like the wild Indians. All the Quakers had gathered around and I remember it as a joyous meeting with much kissing and excellent food and drink out in a sunny day. Every person under thirty in the town must have been there. But Sarah's mother would not come at all and I remember seeing Edmund Freeman dressed in his best with the gold lacing coming to within sight of where they stood, although I think I was the only one to see him. He stood there for a long time by an old tree with the tears streaming down his face and then turned at last and made his way across a field of corn stubble, like some slight acquaintance at a burial who stands for a while at a distance among the stones before the body is lowered so that no one will ask if he is a relative. I wondered as I watched him if he thought about George Barlow telling him that he would regret letting Mary Dyer speak. I thought that bent yeoman's back picking its way among the cut stalks might be father to us all, in a way. I had seen him first on horseback in his pride and here he was now come to this.

It is hard to describe, however, the feeling of the Quakers at that time. It was a newness of spirit I will never recapture. No one will ever recapture it. Even those of us who were not ready to commit to the Friends felt a family tie to them; but more than that. We suddenly realized that we had been closely penned up all these years unaware, so tightly penned that we could not breathe and could not see the outside world. This imprisonment had been a way of life and now Mary Dyer and Mehitable Gaunt had simply lifted the latch and set the gate of our pen swinging open, and those of us clinging to its beams swung out and were, quite by chance, free. But we were still afraid to run out into the meadows around us, or on to the blue hills we could see beyond them, which only moments before were only in our dreams.

George Barlow still was sheriff in Sandwich and he did still try to suppress the Friends, but the shepherd was gone and he was only the sheep dog running wildly among the flock, out of instinct savaging this one and driving that one, but with no direction in mind and little idea where the wolves might lie. He took Peter Gaunt several times into the court at Plymouth, and once, in that time, he took me.

The case had to do with one of the cows Peter had given him under order of the court. George had been a poor man before becoming sheriff, but he had, through the largess of the court with other peoples' cattle, grown wealthy in livestock. But one of the cows Peter had been ordered to give him had died before it could be delivered. Actually, it was carried away by a stream to the sea and so George was not only without the cow, but without even its skin. He would not have settled for the skin alone, as everyone knew, but he pretended he would have since it was now not Peter's to give. He took Peter to court then again for this missing cow, or its skin. Hardly an issue to shake the foundations of the colony, but typical of the work of George Barlow. Typical also for its meanness. In the progress of this, I came upon him on Peter's land as I had taken to being a dinner guest often with the Gaunts and staying, as you might have guessed, late to talk with Lydia in the darkness, leaning against her father's fence, admiring stars and each other.

Well, one night while Lydia and I were there we heard a commotion in the field nearby and someone cursing. I thought it was some Indian who had been drinking and gone on the warpath and so I set off at a good run to see what was happening. When I got there I found George Barlow trying to make off with one of Peter's cows in the dead of night and well and truly tangled — cow, man, rope — in a bush so that none of them could move. George was still free enough to curse, and from the wild look in the eyes of the cow she regretted her efforts to resist him and would care little now who would be her master if she were only free to move her legs again.

"What is going on here?" I said.

"I am taking this cow which is rightly mine."

"I can see that something is happening with a cow, but what it is isn't that clear to me."

"Thomas Burge, cut me loose at once."

"Should I cut you loose first, or the cow?"

"Damn it, man, I am here on the court's business."

"Are you indeed? Well, I don't want to interrupt the court," I said, and started on.

"Damn it man, I am tangled in this tree and you, as a citizen, are obliged to aid an officer of the court."

"I am not too sure what is going on here, George, but I am sure I don't want to be a part of it. I will be glad to get Peter Gaunt to help you."

"No, no, Thomas, please just cut me loose and we will say no more about it."

"I think I had better get Peter."

"You do and I will have you in court as well for aiding a criminal and not giving aid to an officer of the court in his lawful duties."

"Lawful?"

"Yes, lawful! You will be sorry if you go off and leave me here! Do you hear me Thomas! Come back here! I will have you in the courts for this!"

When I brought Peter we surveyed the situation for a time as to which of the creatures trapped in the bush it would be more dangerous to free first, and then cut the ropes holding George who was by this time almost apoplectic. He demanded the cow all the while we were trying to free her, but in the end Master Gaunt said, "If you want this cow to add to your herd you should have come and asked me at a decent hour. Now, you will have to take me to court again for her." George stamped off into the night, threatening us with every recourse the law offered.

He did take us to court and we found Plymouth in a very black mood indeed. The Protectorate, then under Master Cromwell's son and the parliament in England, had fallen, and Charles Stuart, the son of our last king, had been invited to return from France and rule again. He was a papist in their eyes and the last man Plymouth would have wanted on the throne. He had been crowned Charles the Second just to top off their anger, as though his father had been a proper king of England and his execution a crime of regicide. They were in no mood to treat lightly with the matter of a cow and spent close to an hour lecturing Peter on the respect due one of their officers and the majesty of the law which had found him guilty and fined him to that price.

John Alden himself sat on the bench in the red robe of a justice and when I came before him he said, "Here is a name I never expected to see before me in the docket. Your father is a special friend of the court and of mine and sits with us as representative of your village often, as you know. I sorely regret hearing a case against his son. Surely his son is not a Quaker, as this man is."

I told him I was not, but that Peter Gaunt was my friend and for all I knew George had been stealing his cow.

John Alden seemed annoyed by this answer. "This man is our sheriff and had every right to the cow. The law requires any citizen seeing the officer of this court troubled in the execution of the business of the court to come to his aid, and you did not."

"But it seemed so strange. It was the middle of the night."

"I did not ask for your opinion on the law, Master Burge. I am telling you you should have helped this man with that cow. I wish that I could show my love to my friend by lenience to his son. This is your first time before the court. But I am father to this colony and that duty is above my duty to the sons of my friends. God turn you right and away from this man, Thomas. I find you guilty and fine you twenty shillings, to be paid to our sheriff George Barlow. This case is at an end." He then stood up, removed his robe, and left the court without another word.

When I reached my home at last that night I was tired and glad to think about bed and sleep and not to worry more about where I would find twenty shilling, or even ten. I put my horse in its stall and started for the house. Something was wrong, I knew at once, but I could not figure out what it was as I stood there in the dooryard. Then it suddenly struck me. Smoke was coming out of my chimney. I started running to the house to see who had made themselves at home while I was away and threw the door open, ready for a fight. There on the hearth poking the fire was Lydia Gaunt.

She looked at me with her large eyes for a moment as I stood in the doorway, then stood up, brushed the ashes from her skirt, came to me, put her hands around my neck, and deliberately drew me to her, kissing me with such warmth and fire as I had never before felt. I pulled her as tight to me and we fit together as neatly as I had remembered: as though she were a part of my body. We kissed and kissed in that doorway, as though there could be no end to kissing, and each time I thought I had satisfied my taste for the feel of her lips, I would realize I had not yet begun to satisfy that hunger. We would kiss many small kisses, flirting with our hunger for each other, then we would fall into a deep kiss, deep in each other's taste and smell. Finally, I just held her to me and our cheeks were together, hers as soft as a flower petal and mine rough with a day's growth. I could feel every bit of fatigue and worry sucked out of me by this sweet creature's body and youth. I put my arm beneath her hips and lifted her off the floor, pulling her even closer to me and turning in a dance of joy until it seemed she would fly out away from me.

"Oh, Thomas, stop. I will get dizzy!" she said.

"I am dizzy," said I.

"I love you, Thomas."

"And I love you, Lydia."

"I thought I would surprise you, but you are not surprised at all."

"Yes, I am."

"Do you know why I have come here?"

"I hope I do."

"I have come here because I am your wife, Thomas, I have come here to marry you."

25

"To marry me? Oh, Lydia. I already have a wife."

"No, you don't. Where is she? I have searched your house from top to bottom. You have no wife, but me. Sweet Christ has told me I am to be your wife. He has said that in his eyes I am already your wife. That other woman, he has told me, is no wife to you, but I am. Can you deny it?"

"Yes, oh yes, Lydia, but there is a law."

"There is only one law. That is Christ's law. By that law we love and by that law I am your wife."

"But you are a child, Lydia, and I am an old man compared to you."

"You are only thirty-five, Thomas. That is not old. I love each line. I will wipe them away," she said, and put her fingers on my face and examined it with her eyes closed as if she were a blind girl searching for its meanings. "There, now you are as young as I am. There, now you are a child."

I had to kiss her again, and she giggled. When I opened my eyes and looked into hers, she said, "I want to make love to you," and she ran her hands all over me. I put my arm around her and we walked into my bedroom. We stopped at the door and she gave me a knowing look and pinched me. I laughed and pretended to chase her. She leapt onto the bed and sat there upright with her hands at her bosom in mock modesty, her skirts spread out around her on the bedclothes. I could just see her white ankle, and I knelt down by the bed and kissed it.

"Come here," she said, and when I did, with my arm just around her hips, she took my hand in hers and put it on her breast. "I love you, Thomas. I love you here." She knew I felt the full shape of her small breasts. "And I love you here," she said, moving my hand down until she dug it into her skirts.

We kissed again, her hands eagerly at work with the buttons of my shirt. Then, looking up at me, laughing with such a light girlish laugh, I thought, for an instant: "Is she too fine a thing to touch?"

"Thomas!" She said in mock impatience. "Don't you know how to untie knots?" And she put my hand again on her lacing. I fumbled with it and she sat still with her eyes closed while I unlaced her, feeling her firm breasts beneath the cloth. When she was unlaced and her dress opened, one of her breasts appeared in the firelight, and the light struck it at such an angle that the nipple seemed exquisitely pink and translucent, so perfectly formed and full that I could not keep from taking it in my hand, feeling her press it against my palm. She opened her eyes and they were still filled with laughter, and moist with passion, hunger, and fire, but not a trace of fear.

Her hands ran up my leg, searching. I got up and removed my clothes and she did the same. We stood for a moment looking at each other like some engraving of Adam and Eve: enjoying just the simple look of our bodies. I kissed her mouth, and then her face, down her neck and shoulders and, at last, her breasts while she looked down at me.

"Oh, Thomas!" she said, and put her soft arms around me, clinging to me, pulling me into her body.

I thought there would be no end to our embrace and we would make love at last standing there, but Lydia broke away, curled herself up on the bed, looked up at me with a mischievous grin, and motioned me to join her.

We lay there deeply entwined, hardly moving, one warmth, our hands gently exploring each new wonder, each new feel of our bodies, bodies which might one day be familiar, but now were full of secrets to discover, this which excited her, this which did not, and she finding the same in me until she was damp with sweat, flushed, and squirming under my touch.

Then she rose up onto me with her hands on my chest, showing me her whole body. She ran her hands over it as though she were proud of it and excited that I was looking at her and at last spread out her arms above her head. Looking at me and resting her weight on her knees, she slowly pushed down onto me, drawing in her breath as I entered her body and letting it out with a sound of release. I could see a momentary flash of pain pass across her eyes in a startled second and then she closed them, turning her face up with a smile as though she were savoring this moment and tucking the pleasure of it away against some winter: a talisman against whatever hard time might come. As she sat there on me with her legs pressed hard against my sides but very still, I had time to realize what I had not seen in my passion: how I loved the shape and feel of her quite apart from our love. In the warm half-light of evening, as I ran my hands up her body, it seemed like the idealization of all that every man would find exciting, like a dream of a woman in some ship's figurehead, rising up from me so still and straight: her gently swelling hips, firm and softer than any cloth; her slim waist, and those elegant small breasts. When I reached her face with my hands Lydia opened her eyes. Her face was lit with a smile which shook me to the core, and she leaned down and kissed me. I put my arms around her and held her until she slowly began to move. Her movement quickened until I felt her whole body shudder in my arms for what seemed a great long time, then she pulled herself up over me on her arms her hands flat on the bed on either side of me and looked down at me. Her face was illuminated with that look of mischief like a little girl who had done something very bad, but loved every minute of it.

I could hold myself back no more and I filled her with the seed which a man puts into the spring furrow, not with the dream of harvest, but for nature's pure joy in the planting. We were surely bonded there and then in that moment for a lifetime as if our bodies had been melded in that one act of love and she was from then on mine and I was hers.

We lay together, and slept, and talked, and laughed in that close darkness until Lydia took my face in her hands and said, "Again." And we made love again: fiercely and gently.

We both woke at the darkest hour of the night. Lydia's head was cradled between my arm and shoulder. I felt her shiver a little. She said in the darkness, "This isn't right, Thomas. We must get married."

"What?"

"Get married, Thomas! Come on!" And both of us stark naked, like children jumping off into a swimming hole, she led me by the hand out into the cabin where I blew the fire up again and put a new log on it. We sat there side by side, arms around each other in the firelight, and Lydia said, "I will swear no oath to you, Thomas Burge, because the Bible tells us we may swear no oaths, but I will tell you that from this moment, in this place and everywhere, I will love you more than I love any person and any thing in this world; and as long as you and I live I will always be at your side whether we are together or apart and no matter what may happen to either of us I will never leave you. You are sweeter to me than honey in the comb and softer to me than the wool of beavers and only when I hold your head to my breast will I be complete. From this time on I will never be alone. I love you now, Thomas, and I promise always to love you."

We looked into the fire in silence and it seemed to leap up as we watched. I looked into her eyes and said, "I now renounce the bond I made with another woman and divorce her, and I make you my only wife. From this moment I will live only for you. When I work in the field it is your face which will sustain me, when I am lost, or in pain, it is your love which will find and heal me. Your pleasure will be mine, and our separate lives will be one. I love you more than any man has ever loved and I will pay any price for that love. I love you more than my immortal soul. I love you more than my life. I am now and forever yours."

The fire seemed to leap up again as wind passed the chimney and we kissed there, beautiful and naked on that hearth.

Lydia put her head down on my shoulder then and whispered in my ear, "Again." And we made love again on the stones of the hearth in the firelight.

26

Here Elizabeth says:

I am sure Thomas has told you things which make you think it was my fault and that his life with Lydia Gaunt was some kind of great and classic romance, but that is not true. He lived with that slut in sin for lust alone and left me at my father's house alone and in pain: his true wife forgotten for that creature. His true wife was left alone and cast off because he was tired of her; cast off as a snake sheds its skin, and blown away like chaff from the grain. He left me like some old plaything now discarded in the dust and completely out of mind. He never even came to my father's house to see how I was, or tell me that he was living with this other woman. I was to hear that from the women in the village. What did they think of me when they found out I did not know? I heard it from the women of the village!

Look at the facts of the thing. He was twice her age. He was a man of thirty-five and she was a child of barely nineteen. Of course, he found her ripe, full, and fresh and me, his true wife, old and spent and stale, but to take her and leave me alone was a bitter sin.

What happens to men at that time in life which makes them go wild and suddenly hope that they are boys again and can take any woman, can take those women who should rightly be marrying their sons? They are overcome with the fear they will have no heritage. But what of women? Fortunately, most young women see them for what they are. They know a red deer in rut after his time. There are some twisted women, however, who will sleep with them. How can they? How can they want the smells of these old men, their bellies and their gray and thinning hair, their pathetic bodies on the brink of decay and death, their last embers glowing with a ghastly memory of their fumbling youth? What sort of young woman would take such a man, and that man another woman's husband?

They say she is with child and I was barren. When you take the devil into you, do you become the devil?

I tried my best to save him and myself from this. He was caught in a whirlpool from which there was no escape, a maelstrom of sin, a terrible time, and I had hold of him by the foot and the devil had him by the arms. Then the devil struck my father with a great illness to distract me and I let my grasp slip and my husband fell headlong into that pit. He will now burn forever in its flaming tar and I will chill here alone in the winter's long nights. I hate the thought of him!

Yes, the curse of the Quakers came upon Sandwich and Thomas was weak to it. I should have seen that. I should have known. It came like some plague on the land that would pass down a lane and take everyone on it and then pass another unharmed. Though we might burn their clothes and mark their doors with crosses so that no one would enter, the pestilence would stalk on unseen from one door to another, gripping some in a house for no apparent reason and sparing others, passing some doors as it passed my father's and bringing its madness to all in some houses as it did to Goodman Gaunt's. The infection passed through the village as if it moved on the miasmas from the bogs in the morning and sent its victims out cruel and mad as my husband was, to do whatever they wished without a mind to decency, or morality, or compassion, or even the commandments of God given to Moses on the mountain. My teeth ache when I think of that man.

The church was empty, the larder forgotten, children sent wild into the woods with the savages. All they cared about when the germ was in them was themselves and their own consuming lust. The fear of judgement and hell fire had been taken out of them and there was only Babylon, red Babylon riding her chariot through the streets, and there, God help him, was my husband lost to a harlot, and through her victory lost to me. He thought only of himself, as that evil teacher, Mary Dyer, taught the children of Sandwich. May she rot in hell.

My father was very ill and required all my care. I tried to be a wife to my husband and a daughter to my father. I should have known that my husband was lost to sin when he attacked me wildly because he would not have me care for my father. He tried to take a scythe to me in my own dooryard. Would you have been fool enough to stay with such a man? He wanted me to leave my father to die while I would only be a slave to him. I should have seen that he was lost to me then. I curse him!

And where am I now? Where am I now? I am a woman beyond childbearing. I am neither maid nor matron, nor widow. Where am I to go? What am I to do? Will I just be a daughter in my father's house for all my life? Then, when he dies, some maiden aunt to my sister Trial's, children, or some recluse living alone in her cabin talking to her cat while the wild rose vines twine across her door and in her windows? Is that what is to happen to me? When I die who will know I have passed? Curse him! Curse him! What has he done to me?

And she was a child of just nineteen. He must be punished. I must punish him.

I must not think of this more. It will surely kill me with the pain of it.

27

I MARRIED LYDIA in the early days of the spring of 1661. What a spring that was! In the cold weather we blessed the coldness because it allowed us to close ourselves up in the cabin and chink out the rest of the world like bears in their winter lodges, sleeping and loving and laughing in our tight little home. I had not set by much in the bitter end of that winter when I had cared little about what would happen to me. But with Lydia that want was a joy. We would laugh about it as we sat on the hearth enjoying a thin broth, finding bits of fruit I had hidden away, and chewing on every cube of ham fat until we had taken every last squeak out of it. Our love alone was enough to feed us and as for company we were happier to have none.

But old spring would come at last with its bird songs and green shoots breaking through the hummock of earth the ice had raised, its fiddle heads, its trillium and skunk cabbages. Now and then there was a seductive morning when the sun turned ice into jewels and a steady drumming of water, as the earth melted away its icy crust, carried on its moist breath the humus smell of decay, giving itself as a sacrifice to new growth which makes the husbandman restless to break the earth too soon and sets his mouth watering with the taste of a full larder still folded small in the seed. We had killed cattle in the late winter as the old rhyme told us we should, to save the fodder and give heat to those who would survive the chill, but now the young lambs and the calves would soon have fresh hay to fatten on and we let them live.

You cannot help but love the spring. You cannot help but feel its sap rise in you, but I was sad to see it come this year. I was jealous it would take me away from Lydia's arms, and jokes, from her bright busy, happy talk. I regretted that I would be again out in my father's fields when I wished to be always, arms behind my head, lying in that bed with her. I could live on acorns and ground nuts and I suggested that we might just run away and live as the Indians do in the woods for that spring and summer. Let the conventional world go away and let us live on what nature grows in her garden without the hand of man, but she only laughed, and at last I made the walk to my father's to plan what fields my brothers and I would plant and what we would plant in them. We would then pool our seed, set out the draft animals which had survived the winter, and decide who would do which of the chores and who would share in the harvest in proportion to our work.

My mother was unusually silent with me except once when we sat together for a time and she cried and said, "What can I say, Thomas? How could you?" and I could think of no proper answer for her, but that I would go away into the woods if I could and she did not want to hear that. My father and brothers were simply silent. They said nothing about Elizabeth, or Lydia, or where or how we lived. There were no questions because there were no answers. There was no talk of rope in a family where there had just been a hanging, and there was no talk of families, love, or marriage in that house when I was there. But I knew that with the new growth of the spring there was a new growth of interest in what was happening in my house. I did not care. I loved Lydia more than anything in the world. I didn't care what they said. What they said was irrelevant to our love. Our love was a pure thing; it could only grow. It could not be cut in its sprouting. If there was punishment for loving, what could it be? What punishment could be harder than the bond of our love? I would take whatever they wished to give. If silence was the price I would have to pay, that was a very small coin indeed and I would gladly pay it many times over. If tears were the price, then let there be a spring freshet of them and that would be small cost. If the price was that we would live hermits to the world — then our very own desire was a price we would pay happily every morning, three hundred and sixty five mornings in a year.

As the still wan sun reached its zenith in the fields where we were putting in the peas Lydia would come with a basket full of the best she could find for me, lean over the fence rails until I saw her there swinging them, or if I were near enough she would pick up old chestnuts and pitch them at me until I saw her gaily wave. My father and brothers would take no notice, but continue their work as though she were as invisible as a ghost which haunted only me, or they would take that as a silent signal to make their own ways back to their cabins. Lydia and I would make a picnic of it, and I have never eaten so well, nor drunk so deep with such good company, as by those hedgerows with my little wife in the sun: I, caked with mud, but as bold as any gentleman in lace and velvet and she pulling her shawl around her against the brisk chilly wind, full to bursting with the talk of the small things which were large to us.

One day when she came to me she had special cakes and she said very solemnly, "Before you eat those, Thomas, I have something to say to you. I read the Bible this morning when I was baking them. Now the text I read was from Genesis. Do you remember what God promised to Abram when he asked 'Lord God what wilt thou give me seeing I go childless?' What an impudent question that was he dared to ask the Lord God! Anyway, God answered him and God said to Abram, 'Look now toward heaven, and tell the stars, if thou be able to number them: and He said unto him, So shall thy seed be.'" She kissed me on my muddy cheek. "Thomas, God has put his seal on our marriage as I knew he would. I am carrying your child here in my stomach." She put my hand on her stomach, and we both laughed and cried.

Like Abram, God had given me a miracle of children when I had thought there would never be a child of mine in this world. When I went back to the field it was with a whistle and a song and as I knelt down in the furrow I thought that that soil I was now holding in my hands would one day be held in my son's hands and some part of these fields which gave life to me would give life to him and his son, and his son's son, amen, amen.

As the afternoon spread on into evening I grew more eager to be home with Lydia and so I was really angry to see George Barlow and his deputy Thomas Hinkley clumsily stepping through the field toward me. From the arrogant look of them I was sure they were about their usual business of harassment and had found some trivial business to take me away from Lydia. I put down my tools and waited for them. I was not about to give them the satisfaction of calling me out of the field, although George was motioning for me to come to him. When they came closer I was sure my suspicions were correct for George had a paper from the court in his hand.

"Thomas!" I could hear him shouting.

"What is it now, George?" I said as he came near enough to hear. "I haven't time for another of your charges, nor cattle to spare to you. I need to get home to my wife."

"Where is your wife?"

"What? She is at home."

"No, she is not," said Master Hinkley, "No, she is not. I know that because I have just spoken to her in the village. George Barlow and I come to you from her."

"What's this about? It's late. If you have something to say, say it."

"We are not here to say anything. We are here to serve this warrant on you to appear before the Court in Plymouth."

"Then serve it. When am I to appear?"

"June tenth."

"And on what trumped-up charge this time?"

"On a true bill. You can read it there."

George Barlow stepped forward then: "The charge is adultery."

28

I READ THE paper. It said, "Thomas Burge Junior of Sandwich acknowledges to owe unto our sovereign lord the King the sum of one hundred pounds sterling. Thomas Burge Senior the sum of fifty pounds, and Ezra Perry the sum of fifty pounds. The condition that if the above bound Thomas Burge Junior shall and do appear at the General Court of our said sovereign lord the King to be held at Plymouth aforesaid the second Tuesday in June next to answer for a fact of uncleanness by him and in the interim not embezzle away his estate and not depart the said Court without license." There was more but I did not have the spirit to read further.

"I will come to get you in the first week in June, Thomas. I trust you on behalf of your father's good name and not on your own word. But if you are not there I will find you. You can be sure of that."

I could not look up as they made their way across the field and when they had gone I sat down in the mud there with the warrant in my hand. The wind was moving high in the trees, just moving the highest branches, and the trees had turned their leaves with the light sides to the sky as though they had grown pale. There would surely be rain.

After a time I realized I was sitting in the field alone and banks of clouds were growing in the evening sky like blue hills covered with dark forests.

I knew that Lydia would be looking for me, but I was not ready to show her this warrant until I had some other answers for her. I slowly stood up and for the first time in my life I felt old. My muscles seemed not to respond. They had stretched and would not spring back. They had labored and there was no resting. No beginning again. I stood there for a time shivering in the changed wind. Then I walked on to my father's house very slowly so the steps would not tire me: a ship riding on a coasting wind, wary of the shore, light in its sail, and ready at the dead man's anchor. As I came into the high field I could see my father sitting on his porch and Ezra Perry sitting beside him. Ezra watched me as I came across the field, but my father looked up into the expanse of the sky and clouds behind me. The shadows of the rain clouds overtook me as I crossed the field and I could feel a moist breath blow up onto my back. When I reached the porch I stood for a time on the earth looking at him, not an arm's length from him. I remembered all the times, as child and boy, when I had stood before him as I stood now, and all those memories welled up in me as the clouds had welled up from the dark earth.

"And now you come to me," my father said. "And now you come to me." He still sat impassive, looking out past me across the field to the clouds. Ezra was uneasy. They had been talking about me, certainly.

"You know it isn't easy for me to come to you, Father." I stepped up onto the porch as I felt the first drops of rain. My father was dead silent as though I were not there. I thought about sitting in the chair beside him, but that would be a small surrender, a little vulnerability I was not yet ready for and so I stood and turned out to parallel his gaze across the empty, cold, dark field, making it seem less like I was begging him. A stranger hurrying along the path before the storm might think we were in ordinary conversation. Talking about crops we might plant, or the weather. "I know I should have come to you, told you what was happening, at least. But I was sure you knew."

"And your mother. Did you think of her?"

"Elizabeth left me, Father. I did not leave her. It was her choice. She left me long ago. That marriage is over."

He was silent still, but now looking down at the blisters on his hands. They were dirty from the fields.

"There is no hope that marriage will ever revive, father. She is dead to me and I am dead to her. I have repudiated that marriage in the face of God, and Lydia is now my wife. I have married her in the face of God."

He laughed and looked up. "What God is that?"

"I am sorry, Father. I am sorry. But Lydia is my wife."

"I witnessed no such marriage. Your sister is married to this man here. I witnessed their marriage. But I witnessed no such marriage as you describe."

"It took place, father."

"You are telling me, then, that my son is not just an adulterer, but a bigamist as well."

I tried to control the anger my father always caused in me. Ezra seemed eager to leave, but didn't. I wished he would, but said nothing.

"Thomas, what do you want from me?"

"I want your help. You are my father. I should be able to look to you for help."

"I have always been wrong in your eyes."

"I have come to you, Father, and I am asking for your help."

"What help could I possibly give to you now?"

173

"You are a friend of all those men who will judge me in Plymouth. Come with me. Help me explain to them."

I saw his jaw tighten and his gaze move out again across the field. There was lightning far off. Not a flash, but a double palpitation of light in the body of the cloud like a heartbeat, and no thunder followed, although we waited for the sound. "You have disgraced me before the court. You have disgraced me before my friends, Thomas, before the men I respect and who respect me. How can I face them now? You have disgraced me, and this house."

I was begging for help, but all I could say was: "Father."

"What help can I give you? I can tell you to let this little child go. I can tell you that. Send her back to her father. Beg Elizabeth to come back. Beg her on your knees. I would not come back if I were her. But women are different. She may. That is what I can do to help you, Thomas."

"I won't do that, Father."

"Then damn you!"

"You are my father, not some casual acquaintance, and you owe me more than that."

"You can speak of owing? That is why I tell you that, my son, because I am your father."

"I will not."

"You have ruined me and you ask for my help."

"If you cannot find it in your heart to help me now, Father, then tell me and I will leave. I will leave and never come back."

"You say you must have my help, but what thought did you have for me, or for your mother? What thought did you have for anyone? I have other responsibilities in this world than just to be your father. I am a representative of Sandwich to the General Court. I am a husband and a father to my other children. I am an elder in the church. I am a citizen and founder of this village. What I do is an example. Do you think it is easy to say no to you?"

"I am sorry about that."

"You have ruined us, Thomas, and what for? For your own pleasure."

"You couldn't understand, Father."

"Why not? I am a man as you are. I can understand adultery."

I turned and stepped down from the porch. The storm had passed on now into the bay. "Why is it we can never talk together, father, little things, or great matters, we can never talk?"

"Even if I were of a mind to speak to the court, and that I am not, it would do no good, Thomas. Master Alden has his own mind."

"How can they punish me? Can they kill me for this? I don't care. Lydia and I are now husband and wife and Elizabeth Bassett is nothing to me."

"They will break you, Thomas, like kindling. And what will happen to me and to your mother, and to your brothers in the process? Be a man, Thomas."

"We can always run away."

"Then run, and good riddance. Run if you must."

"I should have known there would be no help here."

He looked at me at last and I could see he was crying. "Yes, there is no help for you here." I had never seen him cry.

I started to walk away, but Ezra ran after me and caught me by the arm. "Thomas, please, you won't run away, will you?"

"What is it to you if I do, Ezra?"

"The court has bonded your father for fifty pounds sterling as a bond of your appearance. Perhaps he can pay that, but it has also bonded me for a like amount, and I cannot."

"Oh, yes, I saw that."

"I cannot raise fifty pounds sterling, Thomas. I cannot raise a bit of it. If you leave, Elizabeth and I will be ruined. You will have ruined your sister. I am sorry, Thomas. I can understand your position. But I beg you not to run away. Please! I would lose all the land my father left me."

"Never mind, Ezra, Lydia and I will not run away." He watched me as I went away, and called after me, "I am sorry to ask that, Thomas." But I gave him no reply.

When I reached the marsh I turned and looked back. There was the sloping field as we had planned it all those years ago, and on the hill a cabin, and on its porch an old man who was a stranger to me and a young man standing who was more a son to him than I would ever be.

I knew that Lydia would be worried that I had not returned with evening coming on. How could I tell Lydia? I needed time to think. What would this paper say to her and to the child she now held firmly in her womb?

When I reached the bog I turned into it though my boots sunk up to their tops. If I should stick fast, or sink away what would it matter? I made my way across it to the tidal stream which curves away like a great bow across the sand beach, past the ruins of the old trading station, and then out in a curving spit of sand into the middle of the bay: a farmer's scythe into the fishy sea. I was overcome by the majesty of the view in the first lights of sunset: the sea and sky so vast and the cloud bank going up thousands of feet and all a pure pink wall. High above, some lines of cloud were thin and ghostly, just turning color. I was so blinded by the view that I did not see a figure sitting on the sand in the middle distance until I came quite near him.

I started to turn back, but then grew curious because I could see no footprints on the sand to tell me how this person had come out there in the middle of the waters. It may not be a person at all, I thought, but some large piece of driftwood, or perhaps a mariner washed up on the sand.

As I got closer in that strange pink light I could see it was a personage in a broad-brimmed hat and a long belted coat, but barefoot: a dark figure suspended in a luminous scene. As I drew closer I realized I knew who it was. It was poor George: the sagamore of the Nauset sitting there alone on my father's beach.

"Hello, George."

"Ah, yes. Who is that? Thomas Burge, isn't it?"

"Yes. What are you doing here alone?"

"I am doing a duty here. I am doing what my father did and his father and his father's father."

After a while I realized I was required to keep this conversation going and so I asked, "What is that, George?"

"I am guiding the geese and the eider ducks."

"Guiding them?"

"Yes, yes, they are going north again. This is not an easy world to find your way in. There are six directions in it, you know."

"Six?"

"Yes, yes, there is north, south, east, west, and up and down. Now these geese, they are foolish, dumb creatures and they would not know which way to fly if I did not watch for them and call out to them which way they should go. They would get lost, you see."

"Lost?"

"Yes. My father taught me their language and I call to them." He made a call as much like that of a wild goose as any I have ever heard as I stood and watched them in their ragged V's across the sky from the bog.

"What does that call tell them?"

"I tell them where their paths are in the sea, and where there are men waiting to take them. I say this way is safe and that is not. When they can see no sun to guide them I point out which way it would run if the sky were clear. When they are lost I guide them so they do not just fly this way and that around the sky wildly searching for their way. I say fish will be here and storms will be there. You can learn their language without me. Just listen to them as they speak to each other. When they have heard what I have to tell them my brothers the geese fly on beyond the place you call Labrador, and the place you call Newfoundland into the white eye of the sun in the far north where they will live for the summer with my kinsmen there, and then one day as they walk in the reeds, one of them will lift his leg and stand for a time poised on it and the others will all say to themselves, it is now time to return to George, the sagamore of the Nauset, where he sits on the beach; and they will fly over just this spot to hear from me how they should fly to Virginia."

"Do you really think they would get lost if you were not here to direct them?"

"I cannot say. I have always been here to tell them. It's better not to take a chance, don't you think?"

177

I sat down by him and we both spread our feet out on the sand. "And how are your people, George? How are the people of the Kingdom of the Mashapee?"

"They are not too well, Thomas. Ah, yes, they are not well. They are very weak after all, not like me. I did not think they were so weak. You see, they are too weak to hold the white man's religion inside their bodies. They cannot hold your powerful god. He burns inside them until they are hot to the touch. That is how they feel when they take him in. Many of them die from the heat of him and those who live. . . you can see their bones, as though they are the walking dead, but they are very happy with him in them. They have little holes in their skin where your god burns. It is very sad in a way, Thomas. If they should all die I would be very lonely. They are my children. But I am strong enough to swallow the white man's god right down. See!" and he pulled back his sleeve to show me that his arm was unmarked. "Touch it! Touch it! It is cool as a fish." I felt his arm. "You see. It is quite cool and yet I have the white man's god in me if any man does. I have swallowed him and he sits in there and is very happy in the body of this sagamore."

"I am very glad about that George, but I am sorry about the people of the Kingdom of the Mashapee."

"Don't be. That is the way it is. Are you sorry when the leaves fall, or when the old deers die in the forest in a hard winter?"

"Still, I am sorry."

"Ah, yes, but there is something else which brings you out to this beach with George. You did not come here to call to the geese, I think."

Some gulls appeared out of the vast dome of the sky and began wheeling above us, hoping that we were fishing and we would share our catch with them. Then, with their hard, sharp eyes they saw we were just roosting and flew on.

"Are you also having trouble with your god?"

"Yes, I suppose, in a way I am."

"You are strong enough for Him though, Thomas."

"I had a wife, George, and she left me."

"You must go then and find her again."

"No, I wanted her to leave, and I took another woman for my wife."

"You are very fortunate, Thomas."

"No, you see, God does not allow a man to have more than one wife."

"Ah, yes, I had forgotten that. Now I remember. How foolish that is, though. God should think about that again. One woman may make excellent cakes, another may know where the best place to plant the corn is, another may sew fine seams which will keep out the rain and another make love so well that your toes curl when you lie with her. Why shouldn't you have all these women if they want you? Why not? Didn't God make them too? If they want you why shouldn't you want them? It is like Blue Corn Maiden and the White Corn Maiden."

"God says you may not, George."

"I wish I had my mask."

"What?"

"My mask."

"Oh."

"You have seen my mask. I had it when you visited me."

"You had a wooden scepter."

"No, no, that is a mask."

"The one you had in your hand when Richard and I visited you at the Kingdom of the Mashapee?"

"Yes, that is my mask."

"No, I am thinking of something else. It wasn't a mask. There were no eye holes in it. I remember it."

George laughed. "The eyes are inside. They are inside the wood, you see."

"What?"

"That is why you could not see them. They are inside the wood."

"Oh."

"It was made by a very clever sculptor, and he carved the eyes inside the wood."

"Oh."

"Yes, you see, I am only a poor Indian after all and I think as an Indian. I have no understanding of how the white man thinks after all. I often hear him talk and it sounds like absolute nonsense. But I am a Christian. I had to know what they were saying. So many years ago I sent a request to a great shaman of the Pequot people and he took mercy on me and carved this mask for me out of a single piece of white birch wood. Now, when I put it to my face and look through the eyes which are inside it I can understand just how the white man thinks. It all becomes perfectly clear and I say to myself, what a fool you were, George, not to see that right away. You didn't know that? Richard Bourne didn't tell you? Why did you think that of all the sagamores of the nations of the Wampanoag I alone can talk with the white man and understand what he is saying? I alone can hold the white man's god in me and understand him. None of the others can, you know. None of them."

"And you think you could have understood about my wives then if you had your mask?"

"Perhaps, I do not know. Perhaps if I had my mask I could."

The high wispy lines of clouds which had at first been almost invisible now shone out brightly as if the light came from them, and it changed the whole shape of the sky. The bank of clouds had moved farther away across the water and it was now all dark, but for the very tops which still were just touched with pink.

"Well, I wish the men of Plymouth had a mask like yours. Without it they surely will not understand me."

"Why don't you just live with these wives? The men of Plymouth will not kill one of the wives for you, will they?"

"No, they will not kill one. One has left me anyway."

"Ah, yes, then your problem is solved. I am sorry that one of your squaws is gone. But why not just live with the other one?"

"They will not let me."

"They would want you to live with no wife at all? How would you live?"

"Yes."

"Ah, I have it! Take the one squaw you still have and go with her to my brothers in the nations of the Wampanoag. They are such savages they will not even know that is not the wife God has given you. No one will be the wiser!"

"I wish I could do that, George. I wish I could."

"You can! You can!" and he dug around in his greatcoat pocket and pulled out a beaver skin bag with a pattern worked on it in wampum. "Here! Take this with you to my brothers in the nations of the Wampanoag. They will know it is from me and hide you from the men of Plymouth."

"No I can't."

George looked at me very seriously and put the pouch in my hands, closing them around it. "Take it. You are my brother. I will not have the men of Plymouth hurt my brother. I see in these clouds, which we have watched, that you will have great need of it. I do not need my mask to tell you that none are sweeter in repose, nor fiercer, nor crueler in wrath than the tribe called English. Take this, my brother Thomas. God bless you. Go with the squaw who is now with you to my dark brothers in the forest. When they see this they will care for you. These white men are very unpredictable and they may kill you, or kiss you on a whim."

29

WHEN I TOLD Lydia about the order of the court as we lay in bed that night she did not cry as I had thought she would. She said, "We must run away, Thomas. We must run to my sister and brothers in Rhode Island." I then told her about George's pouch and she said, "You know he is right."

"But, Lydia, I cannot."

"We must run away, and quickly. We will be safe in Rhode Island. The governors are all members of the Friends and they will protect us. I will start packing now. You must get a wagon from your father."

"He won't give me a wagon."

"What?"

"And I cannot go."

"Why not?"

"There is a bond for my appearance against my father for fifty pounds, and another against Ezra Perry which would ruin him."

"What has that old man ever done for you that you should put your life in danger for him?"

"But what about Ezra?"

"What do you owe that boy? He is nothing to you but your sister's husband. Your father will look after him and your father can afford the loss."

"I can't do it, Lydia."

"I am disappointed, Thomas, but it must be your decision." She pulled herself very close to me with her head against my chest. "I am afraid, though."

"There is no reason to be afraid. What can the punishment be?"

"It is not that I am afraid of. I am afraid they will force you to go back to Elizabeth, and I could not stand that."

George Barlow and Thomas Hinkley came for me early on a June morning. I was ready for them.

They held their horses by the gate and looked away as I kissed Lydia. "What can they do, Lydia?" I said softly to her.

I decided to ride my old sorrel mare with the white blaze. After all, it was a warm day and a long ride. She had the gentlest gait and a quiet disposition to match the weather.

It was a lazy, early summer day in Plymouth. As we road down Leiden Street to the General Court it almost felt like a county fair was in progress. The streets were full of dust, horses, and people of all descriptions. Produce was spread out for sale and children and Indians were everywhere. It was full of noise and color, but there was also languor about the place. It was after all now a backwater of the colony. Boston was the center of trade and Plymouth, with its old shallow beach, strict mother church, and poor sandy soil had become little more than the place where the General Court sat: the old capital, America's Winchester, while a busy London was growing to the north. When the court was not sitting it almost had the feel of a village. But this was a court day and it remembered on these days what it had been and the hawkers came out, ladies in their aprons and broad-brimmed straw hats, and every dog in Christendom with a tail to wag.

The court was a busy place with a small herd of horses whinnying and prancing on their tethers as they waited for their masters within to finish their business and set their heads home to the barn in time for their evening oats. There was dust everywhere and people of all sorts, their petitions in their hands, or there just for the fun of it, sitting all about the entrance so that you had to clear a path to get to the door with many a questioning look to see if you had authority to displace them, or if you might be someone notorious coming past them on the way to the gallows. Those who were not there early enough to find a place on the benches in the court, or at the courthouse door, would set themselves up on the grass, or up the hill where the meeting was and the burying ground. It was the sort of crowd which was in need of the loaves and fishes, but there was no Christ to provide them and so they waited the pleasure of the court to provide their entertainment.

In the courtroom itself the members of the court sat on a sort of stage in rough wooden chairs and behind quite ordinary tables. I remember marking where the adz had been at work on the table fronts as though the carpenter had been too busy to properly finish his work. Below them, in a great mess, were set out the places for the clerks and secretaries and all the papers which would be needed for the presenting of cases and for recording how they were resolved. This space was full of the officiously busy little major-domos who push the work along, the studious looking up over their books at us, and the nodding non-participants who may be asked to call the "oyes" or carry a prisoner, or a Bible, to the bar. Like any court, the business was always behind its agenda and justice sat there with its shirttail out. Apart from this business the place was just a large, bare room with its plank floor liberally sprinkled with sawdust. Large windows on the south filled the room with blinding sunlight and invisible black shadows. The time of day might be told by the movement of the sunlight from those windows, as I have been told it was at the Pantheon in Rome. And that sunlight fell now on every kind of humanity you could name: some dressed elegantly and smelling of rosemary sat beside the slovenly with their hair in black strings and smelling of the privy; myself, George Barlow, Elizabeth, and her father among them. What a place to resolve so tender a thing I thought, as though we were here about a contract for the sale of sheep, or a profanity shouted in the public street.

The members of the court were generally dressed as any well-to-do merchant might be on the Sabbath – that is decently, and quietly, but John Alden as master of the proceedings was wearing a red robe and sat at the center table, though not above the rest.

There were some who brought others to speak for them, and among those in the seats there were those who would argue your case for you for a price, but most spoke for themselves and plainly. Every shire of England lent its own special dialect to the proceedings.

Somehow I could not keep my mind on the court. It was as if I were only a spectator, not a participant, and there were so many things to see I had to labor to see any one of them. Then again, the heat, the hubbub, the dust, the atmosphere of a fair made it seem less than I had expected. There was no severity, nothing seemed sinister, or awful; it was just a room full of people carrying out their routines. Nothing could come of this but a few shillings here and a piece of paper there. After many cases resolved with fines, which to my lights, seemed to make no sense at all, the clerk stood up and called out: "The case of Thomas Burge of Sandwich in a matter of uncleanness."

It took me a moment to realize this was my case. It certainly did not sound familiar. I did, however, stand up when I saw no one else would.

"I see you are again before me," John Alden said. "I expect you thought I would not remember. Come forward! Come before the court! Bailiff, read the crown's charge against this man."

The clerk sorted through his papers, pulling one from the pile at last and giving it to the bailiff. This man scanned it before he read it.

"Are you here to speak before us on your own behalf?" John Alden asked.

"I expect I am. There aren't any others. I was not aware . . ."

The clerk was now ready and he read out the charge in a dry, matter-of-fact voice: "That the party, Thomas Burger, here present, the husband of Elizabeth . . . ."

"The name is Burge, sir," Mister Alden corrected. "You know his father."

"Oh, yes, . . . did commit unclean acts with a woman by the name of Lydia Gaunt, and is now living with this woman in a state of sin. The plaintiff, the aforementioned Elizabeth, asks for a divorce from Thomas Burge on these grounds and the division of their goods. Our sovereign lord the King does ask punishment for the aforementioned uncleanness committed in this colony."

"Thank you, William. There has been no act of divorce in this colony and I hope there will not now be. How do you plead?"

"I beg you pardon?"

"Do you tell this court that you are innocent of this charge or guilty?"

"Not guilty."

"You plead not guilty?"

"Let me explain."

"It is not your time for explanations, Thomas. We must have some evidence presented against you first. I will hear the case of the prosecution. Who speaks against this man?"

"I do," George Barlow replied.

"Very good, the court recognizes the sheriff of the town of Sandwich, who is known to us, to speak for the crown."

"I say of my own personal knowledge, and that it is common knowledge in the town as well, that this man has lain with the woman Lydia Gaunt and that she now lives with him at his dwelling place as if she were his wife. She was there when my deputy and I arrested him."

"Yes, I do not deny this."

"What? Are you changing your plea to guilty?"

"I do live with her."

"And is there carnal knowledge between you?"

"Yes, there is."

"Then how can you plead as you have?"

"I have divorced my wife Elizabeth and married Lydia by the manner of the people called Friends."

"I would not bring the abominations of those Quakers into this court. I am not surprised their false teaching has brought you to this bar." There was a silence in the court. "No such contracts are known to this court. We have in all the years of this colony declared no persons divorced, but I am sorely tried here in my patience. Such an action is as grave a thing as has ever come before this court, and you, sir, will admit this sin out here? That you have broken the commandments? Did you not covenant before God with this woman Elizabeth for life to be your wife?"

"I did, but I considered that bond no longer in force. We have had no children, but Lydia carries my child."

"Are you mad, telling us that? What was the duration of this marriage?"

"More than ten years," George said.

"You considered it no longer . . . marriage is a contract entered into in the face of God. It is one of the most sacred of the sacraments, and you believe that you can sunder it at your pleasure?"

"May I speak?" asked Elizabeth.

"Dear woman, you surely may if you wish, but there is no further need for testimony because this man has accused himself and convicted himself with his own words."

"I am disgraced by this man. No other man will ever have me because of what he has done to me. This man is no husband to me, and I pray you whatever you may deliberate that this man no longer be my husband when you finish. I wish to be rid of him as much as he wishes to be rid of me."

John Alden sat back in his chair and closed his eyes. He thought for a time and then leaned forward to listen to the advice of the other members of the court. They spent some time in animated whispers. At last he passed his left hand across his eyes and looked up. "We are agreed that adultery is truly a sin for which a marriage can be dissolved. But I beg you to reconsider, good woman. What is your father's opinion?"

"My father is here and he agrees."

John Alden sat silent again, then turned to me. "Thomas, after this are you not repentant now and will you not return to your wife and beg her forgiveness? I could order that in this case."

"No."

"God often comes into this chamber to see what we are about. I pray he has not visited us today. I beg you both to reconsider."

The courtroom was absolutely silent for a time until the silence was broken by the sound of a baby crying. Its mother took it from the court.

"Very well. What is the property here?"

Elizabeth's father said, "I have at my home an old cotton bolster, a pillow, sheets, and some other things."

"Is that all there is for ten years of marriage? What value do you put on these things?"

"About forty shillings."

"Forty shillings. What other property does Thomas have?"

"Some land, his home, cattle, what you might expect."

"Is that the extent of your estate, Master Burge?"

"It is."

"You are aware I will divide that. Do you have objection?"

"I do not."

Mister Alden sat in thought again. "I ask the secretary of the court to write the following in his clearest hand, that it will be an example to all the generations; and I proclaim it here and order that Master Barlow will also proclaim it in the town of Sandwich. Before I do, however, I advise you, Thomas Burge, that it is the law of this colony that any man or woman convicted of adultery will wear on all his garments a letter as a sign of that sin so that those who meet him may be warned of his character and so that his example will keep others from breaking God's commandments. I am, and many here are, friend to your father and know him very well, because he has sat with us here. He is a wise, humble, and good man and I would not hurt him for the world. Should you walk the lanes of Sandwich with this mark it would, I believe, punish him more than it would punish you. I, therefore, ask you, for your father's sake, to leave this colony and spare him that shame. Will you do that?"

"I will."

"Yes, well, then there is some vestige of humanity left in you after all. Clerk, here is how the order shall read: Thomas Burge Junior, being bound over to the Court to answer for an act of uncleanness committed by him with Lydia Gaunt, he was sentenced, according to the law, to be severely whipped, which accordingly was inflicted while this court was in being, and a second time to be whipped at Sandwich, at the discretion of Mister Hinkley, on the first Monday next after the date hereof; and as concerning the capital letters to be worn according to the law, it is for the present respited until the Court should discern better of his future walkings. And whereas Elizabeth, the late wife of the said Thomas Burge, did urgently solicit the Court for a divorce, the said Thomas Burge manifesting little dislike thereof, and some of her relations concurring therein, the Court, considering the nature of the fact, together with the particulars mentioned, did see cause to grant the said Elizabeth her desire, and therefore do hereby declare, that henceforth they, the said Thomas and Elizabeth, are not to be reputed husband and wife each to other, but are cleared of their marriage bond, and are fully and clearly divorced; furthermore the Court doth allow and determine, that the said Elizabeth, the late wife of the said Thomas Burge, shall have and enjoy one part of three of all his estate, viz: lands, goods and chattels, as her proper right forever; as also, the said Thomas Burge consenting thereunto, at the same time the Court did allow her an old cotton bed and bolster, a pillow, a sheet and two blankets, that were with the pair of sheets, with some other small things that are in William Bassett's hands, to the value of forty shillings."

He spoke to the others for a moment and then he spoke to me. "I hope that I will never try such a case again. Should this become common among us, where would we be? This would be a colony of fornicators and adulterers without the law of marriage. When the vow of marriage might be taken as nothing, but a pledge that a man would lie with a woman only as long as it pleased him, who would look after the mothers and children? It chills me to the bone to imagine such a world. And if a sacred vow of marriage taken before God and witnesses is so lightly valued, what other vows might lose their substance? I am much troubled by this, Master Burge.

"We will adjourn now for a midday meal, Master Burge, and when that is done we will assemble again at the place of execution and the public hangman will execute the punishment of this Court upon you in the face of this Court. I would make yourself ready for that with whatever prayers you may still have. We will see you at the whipping post, Sir."

30

QUITE A CROWD had gathered. I stripped off my white shirt as I did not want blood on it, the shirt which Lydia had laid out for me just that morning, and the hangman came up to me with his black hood hung over his arm. He tied my hands firmly, asking if the knot was too tight. I thought it ironic that before he would lash my body with his whip he would inquire politely if I was chafed by the rope which held me.

With his helper he strung the rope up to the scaffold and pulled it until my feet were just touching the ground. It is always interesting to watch a man at the work he knows well. There is an economy of motion and a precision in his every gesture which is pleasing.

"You will feel the lash less if you dance a bit with it, Sir," he said.

The crowd was getting louder behind me and they were so close I could smell their sweat. They shouted "Adulterer!" and other things I could not make out. There were women's voices and even children's among them. I could hear this, but I could not see them as they were all behind me. I felt the hair on my neck rise and a chill run thorough my body as they loosed their accumulated anger at my bare back. From the sound of them they seemed to press so close in upon me I felt defenseless, trussed up against the scaffold with neither hands nor feet free. What did they know about me, or about Lydia, or about Elizabeth that they could make me such a subject of their rage, or such a toy for their entertainment? I could hear some of them laughing and others inquiring about the details of my crime. The speculations on that ran from theft to murder until the cry went up again: "Adulterer!" All that I could see were the rough underpinnings of the scaffold. On the other side, quite a way away, the dirty faces of some little boys who had crawled unnoticed up inside the structure looked out and were now nested there, making faces and sticking their tongues out at me. They giggled quietly to each other, afraid they might be heard by the hangman or his assistant. The hangman put his face close to my ear so I could hear him over the rising noise of the crowd. "You had better put this in your mouth and hold it fast between your teeth." With that, he forced a piece of old leather like a horse fitting between my teeth. I thanked him with a muffled word into the leather. He laughed, "You have no business thanking me."

It seemed that hours passed like this, with chills wracking my body, praying that it would begin, and the sweat so flowing on my face that it blinded me no matter how I shook my head to clear my eyes. Each time I shook my head it started the crowd anew. I wondered if I would have gloried in another's punishment as these people were in mine. I wondered if I would know that each crime is singular and its punishments unique. It was a mercy, I thought, that I was in the hands of the General Court and not of those who shouted out behind me for my blood. Some of them shouting out without any knowledge of the crime at all. Do you rejoice that your brother is beaten because it reassures you that you will not be beaten? That you are that little less with sin, or is it just revenge on some other back for all the punishments you have endured? Or do we simply let our beast out for a walk in the common on a bright June day so that it may be sated and rest easier at home?

Finally, a great cheer rose up from the bystanders, and I was sure the members of the Court had come.

I hung there another agonizing time while they read the charge again.

If I turned my head I could see the hangman now in his black hood. He leaned over to me again: "Prepare yourself. Remember what I have told you. I will try not to hit your face with the whip, but you had best keep your eyes closed. I have plucked out an eye with old Bathsheba here and not known it until the prisoner was cut down."

I could just see him swinging the whip beside him as the crowd hissed and drew its breath and then they cheered as it began to crack. I could see he laid his whole weight into it, swinging as though it were an ax and he would cut me in two. I cannot describe the pain. No words can tell. The only consolation in that world of shimmering pain was that the crowd disappeared and I was alone with it. The whip was whirling and spitting and coiling all around me, finding tender places I had not known before, so that I bit down as hard as I could on the leather, again, and again, but it was little help against the magnitude of that searing, coiling pain which seemed to be all around me and within me, not just on my back. I did dance. I danced wildly since I could not cry out. I hoped that the lashes which came after the first would hurt less as I became used to the pain, as your hand can become used to frozen water, but that was not so. When the whip had torn my skin away it found flesh infinitely more tender to work on and it was like bands of red hot iron coiling around me, and as the whip was rudely yanked away it was as if tongues of flame came out from deep in my body through every wound.

I prayed as I had never prayed before that each lash would be the last, but they came on and on, each more fierce and probing than the one before, as though the arm of the hangman would never tire and the lust of the Court never be satisfied. I could not cry out because of the piece of leather between my teeth, but with each lash I silently cried in my mind, "Enough! How many more? Oh, Lord God, how many more?" Then another blow would come with such force I could taste the salt blood in my mouth.

At last I could not distinguish the real world from fantasy, except that in both my body was on fire. I did not even have the small mercy of knowing when the ordeal was ended for I was unconscious long before that, hanging like some side of raw meat on a rope, dangling from the scaffold, surrounded by the flies which smelled their feast and a nursery for their eggs.

When they cut me down, though, they threw the pint of salt on my back and I awoke grabbing at my body, crying out and writhing on the ground.

Of the trip home I remember only moments through a red haze. They had lashed me, belly down, with my arms across my mare's shoulders and my hands at her breastbone and with my feet lashed at the stiffle bone. When I would wake thinking some devils were gnawing at my back and sides, I would feel my cheek rubbing against the sorrel hair on her withers. If I cried out I could feel her crupper shiver and she would dance for fear of the unfamiliar load, the command she did not understand, and that would hurt all the more for the stretching of my wounds. When she started I am sure she could also smell the blood which was all over me and would begin again to flow. I rejoiced that I had chosen this gentle horse that morning. Any other would have long since run away with me on it.

They left me alone, still lashed to my horse, at my own gate where Lydia found me at last and cut me down. I had not been able to find enough voice to call to her.

But for all the pain as I fell from the horse and her trying to find some way to lift me, as I could not walk, I felt a joy and release in her arms and from her kisses I knew my torment was ended and I was still alive.

31

I KNEW WE had to get away from Sandwich, and as fast as we could. I knew I could not get a message to Mehitable, Zachariah, or Hannaniah in less than a week by sea, but I was sure they would make a safe place for us among the Quakers in Providence Plantation if I could only get Thomas there. I would catch myself staring into the whorls in the glass in our windows, at a mad world which might take us at any moment like a savage dog with a rabbit, or I would be stirring a pot on the crane over a low fire and suddenly realize I was crying, weeping, when I realized I had allowed Thomas to stay in this vicious place, and in my pride, or weakness, let them do this thing to him for my sake. What had it been for? To protect that old man's wealth. To protect that old man who could have lifted a hand at any moment and stayed the brutal hand of the court, but who did not. For the sake of that man's pride. God forgive him that he would have done that to his son to save his fortune!

I knew we had to leave and was desperate to get Thomas out of their clutches. I could think of nothing else. I would stand there wringing my hands and weeping for days and it would mean nothing. I had to get him away! Thomas was still feverish and his mind unhinged. He would talk at great length and I could not understand a word he said. He would wake in the night and roll onto his side, staring at me with eyes glazed over with pain as though he did not know me. Some company was around him I could not see. He would cry out to them.

I dressed his poor wounds as best I could, but he could not stand, much less run, or ride. No one came to our aid. We might have been lepers.

Who had he hurt, this sweet gentle man, that they should do this to him?

One evening I woke beside him to the sound of his groans, my hands still slick with the grease I had used on his back. All I could do was kneel down by the bed and pray to God that he would spare this poor man's life and bring him back to me. I dared not pray that God would relieve him of the pain. I was not brave enough to face that. I was not brave enough to think that God might take him from me even to save him that torture. With tears streaming down my face I said to the darkness, "Dear God of mercy please make him well. Please God, now that a light has come into my life which illuminates it, do not take that light from me. Do not take him from me. Look down in mercy, dear Jesus. You know I do not ask anything of you for myself. But now I beg you. Do whatever you wish to me: kill me, revile me, send me out into the wilderness without a home, even take your love from me if you must. God spare his life. I will give him back to Elizabeth. I will go away. Anything if he will not die. God, I give meaning to my days by the thought of him, by his smiling face, his laughter, by his solidness, by his true love for me, but I would give that up rather than to see him dead. Save him! Save him! When I think of him so full of life and now so still and far from me I cannot stand it. Spare him good Lord. I will pay the price."

I lied in that prayer. I would never give him back to Elizabeth. Perhaps because of that lie God answered my prayer in his own way.

The next morning Thomas knew me. He was able to stand for a moment. He could speak again. By the evening I was able to bring him to the fire.

I dared to dream that I might yet get him away.

I brought smoked ham, some parched corn, all I felt we could carry, and put it in anything I could find to strap onto a horse. I went quickly to the barn and saddled two horses: my black and Thomas's dear old sorrel with the white blaze which had brought him home to me from Plymouth. I then selected a heavy bay to carry our provisions.

I led my black out into the dooryard, and he flicked away the flies with his long tail, reluctant to be saddled again. As I struggled with him, here came George Barlow and Thomas Hinkley like the hosts of Perdition.

George said "Woman, where are you going with that black horse of yours?"

"You know my name perfectly well, George Barlow."

"I asked you a question, woman."

"You just get away! I have a right to saddle my horse and go wherever I wish."

"You may, woman, but the adulterer, Thomas Burge, has no such right. He has a charge of the King to answer to."

"Leave him alone, George! Leave him alone! You have almost killed him already. Only God's mercy has saved him. Now go and kill someone else and let him be."

"Where is he?"

"I don't know."

"Where is he? We have business with him and it is the King's business."

"He has gone, George. Maybe he has gone to Rhode Island. I don't know. He just rode off without a word to me. That's why I am so angry. He just rode away. If you are quick you may catch him before he gets to the Old Bay Path."

"I don't believe you."

"Well, what do I care what you believe. It is the truth."

The two men moved their horses as though they might start off.

"It sounds true to me, George," said Thomas Hinkley, "Let's ride on and try to catch him. We can always come back."

"I think she is lying."

"I don't," said Master Hinkley and turned his horse. George's horse instinctively followed.

"We will come back for you, woman." George said over his shoulder as he started after Master Hinkley.

Just then Thomas called me from the house. All these days he had not spoken, but at this time he called me. Had it been another time I would have run to him in joy and wept. I felt the tears well up in my eyes again, but I turned my head so the men could not see them. What a trick; God did this to punish me for lying to him.

"Not here, is he? Then who is that calling you, woman? Have you given over so fully to sin that you keep the house full of paramours?" And George yanked his horse's head and swung down, letting loose the reins.

"You have no business here!" I shouted, and went at him with my bare hands.

He started back calling for Master Hinkley, who let his bridle drop, and jumped down from his horse.

"I don't want to hurt you," said George, as he was retreating halfway up the stile. When Master Hinkley joined him the two went over the fence like two old hounds after the hare and spread out in the dooryard, but keeping their distance from me all the time. I began looking for something I could use to stop them and I saw out of the corner of my eye an old ax stuck in a stump. I grabbed it out with all my might, and the weight of it coming out, sent it flying over my head, pulling me back to the cabin wall. I gave it a mighty heave, swinging it out at them in a long arc, but it had control of me and I had no control of it. It pulled me around with my back to the men. Thomas Hinkley took this opportunity to jump up onto my back. The two of us went sprawling on the ground with him coming down on top, knocking the breath out of me. I let the ax go, as he was holding it down so I couldn't budge it, and I squirmed around underneath him and got a good fistful of his jowl. I dug my nails in and pulled with all the strength I had. The blood came out all around my nails.

"Oh God!" he cried out in pain, "Oh God!" and as he grabbed at his face to stop the blood I had hoped I might get my hands on the ax again, but he knew what I had in mind and let fall with all his weight onto me. He then held my hands down, his face dripping blood on me, as George ran into the cabin to get Thomas.

When Thomas came out he managed to say, "What are you doing to my wife?" He started away from George as if he were about to save me. I hoped he had not seen Hinkley's blood on me and thought it mine. George got a good grip around Thomas's waist and, swinging him round, clipped him with his fist, which sent Thomas sprawling on the ground unconscious.

I was much more worried about Thomas then, as he had just walked that morning for the first time, than I was about my tormenter, so I just went limp and said, "I'll be good. I'll do anything you say. Just let me get to him." Thomas Hinkley, cursing, reluctantly let me up, rubbing the blood from my scratching on the side of his sleeve. I ran to Thomas and cradled his head on my lap until his eyes opened.

"I'll bring him in, George," I said. "I'll bring him in, I promise."

"There is not a chance of that, woman. I may be a fool once but not twice." Of course, he was right, for if George had let me we would have been gone. It was times like these I wished I were a man. Damn them for their swaggering and brutality, but I would have been the brute with them if I had had the chance at that moment.

"Look, George, look at this man. You have nearly killed him. You can do him no more harm. Are you proud of yourselves for your victory over him? Why, this is a man who can hardly stand. He cannot defend himself. What sort of man would take a man in this condition? What sort of man are you?"

"It is the law, and the law is the law, Lydia!"

"It isn't the law. You just love to hurt other people, and the weaker the better. If Thomas were well you wouldn't dare to try to take him."

"We must take him."

"You will take him over my dead body."

"If we must we will," he said, and Thomas Hinkley grabbed me again and held me while George manhandled Thomas, still unconscious, up across the neck of his horse, and began to lash him there.

"Damn you!" I said and stamped down on Thomas Hinkley's instep as hard as I could. He cried out in pain, but did not let me go. He put his other arm around my waist, fumbling to get his leg around me until he had me off balance and then, throwing his weight forward, he again brought me face down in the dirt. He held my face down with all his strength.

I could hear George shout, "I am going on with the prisoner, Master Hinkley."

I felt Thomas Hinkley's body tense. "Don't you leave me here with this panther by the tail!" But George just kept on riding with poor Thomas in front of him.

Thomas Hinkley pushed himself up abruptly and made a run for the stile. I had the ax in my hand in a moment and was after him, swinging it above my head, and him scurrying to get out of my reach. The head of the ax came down sharply and bit into the stile where his foot had been and I saw him go pale. "Jesus save me," he said under his breath. I was yanking at it trying to get it loose again as Thomas Hinkley pulled himself up on his big bay and was off at a brisk trot down the lane toward Sandwich, still struggling to get the reins he had dropped in his haste.

I stood there in despair with the tears streaming down my face. God had not heard my prayer after all, I thought. It had just been a cruel joke. They were taking my Thomas to the whipping post where he would surely die under the lash. I could not see where I was going, but somehow I made my way to the barn for Thomas's horse and the bay. My own horse had been startled by the fight and he put his big nose over to nuzzle me as I passed. I had a great deal of trouble saddling the horses and could not seem to make the buckles work or pull the cinch. At one point I simply sat down in the dirt and let myself cry while the great horses' feet moved uneasily around me. When I had control again it was no better because the horses were now so skittish that they moved around in worried circles while I tried to get them ready.

Finally I finished and mounted my black gelding, taking the others on a short tether. I rode on, leaving the gate swinging open. I would never come through that gate again, I said out loud to the empty sky; George Barlow, or the Indians, or wolves, or God only knows who could take all the livestock for all I cared.

As I rode into town with the two horses behind me and still crying, those who saw me on the road turned away and I knew then that they knew and I surely must be too late. They dared not meet my eyes.

I could see Thomas still strung up from a good distance away and Master Hinkley still at him with the whip so that his whole back was a bright covering of fresh blood, the blood soaking his trousers, but still Master Hinkley was at him with the whip.

Half dismounting and half falling from my gelding in my haste, I struggled to untangle myself and ran as fast as I could, sure I would grasp that whip out of his hands or throw myself between it and Thomas, but George Barlow stepped out and caught me. I was hysterically mad, and heaving with uncontrollable sobs. I managed at last to say in a hoarse whisper, "George Barlow, you stop him! You make him stop! The court did not give you leave to kill him." I fell down on my knees before him, convulsed with sobs, for I could see Thomas was hanging there limp, swinging with the whip, and was surely already dead.

Only a creature of iron could look on that scene and let that whipping continue, and George finally relented. I had never seen him do one good thing in all his wretched life until then. He came up to Thomas Hinkley, took hold of his whip hand, and when he had stopped him, pointed at me on my knees in the dust sobbing. I don't know what George said to him, but it was an act of mercy, as sure as any in history, because Thomas Hinkley then cut my

Thomas down. Thomas just slumped to the ground with his jaw slack like some poor deer an Indian might have brought into Sandwich for a feast.

There were a few people gathered around, but they had been very quiet and now they started to move away. Those who did stay did not make a move to help us, but just stood about watching in horror, or fascination, wondering perhaps if they might ever face such a fate. They knew they were there just to observe, not a part of what they had seen, not our dear friends, just bystanders. They were neither perpetrators nor victims.

I got up, wiping the tears from my eyes with my sleeve, and when I knelt down beside Thomas I was sure he was dead. I tried to lift his lifeless body, but I lacked the strength in my arms to move that dead weight. How could these people just stand there watching me struggle, laboring to lift him with his blood all over me? They had known us all our lives. How could they? I could not budge him. I would try to lift him, dragging him by his arms, but I could not move him at all and I was frantic to get him out of there. The horses were all prancing and wild with the smell of his blood. When I did manage to pull Thomas's body to them and tried to lift him onto the horse, it would shy away with a wild look in its eye. Finally, I got his horse quiet enough so that with a superhuman effort I could get his arms up onto the saddle. I tried pushing him up from there, but I could not lift his feet up off the ground. Keeping a hand on him as best I could, I went under the horse to the other side, and although I thought it might break his arms, I tried to pull him across the saddle by his hands from that side. The horse then moved again and his body, slippery with his blood, slid down to the ground. I sat down in the dust under the old sorrel mare and cried. At last, a man came up to us and lifted Thomas up onto the horse, unhooked the rope I had put on the pommel, and started tying Thomas onto the mare.

I had only seen his boots, but when I had my hair and tears out of my eyes I saw it was Richard Bourne, and I said, "God bless you, Richard. Thank you." He didn't look at me at all. He just kept tying

Thomas's body onto the horse. At last he said to me, "Don't you thank me, Lydia Gaunt." When he was finished he just stood there for a few moments with his hand on Thomas's arm, then he walked off without looking at me at all.

I got up on my own horse, gathering the leads of the other two, and started off. No one watched us as we left. Sandwich might have been a ghost town. Thomas's ghost would surely haunt it, I thought. All my life I had lived here. The people of this town had known me as a baby in arms, as a rag-tag little girl with my hair all filled with snags, as a young woman freshening and flirting for the first time with the boys: those boys who were now so stiff-necked that they were hiding in their houses lest they might catch our sin. Now all those who had known me, who would have risked their lives to pull me out of the sea, or out of a field with a bull, or whatever I might have needed in that little world, closed their doors and shutters fast against me and not even an old man would come to his gate post to take off his hat in farewell as we passed. Not a one!

But my father had not raised us to be cowards and I rubbed my tears away and straightened my hair as best I could and rode out with that poor load behind me, sitting as tall in the saddle as ever a queen of England sat her horse on the way to the block. I didn't have the slightest idea where I was going, or how I would ever get there. I had never traveled more than five miles from my home, and to leave the Cape was beyond imagining until now.

I rode on and on, as though there were nothing else in the world but my black horse and the body of Thomas Burge. I figured this lane must surely lead to another. Then one day if I just rode to the west I would surely come to the Old Bay Path I had heard about, and that would surely take me south to Providence Plantation. Nothing, however, is as simple as it seems. I had no idea of all the lanes there could be in the wide world and as I rode they just kept coming apart and coming together by the hundreds. Any one of them might be my way. I lost track of what direction I was going in altogether. Was this crossing the Old Bay Path, or had I passed it as it crossed? In and out of woods, up and down hills, circling around meadows, dead-ending in marshes so that I had to turn back and hope to find the road I had left: I was surely quite completely lost. I was certain the lane I was on was wrong when it started to get narrower, and with night coming on I could barely tell where the lane was at all. There was the hoot of an owl far off in the twilight. I wished I could sail as the owl did on that invisible road south. I could not see the stars because the forest had long ago closed above my head and I had to ride slowly for fear of low limbs, but I could see the moon skulking along beside me and now and then flickering down where a stream cut some trees away. There was not a soul, or a sound, anywhere but the thudding of my own heart. There was not even the palest wink of a fire. I was now beyond that vague line which marks the mapped world from the featureless wilderness where only wild things live and where no person dare walk alone. At last I came out into a little clearing in the woods and got down from my horse, straining to see where the path might be on the other side, but there was no path out of this clearing. The path just came to an end. Why should there be such a path, I thought, if it leads to nothing? I could feel my flesh crawl. There was no turning back. In the dead of night I would be more lost than I was here. I was so frightened I was trembling all over, and when I touched the horses they were trembling too. I should have stopped when there was light. What sort of camp could I pitch here in darkness so deep I could not see my feet in the thatch of leaves beneath me?

I felt my way along the side of the old sorrel to touch Thomas, expecting him to be cold, but he was burning up with fever and I began crying again, praying as I stood there. I couldn't think of anything to do but stand there in that clearing crying, crying in the middle of the forest with the only family I had – a tiny speck in my womb and a man burning with fever laid across a horse – and all of us sure to be killed now. The air was dead still, but I sensed a movement and held my breath, trying to slow the beating of my heart. It was pounding so hard in my ears I was sure it could be heard. I stood there still as a statue, straining to see into the heart of that black forest. Then the moonlight came slowly down around me and across the clearing and I could see and I wished to God I had not. I suddenly saw twelve black figures standing around me. I had walked into their silent trap and there they stood with their hatchets and scalping knives looking at me. Waiting in that woodland clearing like pigeon hunters with their net.

The moon shone chalky white in the clearing and I could see their painted faces, all stripes and dots, watching me, the moonlight in their eyes making their faces look like ghost masks. Then, one at a time they began to whoop, softly at first and then louder, building on each other like the calls of the wild wolves. Wild, spine-chilling cries, high and clear, as if they would call all the others around to the feast. They started moving slowly in on us on moccasin feet. I prayed to God they would not rape me before they killed me, because I had my baby in me. You think mad thoughts like that at such a time.

When they put their hands on me I knew I was surely dead. I did not faint, I have never fainted, but I did lose consciousness for a little time.

32

WHEN I WOKE up I was all alone in a wigwam and there was nothing else in that small space but dirt and a corn leaf basket. Through the opening I could see there were many fires outside and the Indians were dancing in the spheres of light around fires in an otherwise pitch black night. I was sure they would soon come for me so I lay dead still hoping, like the quail, that in that stillness there might be invisibility. I listened to the strange music and the beat of their feet like lost souls alone in the forest, cursing their fate.

At last I screwed my courage up and crept to the wigwam opening. What I saw bore a lively resemblance to hell. It struck me through and through with fear. There must have been a dozen great bonfires with tongues of flame leaping up to the highest tops of the trees and hundreds and hundreds of Indians around them — most of them naked and greased, all of their faces covered with such paint that they were not recognizable as human. Some were dancing wildly and some kept time with little bells attached to rings around their ankles. In the midst of them there was a deer skin laid out and on it a man knelt with his body all painted black as the devil. I did not know it then, but this was the great prince sachem Phillip who called himself Metacom. Many of the others were around him in a ring, some with their faces visible to me, and some just naked black bodies between me and the scene. They were all striking on the earth with their hands and sticks, muttering or humming with their mouths. Another man stood beside Phillip with a gun in his hand. Phillip made a long speech, then held his hands, palm out, before his eyes, peeking out between the fingers and making a cracking sound. With each word he uttered in the Wampanoag language the others nodded assent and the man standing beside him with the gun urged him on. Once, the man with the gun tried to leave the circle, but they all stopped him. He tried to make a stand against them, but they forced him back again. Then they all sang in a wild running rhythm, tore at their hair, and beat the dirt. They passed a second gun to the man and the kneeling man on the deer skin began a low sad singing speech again, the rest assenting, humming, and muttering after every phrase. The man with the gun had left the circle, but they called him back with such force that he returned, and when he was in the firelight again he spread out his arms above his head with a musket in each hand, and began swaying and turning until the man kneeling on the deer skin began to speak again in the orange light of the fire.

I woke up the next morning with pains all over me. I had slept there through the night on the earth with my head at the door. It was very early, that opalescent hour when there is light, but the sun has not risen, and no one is stirring, and there is great silence upon the world. I crept out past the smouldering remains of the fires and past the deer skin still stretched on the ground. To my surprise no one seemed to be guarding me and I was quite alone. I thought of running, but Thomas might still be alive and to search for him among the wigwams would surely raise the camp. I came at last to a brown stream with some brush on its verge and did what toilet I could. The cold fresh water on my face made my skin tingle and I wished the surface had been smooth enough for me to see my reflection. When I was through I sat there in the bush for a long time, wondering what I should do. The woods looked inviting, but at last I returned to the wigwam where they had put me like some pet animal, more frightened of the world than yearning for its freedom. I lay awake in the darkness of the wigwam listening to the sounds of the morning: first, there was the sound of wild birds, then one lone dog began to bark, some others joined him, a child began to cry until it was comforted, then the sound of voices speaking in the soft, sibilant tongue of the Wampanoag, and finally the smell of smoke and women's voices as they began a morning meal. I wondered if they would come for me, or if I was now forgotten. At last, I could see movement at the entrance to my wigwam. I could see a woman's legs, but she was talking to someone before she entered. I sat up tight against the back wall, waiting and bracing myself for what might come.

A young squaw crawled in and sat on the earth by the door. She looked at me for a moment and then down at the earth. We sat like this for what seemed to me an hour, until I could stand it no longer. I wanted to scream at her, but I only said, "Where is my husband?" Simply saying the word brought it all back and I felt a lump in my throat and the tears welling up. I held them back in fear what these savages would do if they suspected my weakness.

"Husband," the girl repeated, and then was silent. I began to wonder if she was simple-minded and that is why they had sent her to guard the white woman. Then her face brightened. "Sannup?"

"Is my husband here? Is he still alive?"

"Still alive," she said.

I was not sure whether that meant that he was alive, or that she simply did not understand what I was asking. I went to her and grasped her hand. "Yes, Please! Is he alive or dead?"

She seemed frightened of me and pulled away.

She was very young, dressed in buckskin with many bead necklaces and dozens of bracelets of all kinds and descriptions. Her eyes were very wide and dark and she looked at me quizzically. Her long, straight, jet black hair hung down her back unbraided and she had carefully marked her face with delicate, graceful finger marks in red ocher. She seemed so delicate and well bred I was sure she must be related to the sachem. I grasped both her hands, hoping to appeal to her as one woman to another. "Please, my husband: is he alive?"

At last she said, with some difficulty like a stutterer, but I was sure the problem was that she was uneasy with her English, "You come. I show."

She took my hand in hers like you would a friend or a child, and led me across the camp. As we passed, the dogs barked and the men stopped to look at us; she turned back to see if this had frightened me. The women of the camp went on about the chores of the morning without a glance toward us.

We entered a much larger lodge, and there on a raised cot Thomas lay on his stomach. I threw myself down beside him, kissing his hand and brushing the hair away from his face. He was breathing, though still unconscious, and when I touched his face I was amazed that the fever was gone. The Indian woman watched us in surprise. I had a feeling that if she were in my position she would not have shown this emotion to another woman to whom she was not closely related.

I drew myself up and made myself look at his wounds. The Indians had dressed them and I only hoped that their primitive cures would not make them worse. His whole back was covered with oak bark and leaves in a thick poultice.

"Prisoner of your enemies?" the young squaw asked.

"What?"

"Take him prisoner?"

I thought for a moment that she was telling me that we were prisoners, but then I realized that it was a question.

She thought for a moment, then said, "Tortured?"

"He was whipped."

"Terrible enemies. Must be Mohawks."

"No. He was beaten by order of the General Court in Plymouth."

She looked puzzled, "Court?"

"Yes, they did this to punish him."

"Nux!" she thought for a time, "Your own people do this to him?"

"Yes."

"We do this to matchit Indians: Narragansett, Mohican, Mohawk, not to Wampanoag."

We sat in silence and I began crying again, patting and kissing Thomas's hand. She watched for a while, then began to croon a slow tuneless melody. At first I wondered how she could sing at a site like this, but then I felt she was trying to help in some way.

At last she said, "Very sick. Not die."

I embraced her. She seemed very surprised and pulled away at first, but then she patted my hair and said, "Not die."

I sat by Thomas all morning while the young squaw brought me some little cakes about the size of two fingers, made of wheat and fried in bear grease, she said, and also some meat which she showed me with signs I was to chew. How sweet that meal tasted! I realized after I took the meat between my teeth that I had been a day without food.

In the afternoon a delegation came to visit us. It certainly was the strangest visit I have ever had. The visitors were an older Indian and two young braves. They came in as the young squaw had and sat by the door in silence until I could stand it no longer and had to speak to them. The older man was outlandishly dressed. He was obviously an Indian, but he wore his long graying hair down his back and not cut short as was the style among the others. He was dressed as I have never seen any man dress. It was what I had dreamed an Englishman might wear at court with petticoat breeches of a light brown trimmed with a wide ribbon of sky blue cloth arranged in overlapping loops. His doublet matched the breeches with half a dozen slashes in each ample arm, showing sky blue silk through them and all turned with loops, braid, and buttons of the same. His collar was of white linen and lace of such quality it might have lain at ease on the breast of any English lord. It was turned down across his coat in a multitude of lace flowers that would shame the King's gardener. The lace was so full under his chin as to need to be laid out in box plaits. The shirt was of Holland, so long and fine that it hung out beneath his coat. Over all of this he had a full dark blue cloak (although it was a warm day) gathered in a rolling collar and with gold braid hanging down to close it. The hat above all this splendor was of a low round beaver in the Flemish style with a broad brim, and that brim full of sky blue plumes like the nest of some exotic bird. To finish off the effect, he had French full boots with buckle tops. All he lacked was a powdered peruke, and for all I knew he had one of those tucked away in one of his great pockets. I could not take my eyes off him.

The two young men with him were, in contrast, so close to naked that I was embarrassed to look at them. Even their heads were shaved.

"What cheer, good lady?" said the older gentleman. "I am Wassausman: the teacher of these two young gentlemen. They are the King's grandsons: Wansuta and Metacom. Your people prefer to give them names in English which their grandfather Missasoit chose for them at the General Court: Alexander and Phillip. The Great King Sachem has one other grandson, but you will not have the pleasure of meeting him on this visit. He is Sonconewhew, who is now a student at Cambridge University. I am only recently returned myself from that august institution in your beautiful England. I studied there for several years, primarily in history and rhetoric. I am particularly charmed to be again in the company of a lady of your civilized nation, and particularly one of such beauty and grace, though I regret it is such a sad occurrence which brings this meeting about. Have you been well-treated?"

"I have."

"Perhaps you are surprised to find such hospitality in the forest, and in the very camp of the Sachem of the Wampanoag."

"I did not know what to expect. As you can see, my husband and I had little choice."

"Yes, well, dear lady, an article was found on your person as you slept, and, begging your pardon for the liberty, I have it with me. If I may?"

"Yes, please."

"It is a small talisman from the hand of our dear brother George: a sagamore in thrall to the sachem, and his dear friend. It advised us you were a friend of our people, and so the great sachem Missasoit has ordered that you be treated as though you were his own kin. I hope that when you left the Nauset people they, and our dear cousin George, were well?"

"It is my husband who is a friend of the sagamore."

"What a pity. I should have enjoyed news of him. George is a man of many parts and I love him; although he is sadly uneducated. I must wait until your good husband recovers then to find how he is faring." A pause followed, but this one was not an uneasy one, rather a moment for Wassuasman to collect his thoughts. "I am very fond of your England. Did you come from there?"

"No, I have never been away from Sandwich."

"What a pity, dear lady, the world is truly full of wonders. I am particularly fond of your pastries and fruit tarts, your learned scholars of ancient history and, of course, my great passion: angling."

"Angling?"

"Oh, you are not familiar with that, then?"

"No, I have never heard of it."

"It is a special means of fishing I have particularly enjoyed with the chaps on the Cam. Now, our benighted people just go out with a spear, wade out into some river, stand very still, and when a fish comes by they kill it and eat it and that is that. You see, we live in nature all the time and therefore take it for granted. We get no special enjoyment from it: no intellectual enjoyment from it. We eat it, you might say, rather than taking pleasure in it as you do." He laughed at his little joke. "Now, the true English angler: he is a very different sort indeed. He puts a cleverly made little hook of metal on the end of a string, just so. Then he hangs this string on a long stick and casts it out upon the waters. He proceeds to the significant part of the business. He sits or lies down upon a sweet bank of flowers and herbs and muses."

The boys looked quite bored, as though they had heard this lecture before, and one of them stared at me with such a searching look it sent chills all over me. I was glad I was not alone with that one.

"He muses, you see, on whatever might come into his mind: the Pope, the Lowland Wars, the essentials of commerce, the very nature of life itself. And then, by and by, along might come some little fish and nibble on his hook. Then begins the activity itself, quite apart, you understand, from the purpose of angling, which is now fully and sufficiently satisfied. Now some common people may think the purpose starts at this point. They are quite off the mark, for it is here that the purpose ends and the activity begins. That is the delicious subtlety of your civilized man. Well, here we are with a little fish considering what you have offered him. Now, fish are not the fools you might think they are. They will not strike at just anything. They are aware that some things dropped into the water may not be put there with their well-being in mind. So we find him gently taking it in and out of his mouth to see if it fits his mouth or is soft enough for his taste, but ever so gently so it will not arouse whatever might be attached to the other end of it. The ever-vigilant angler now begins a game of infinite wit with this little creature, which he knows is wise beyond his size. He moves the prize he has put on the hook ever so slightly so that the fish will be assured it is a living thing. It is quite a skill to move it just so, so that it seems to have the spark of life in it, but does not seem to be dangerous. Perhaps you may say the fish of our waters are not as wise as the fish in the River Cam. But that is not my experience. If the angler has been wise and cunning the fish will, at this juncture, strike the bait, and now the angler is busy at war, and for his small size, the fish is very clever and very strong. The angler must outthink him: as keeping him away from tangling weeds, or from just running away and spitting out the hook. If he is skillful he may bring this fish to ground, and there is a metaphor indeed. But does he eat this little chap he has had such good sport with all the afternoon long? No he does not. Well, sometimes he may, but more often than not he lets the little fellow go again to raise his little ones and give some other angler such good sport another day. Now, that is civilization for you of a fine sort. I do love civilization. I am surprised you have not done this. Well, perhaps there are no good streams for it in Sandwich."

"I am sorry, Wassausman, but I can only think of my poor husband."

"Oh, pardon me, dear lady. Quite so, quite so, it has been beastly of me to prattle on, not thinking of that poor man. Well, Watamoo tells me he is recovering very well, and whatever fierce beast so savaged him in the forest we will surely find and kill."

"He was whipped on the order of the Court."

"Ah, I didn't know. Well, the law is the law. God be thanked he has survived and come to us. Now, what was it I came here for? Ah, yes, I remember now. I came here with these fine young princes to invite you to join us and the great king sachem Missasoit this evening. It is a poor table at this time of year, you must understand, and uncivilized, but it will help you keep your strength up."

"Thank you."

"I will come, then, at midday and be your interpreter. Boys! Bow to the lady." The two fierce, naked men stood up and, with some obvious reluctance on the part of one of them, made a formal bow to me together with all the flourishes you might expect from young princes.

I was amazed but, not to be outdone, I rose and dropped my best curtsy in reply. One of the boys gave me a sour smile, but the other remained stony-faced.

As they left the young squaw reentered and sat with me in silence all the morning long while I held Thomas's hand. His breathing seemed better to me and he even made a sound in his sleep, to my delight. It was the first sound I had heard from him that day and the tears that came were tears of joy. Once, he even opened his eyes, but could not see me. God had answered my prayer in his own way and in his own time.

With all these good signs, when Wassausman came for me I was not willing to go and I begged him to excuse me and let me stay by Thomas's side.

He looked at me very gravely and warned, "The lord Missasoit is a great king, dear lady. I have had much experience of kings. I have even met the King Charles, though he was in exile in France at the time. It is my experience of these great kings that they may refuse invitations themselves, but they do not issue invitations lightly and are quite unpredictable in their behavior toward you, should you choose not to come to them when you are bidden. This squaw will watch over your husband for you and do any services he may require should he wake."

"I know she will. But what if he should wake and not see me?"

"Well, I am sure that would be very sad for him, but it might be sadder if that condition were more permanent."

In the end I did go with him. When I reached the great lodge, however, and saw the crowd gathered there, I could not imagine how anyone would have even noticed my absence, except that there were few women. Those who were there, I was surprised to see, were sitting with the men as if they were their equals.

"I will tell you what is happening and being said, dear lady," he said, close to my ear so that he could be heard over the chattering crowd.

After a long wait, four strong young braves came bearing an old man upon a litter. This was surely Missasoit himself. He seemed very feeble and was propped up against many blankets and furs and held a stick with eagle feathers hanging from it. From his necklace hung what looked like a complete bear claw. But for all this savage show he seemed a man of great dignity and surely did have the presence of a king. When the litter was put down everyone in the lodge stood and whooped and cheered.

Wassausman whispered in my ear, "It was not our custom to stand when the sachem entered until Missasoit visited the General Court and saw that it was done there." Very slowly the four young braves raised the old man and supported him as he slowly made his way into the lodge. Although his steps were uncertain, he stood as straight as a javelin and never once lowered his head to look down at where he was stepping. I could see his hand trembled, though, as he signaled for the company to sit.

"We have come here to eat with you, our children. Where is the white woman who has come to visit us from our dear brother of the Nauset?"

Wassausman led me to the old chief's side. The sockets of the sachem's eyes were dark, but the eyes in them were bright. His skin seemed dry and papery and he had the smell of death about him. "The spirits let you pass through the forest to me because of the charms of our brother George, and you are welcome. George knows that I have always taken great pleasure in the beauty of the women of your race since that first time I saw them at the place you call Plymouth when I was a young man out hunting. In sending you to visit me he has sent a great gift to this old sachem in his last days."

One of the young princes stood up. "I will not sit at your table, grandfather, if this white squaw is to sit here. She dishonors the memory of my mother."

"I say to my grandson, Phillip, that he has many more meals to eat, at many more tables, than his grandfather Missasoit. Let him choose the guests for all of those meals, at all of those tables, but let me eat this one in peace."

Phillip sat down again.

"Come and sit by me," said the old sachem.

I thanked him and curtsied.

Wassausman had been too modest in his description of the meal, unless it was my hunger that added spice to it, because its taste seemed excellent to me. There was a great side of venison from which each person cut a chunk. They would cut into the meat with their scalping knives, take that piece between their teeth, cut it free with the knife, hold the chunk on the end of the knife, and take additional bites from it there until it was gone and the time came for the ritual again. Wassausman cut a chunk for me. I accepted it in my hands and set to work eating it that way. This was amusing to the company and they laughed heartily at the idea of eating meat with the hands, and a woman doing this made it doubly funny. Succotash was served in finely shaped stone bowls. This was followed by deer's blood served in its own paunch, sampe, lily root, the little knobby roots of a wild daisy which we sometimes call artichoke root, and what, as I think back on it, might have been frogs. Much as I disliked the idea of eating frogs, I was happy it was not horses' hooves, which I had been told were a delicacy among the Indians. They ended the meal with a delicious mix of hirtleberries and chestnuts.

Once I felt at ease, I took the time to look about the company and realized that, although Wassausman was more elegantly dressed than the rest, he was by no means unique. Others of the company had white neck cloths, sashes, and even ribbons on their shoulders.

"I ask you a question," Missasoit said to me in a high voice with only the hint of a falter. "We are very much the same. The English of Plymouth, which did such an injury to you because you would not obey their rules, have said to me as well, 'We English are too strong for you, and so you must do such and such!' When I came to them when they were a tiny tribe, the least of all the villages of the Wampanoag, and dying every day of the fever, as we now die, did I say that to them?"

"It is because you were willing to speak to these little men," said Phillip.

"Perhaps you are right, my grandson, but it is too late for me. I have made pledges to them, and it is the word of Missasoit which rules this land. John Alden and Captain Standish are now my friends."

"And they have lied to you. They have not kept their pledges to Missasoit."

"That they have not does not make it right for Missasoit to break his pledge. Who of all the nations would follow me if I did this?"

"You should not speak to these little men, grandfather. You are the great sachem of the nation of the Wampanoag and you should speak only to their sachem across the sea. You should only speak to the sachem Charles Two."

The old sachem put his small, dry hand on my arm. "My grandson Phillip believes we should make a great war on the tribe of the men of Plymouth and drive them out of our land as we do other tribes. But I say to him, here is the tribe of the English, and if we should drive them out the tribe of the Dutch would come after them, and the tribe of the French, and the tribe of the Spanish, all those strange tribes, and we would have to learn their strange languages as well. Making a war on them is like hitting a hornet's nest with a stick to be rid of hornets."

"It is my belief," said Wassausman, "that we are very like a tribe that once lived in England, called the Anglo-Saxons. They lay upon the land of England as far as the eye could see, as our nations now lie on this land. But they were defeated at a great battle at Synlac by a tribe that came to them, as these people have come to us, out of an eastern sea. This tribe called itself Norman. Now these Norman took the land and ruled it. All the sachems were Norman and all the sagamores of that land were Norman, but you see, my dear lords, the Anglo-Saxons were so numerous on the land that in this day, after thirty generations, the children of England are their children and the language is their language. What I say to the Great Sachem is that is the way it will be here."

"But these Anglo-Saxons did not lay down their arms when they saw these new people, did they?" said Phillip. "I have seen no war here. Have you seen a war?"

"I apologize that I have not taught the young Prince better of the world. We cannot think of war. I say to the great king Missasoit that we should let these English alone. Let them wash over our land like the tide. But when it has washed over us as far as the mountains, where it will meet the fierce Mohawk, then we will come up again out of the sand like the little flower the English call the sea thrift which holds its seeds down in the sand under the tide and when it is time sends up round pink flowers and flourishes again on all the beaches of that island."

"Wassausman has no pride!" Phillip said, standing up again. "We are a warrior nation and that is our way. We are not a nation of flowers!"

"Sit down, my grandson," said Missasoit, and Phillip obeyed, but his eyes were smoldering with anger.

I said nothing at this powwow because I was a woman, and English, and had little interest in these ideas among the Indians, but later I remembered what I had heard and it made more sense. I could have warned Plymouth and saved many lives, but I was only interested in saving Thomas and escaping to my brothers and sisters in Rhode Island.

Later, Wassausman accompanied me to the long wigwam where Thomas lay. It felt very strange walking so pleasantly with this elegantly dressed man with manners as if he were walking with me on the Strand in London. But we were walking through a dusty Indian village, full of naked children and barking dogs. It was unlike London, or Sandwich, because it might at any moment be folded up, like the set of a puppet play, trundled off to be set up somewhere else in the forest. But nevertheless there was the feeling of a royal residence about it.

"I must apologize for my young charge," Wassausman said at length. "He is still so young and knows so little about the great world. I think of myself as Aristotle to both the grandsons of the sachem."

"Who?"

"Aristotle, dear lady: the teacher in ancient Macedonia who taught the young Alexander, who was later to become ruler of all the known world. It was the wisdom of Aristotle, not the might of Alexander's arms, which was carried from Greece to the Hindu Kush and which changed that vast continent for all time. I flatter myself that it may be the wisdom of this Aristotle that will enlighten this new Alexander. One day this wisdom may pass even as far as the Mohawk."

"I love to hear you talk, Wassausman."

"I am deeply flattered. But let me put your mind at rest. You surely could see that the great sachem Missasoit will soon die, but it is his eldest grandson Alexander who will be our next sachem, and not Phillip, who just spoke so disrespectfully to his grandfather. On that I hang my hopes. Alexander has a gentle temperament while his brother is a ruffian. Dear lady, I cannot tell you what pleasure it gives me to talk like this about matters of such gravity with an English lady of such good breeding, and such a great beauty, in this benighted land."

"Oh, I am afraid you are mistaken about me. I am not yet twenty, sir, and I have never before left my village. You are far more educated than I am. I hardly understand half of what you say, but I do thank you." On an impulse I kissed him lightly on the cheek. I would swear he blushed then, this Indian gentleman lost in the forest, dressed as though he were about to be presented at Whitehall. Indians are not as swarthy as you are led to believe. They are simply tanned, or burned by the sun, because they live outdoors all the time, I think, and I was sure this one blushed.

I became used to the food, but I was always bothered by the lack of privacy. There was always someone with you, or if not, just outside your door. The Indians had no sense of being alone, but lived as if they were all one family. Of course, as they could take many wives in some cases they were all part of one family.

When the bark and leaf poultice was removed from Thomas's back I was amazed to see that the wounds had healed and scar tissue had begun to form. I moved into Thomas's wigwam and they gave me grease to rub into his wounds to keep the scar tissue supple.

I dreamed of one day being alone with my husband again, of having him in my arms just once more as we had been in Sandwich. And then one hot summer day it came true. I looked out and the village was empty.

The Indian people all seemed to be off somewhere at last. We were alone.

Thomas was awake. His eyes followed me as I moved about in the dim light in the wigwam. He pulled the folded animal skins I had given him for a pillow, and rested his head on his folded arms. His back gleamed with bear grease.

"Come and sit down, Lydia. Rest."

"You look much better. You look awake."

"I've been awake. Just tired."

He may have been awake, but not in this world. He had drifted, mumbling and shivering, for two weeks at least. Sometimes he moaned in the night. Twice each day, I rubbed the bear grease they gave me into the healing scars on his back. They were healing, but too large and deep to fade. Thomas was marked for all of his life with the price he had paid for me — for our love.

I pulled his fur pillow over onto my lap, and he rested his head there. I stroked his hair gently and ran my fingertips down his cheek.

"Does it hurt still?"

"Not much. At least, I don't think so." I could just see the smile in his dark eyes. It was dim inside this big wigwam. There was no fire at midday.

He took my hand, kissed my fingertips. I knew his thoughts. I ran my hand down his neck gently, down his chest, gently caressing. "Lie beside me."

I stretched out beside him on his pile of furs. I touched his scarred side carefully. He did not wince. I gathered him to me, resting my cheek on his hair as he nuzzled at my breast. My heart was beating, and I could feel his heart, his warm breath coming fast on my breasts. I needed to be free of the bodice. I needed to feel his hands and lips. I pulled at the knot, untied the tight lacing. I lay warm under his hands, in the joy of his touch. Then my skirt was loose, and his hand ran down my stomach, only a little swollen with our child.

"Will it hurt him?" he asked.

"No." I knew it would not. He is safe. It will not hurt him.

He was truly mine. God had made him for me. I had known that ever since, when I was a little girl, I had come upon him lying naked in a water field by his father's spring. I had hidden in the bushes there and watched him. I had known then that he was mine.

33

WHEN WE FOUND our way to Newport town on Rhode Island we found ourselves not just accepted but welcomed as heroes oppressed by the authorities in Plymouth. Many of the people of Newport were Quakers who had fled the colony, or been ordered to leave. What our crime had been was not an issue among them. Lydia joined the Quaker meeting. I did not join; I had had enough of religion.

All the leaders of the community worshiped with the Quakers, and we found that Lydia's sister Mehitable had married into that aristocracy. Her husband was John Easton. John was from one of the first families to settle in Newport. He was also a physician, a great land owner, and one day would be governor of the Island. When Newport was first laid out Easton's Beach was the first place considered for the town. Only its exposure to the sea, its storms, and the shallowness of the draft in its harbor kept it from being chosen. It was with great reluctance that the earliest settlers looked west to a marshy bottom in what was called the Western Harbor, but this unpromising damp thicket did open on a most remarkable seascape. Even the poorest man on Thames Street has the wealth of that view. I must describe it, if only for the pleasure it gives me to think of it.

You look out from a rising hillside to the westward across a great curved cove of gentle water. Along this water's edge, for fully a mile, is a handsome avenue cooled by the western wind across that expanse of water. In the distance the outer harbor is framed by two promontories of land each fully covered with the most amazing great, ancient, black forest trees, with many stooped and made individual by the sea winds. As a special ornament to all of this, the eye might search out an island set in this bay like a beauty spot upon the face of some great lady. It is called Goat Island and is also rich with the same fine old forest. Here it is, often in silhouette against an orange sunset on the water, that nature blushes with passion at the sight of it.

Now, the story is that when the town was to be laid out, the lower part was such an impassible marsh no one could get to the water's edge, and with so few men they could not imagine how to clear it. They were standing on William Brenton's beach as they debated the site, when an Indian came ashore in his canoe. They asked what it would cost to hire him and his tribe to do the work. The Indian thought for a moment, because they are not used to heavy labor, certainly not to change what God had planted in nature. Then he looked at William Brenton and noticed his fine red coat with many large brass buttons on it glinting in the sun, and he allowed as how he would take that for payment. They agreed and the Indians burned all the brush. They knew they could do that because such a fire often happened in the course of nature clearing the marsh on its own. They then had an easy job of pulling the remaining sticks up for use in their village. When it came time for payment William offered the coat. The Indian took it gladly, pegged off the brass buttons, and returned it to him. He took a string, strung the buttons on it as a necklace, and went off as naked as he had come.

They parted company, both the richer for the meeting.

Thames Street then, for all its mile, was set here and there with wooden houses, each far apart as in a village, and looking out through their glasses into the very heart of what has made the town wealthy: a placid basin, a large outer harbor, a convenient roadstead, and a clear offing. By the time we arrived, however, some of these views were already somewhat obscured by the wharves which reach far out from the land into the bay where the deeper drafted vessels may stand to be unloaded. The older practice of carrying goods to them in lighters was almost passed. Behind Thames Street, and up the hill parallel to it, stands Marlborough Street.

The town had fully seven hundred inhabitants when we came to it in 1661, and only Boston and New Amsterdam were larger in this land. As London was destroyed by fire a few years later, Newport was not inconsiderable among the great towns of the world. By the outbreak of the Indian war, Newport had grown to a town of four hundred houses.

Almost all her people now live in wooden houses with high-pitched shingle roofs and very few of the older wattle and daub huts with thatch remain. Most of the houses are town houses for the Quaker grandees, as they are called. These men have estates elsewhere in the island, or in the Narragansett territories. Half the town is Quaker, though all religions are welcome as they are not in other colonies. Even the Jews who fled New Amsterdam were welcomed. The governors have always been Quakers, however.

Our house is above Nicholas Easton's wharf, and Lydia and I can spend all the day long in pleasure, watching the busy commerce of the place from our window when we have no business to take us from it.

Ezra Perry, my brother-in-law, in gratitude for my not fleeing Sandwich, sold all my possessions there and sent me the proceeds as a grub stake. I, of course, could read and write and do sums. This, combined with the generosity of Lydia's sister's well-placed husband and her brothers, helped me find a place as a factor to the Brenton family. My familiarity with the customs and people of Plymouth helped me in that trade and my notoriety among the Puritans made me a person who could bring attention and business to their house. As factor, it was my business to find traffic for the wharf, measure the business passing through that port, and negotiate with the captains for the tariffs. The Brentons sent ships, not just up and down the coast from the Carolinas to Acadia, but as far as Barbados and even London itself.

I think often of the parable of the vine dresser and the fig tree. God cut me to my roots in the soil because I bore no fruit, and in that terrible trimming forced me into flower. And in that flower was fruit in time.

Our son Thomas was born in that bright room that looks out across the town's commerce. Mehitable was midwife and all the fat, richly dressed Eastons sat about for me to entertain with my faintings and fears at every cry of Lydia's in the process.

What sights we saw out those windows, Thomas Junior, Lydia and I, on Thames Street! Newport has no market, and so Thames Street is often impassable for the wares scattered about on it for sale by the farmers. All of this is interspersed with what the merchants bring in for shipment abroad. The famous Rhode Island horses, sheep, and hogs are brought alive for transport to Barbados, the Portuguese Islands, and beyond. The hogs, particularly, are so many in the streets that they are a menace and you always have to carry a stout stick to keep them off. Grain is always abundant at Newport, and a great plenty of timber is cut on the island, although some try to sell it short. You might see a whole wagon so loaded with fleeces it looks as though it has come down from the far north, still carrying a load covered with snow, or another loaded with furs, looking like a brown caterpillar. There are also bushels of peas, firkins of butter, and bushels of sea salt.

As these go out down the narrow wharves, pushed on by the curses of their teamsters, here come back up the same wharves delicious muscovado sugar, rosemary for perfumes, tobacco kegs from Virginia, fine casques of rum by the ton weight, bolts of lace from the Lowlands, fine silk taffeta, striped blankets, kersey green duffles a yard wide, nails, braces of pistols, English furniture, whole barrels of ivory-handled knives and scissors, gray and black casters of every size, pipes of wine, molasses kegs, and common ravel. I must count them all and walk among them like some Turkey potentate in my broad gray Quaker hat and gloves. Now and then a merchant will break open a load of goods and sell it there one piece at a time, or the lot, because it was not the finest, had spoiled at sea, or because the whimsy took him to be rid of it and have some other commodities.

If you look up to the north toward Brenton's Point you will see the shell of a ship being built of more than one hundred and twenty tons, looking like the bleached skeleton of some great whale tormented by carpenters crawling around its ribs.

Beyond that you will see a place where some posts have been set up among rocks on the sand for the fishing boats to moor to. If it is low tide the fishing boats will lie all about them like some giant child's toys or as though they were harbor seals sleeping there on their sides. All about them like a great spider's web the nets stretch out with their owners under them, mending the holes for the high tide. If it is high tide these same fishermen are cursing and bumping each other in their boats, eager to be untied and out to sea again. If you are bound for this place to select some of the day's catch for your pot you will say, "I am going to the Point." If you look the other direction you will see the windmills which give power to grind the town's grain.

When we first came to Newport, the Eastons hired me to oversee the business of their wharf, but there were fortunes for the taking in this town, and as Lydia and I grew richer I purchased a farm across the Narragansett in Little Compton from Mister Wilbour.

It was rich land and I raised horses there, taught them the Rhode Island paces, brought them down to Newport on the Jamestown ferry, and put them to sea on the Easton's ships for sale overseas.

I could not live at Little Compton because it was still in the Plymouth colony, even though it was far removed from Plymouth itself. I was still restricted from travel in that colony. However, it was a sweet time. Lydia and I would walk out in the evening – me with my gold buttons, and Lydia in her gray silk and finely cut lace. I acquired a taste for Virginia tobacco, and might stop at Mahershallalhashbaz Dyer's tobacconist shop to fill my white Holland pipe and light it with a stick from his fire so that it might leave a blue ribbon curling behind us as we walked into the twilight.

At Little Compton we built a fine house of wood with leaded

glass windows and four dormers looking out across the Narragansett and four looking back at our horses in their paddocks. My son loved to hide there in its stone-fenced fields from the heat of Newport; he had his father's love of animals and his grandfather's love of the land.

News traveled slowly from Plymouth to Newport, but it did take passage on her ships. Soon after we arrived, we heard of the death of Missasoit and that Alexander had taken his place as sachem of the Wampanoag. Alexander went, at last, to Boston to the General Court and died there. Some said he had been killed at the order of the court, and others that he had been poisoned there by order of his brother Phillip. I thought the fever, which often kills these creatures of the wilderness when they come into a civilized city, had simply taken him away.

But as the years passed worse news was to come to us. The ketch *Content* brought us the news that Phillip had joined in an unholy alliance with the Narragansetts and, as great sachem of both tribes, he rode with arrogance into Plymouth, demanding to speak to King Charles II and no one else. He brought our old friend Wassausman with him as interpreter, but they had a falling-out while in Plymouth in which Phillip believed that this old man had betrayed him. After they left the city, Wassausman fled in fear to his own people. Years passed before the saddest news of all to Lydia came to us with the ketch *Martha and Mary*: a coaster out of Boston. In that winter Wassausman had been fishing through the ice on Assowomset Pond where his old tribe, the Nemasket, had set up winter camp. While he was fishing three of Phillip's men fell upon him, forced him under the ice, and drowned him. His body was not found until the spring thaw, though his fate seemed well known to the Indians. When it was found, the Court at Plymouth quickly prosecuted the three whom Phillip turned over readily enough. Tobias, Mattaschmanamoo, and Wampapaquin were hanged for the crime on the Boston Common. Two of them went to the gallows proclaiming their innocence, but one confessed, hoping that this might bring him lenience. It did not. Nothing, save rumor, could ever prove any connection between Phillip and that ugly business. Lydia said she remembered how Wassausman had loved to fish.

My son Thomas was already a man when the first tales of Indian raids by the Wampanoags and the Narragansett on the outlying villages of Plymouth reached us at Newport. Soon these were followed, however, by stories of terrible massacres by the Indians among the whites.

Rhode Island was spared because it and Providence Plantation had always treated the Indians well, purchased the land they settled on — and not just taken it — and honored their sachems and sagamores. Roger Williams had been given a pledge by Missasoit that his family would never be harmed as long as he lived, and that none of his property would be touched by an Indian of the Wampanoag nation. Although many think Indians to be great liars, Lydia and I know they are a people of honor, and what the white man may consider a lie is not thought to be such among the Indians. All of the other colonies — Boston, Plymouth, Hartford, and the Connecticuts — united against Phillip, but Rhode Island and the Providence Plantation alone stood aloof from the war. This might have risen in part from the strong admonitions of the Quaker majority against violence and particularly war, but whatever the reason, we remained the only secure haven in all of the land. The raids had taken place so close to Plymouth that the smoke from burning towns could be seen in its streets. Phillip had more men at arms at the outset of the war than the English and many muskets and braves who knew their use. England, however, sent soldiers to the aid of the colonies, and with the militia from all the other colonies Phillip was often surrounded and cut off. He had no reliable supply as the English did and in time missed those killed outright in the field, those felled by disease and privation, those captured and sold into slavery in Barbados. Some of the rest fled to slavery among the Indians to the west. Soon Phillip found himself with only a handful of braves left ready for battle and a company of camp followers. The Great Swamp Fight, as it was called, killed many hundreds of his best braves. Phillip had foolishly taken a stand on an island of high ground in the middle of a swamp where he had built a stockaded village for his people.

A combined force from all the belligerent colonies and the English trapped him there, and burned the village, and Phillip was lucky to escape with his life. He raised another army among the tribes and turned now to Providence Plantation. To honor his grandfather's pledge to Roger Williams, he gave the citizens warning. They had fled in every conveyance they could think of and these refugees brought with them the first smell of burning and death to reach Newport. The refugees from Providence and the Narragansett country slept on every porch and in every shed in Newport. When those were all taken they camped on the ships lying in the harbor, or made houses of their clothing and slept on the ground. It was an appalling sight. In their need they grew desperate so that the town had to double the night watch to two men. These men with their lanterns walked the streets, crying the hour and the conditions on their watch, and raising the alarm if it should be required.

Newport had never known poverty. It had no poorhouse and had never had more need than could be satisfied by taking up a collection at the meeting for a widow, or taking some distressed person into another's home.

The Indians kept their promise to Roger Williams. They burned every house and post in Providence Plantation, but left the house of Roger Williams standing. At one point a Wampanoag came to Roger where he sat on his porch, and told him to go inside as there were many strange Indians among them and he could not vouch for their actions.

There were many harrowing stories that came across the Jamestown ferry. A man named Wright who was neither Quaker nor Anabaptist, but somewhat addled, swore that the Bible alone would be his protection. The Indians, hearing of this, joked that he had the Bible in his belly, and so cut him open and put his Bible there. Another story told of a man fleeing from Providence by boat who found himself surrounded by canoes in the pitch dark. An Indian voice insistently demanded that he pass one of his children to them, where they said the child would be safe and then the rest would be allowed to pass. He passed his youngest son down to them and went on. The child was never seen again.

On Rhode Island, however, all was calm but for the strangers. We were safe and the steady wind blowing from the sea carried even the smell of smoke away from us.

One lovely day I was out upon the grass of the bowling green at high noon. My coat was over a tree limb and I was down to my shirt sleeves.

I was the Second of my Four, the Jack was alive and I had my second bowl in my hand. As I stepped into the rink, onto the mat and set the bowl in course someone called my name. A man in buckskins approached me, and said, "Don't you know me, Thomas?"

I knew that round, cheerful face, though it had been deeply marked by the twenty years since I last saw it, and his hair was now quite white. We embraced. "Of course I know you, William Almy. How could I not? What brings you out to watch me bowl in Newport after all these years?"

"I am a refugee, Thomas, with the rest."

"Well, you must come home with me."

"I have something else to talk to you about, Thomas. I am sorry to say this is not just a chance meeting. I had heard you were settled here in Newport."

34

"VERY WELL," I said, "come along and we will have a tot of rum at Lieutenant William Baulston's Inn." Peter Coggeshall took my place in the game.

When we were well set up in a private room of the inn with rum and tobacco enough, I said, "William, I can hardly believe it is you again after all these years. Where have you been? We have never heard word of you at Sandwich, or here, for all these years."

"You know, I often think of that time we spent together in Boston with the militia."

"And I hardly remember it."

"You remember the sermon we heard together there?"

"Yes, yes I do."

"I think of that."

"Why in the world would you think of such a thing? I don't remember you as a great man of God, William."

"I was just a happy fellow then in that other world. Now I am eaten up with many hatreds."

"I can't believe that."

"It is true."

"What was there to hate there?"

"That sermon was the very example of what there was to hate in that dark place."

"I remember it as entertaining and exciting at the time. I had heard few like that. Mister Leverich gave no such sermons."

"I believe they suffered there a very grievous sin. But then, who am I to talk about sin? I don't know that I believe it even exists."

"Not exist?"

"But I can see now that that was sin most clearly if there is sin in the world. But I don't pretend I can see my own sin. I can surely see that minister's sin as clear as clear, even after all these years. Don't you remember, Thomas? He was without compassion. That is surely the greatest sin. That is a sin our religions do not address. It is a sin without a name. It is the very sin of this new land. It results in judgment without love and law without mercy."

"I am not sure I understand you, William, but I am not one to defend them. They tried to make a state where religion might govern everything: a perfect land. Perhaps it was too perfect for us to live in, William — too perfect for their children. An old Indian once told me it burns you out from within. Perhaps that is our problem, William."

"Worse than that, I think, Thomas. Tell me, did you ever marry that girl you were on your way to see?"

"Well, yes, in a way I did."

"It is hard to marry someone in a way."

"That is another story for another time. Tell me where you went when you left us on the road. You were on your way to the Connecticuts as I remember."

"Well, I never made it there. I married and settled in Lancaster. That was not much of an escape for a man who loves escapes, eh?"

"I thought you would never settle. You always wanted to be up and away from folk."

"Ours was a house away from the town."

"I am not surprised to hear it was. Where is your wife now?"

"She is dead, Thomas, and my children."

"Dead?" I could hardly believe this. In our safe little world now, to think of death was almost beyond belief. "How did she die, William?"

"That is a part of why I am coming to you, Thomas."

"Whatever I can do I will. But what can I do?"

"They were killed at Lancaster by the Indians."

"I'm sorry. I didn't know."

"It was a day like this, Thomas. I wasn't at bowls that day as you were this day. I was out in the fields, but I might have been at bowls for all the difference it made. I stopped by the stream for a drink. I never did that. Why did I stop that day? If I had not, I might have been with them. I might have died with them. I wish I had, Thomas. When I came home at midday I could tell that something was wrong at once, but what it was, was hard to say. Then as I came down the hill I saw the cabin was gone. Only the stone chimney and the smoke was left. My poor Silence was dead there in the ashes and one of our children with her, shot through with a musket at close range. The others . . . God knows where they are. I pray that they are dead." He put his head down on the table and cried as if what he was describing had been only yesterday and not years ago.

"William, William . . ." was all I could say. What can you say to such a story? It is beyond thought.

"I was afraid, but I found a shovel in the shed and buried them as best I could, then lay down there and slept. There in that land with the savages everywhere. I didn't care if they came for me. I could hear the sound of their cries in the distance and my body seemed numb. Finally I got myself up and went on into Lancaster on foot. The Indians were everywhere, but somehow they did not attack me as I walked there along the road, unarmed, in clear sight. I passed my neighbors' houses; all of them burnt. In one there had been five people: the father, the mother and a suckling child. They knocked the child on the head and killed the parents. The other children they took away as prisoners. The houses in the village were garrisoned, though the work had just been done and none of the defenses were complete.

"Richard Wheeler came out and pulled me in quickly. Everyone in the house praised God that another white person in the district had survived. The Indians then came in force against us, and set fire to the house we were in. We could see fire at the Rowlandson's garrison across the way as well. There must have been two dozen of us in that place, but we could not get the fire out and the Indians set up such a volley of muskets that you could hear the balls hitting the wall like a shower of hailstones. First one man, then another, then a third were wounded or killed, I could not tell. Then one of the women said we would have to go outside if we were to survive the fire that was raging above us. I took one of the muskets and followed. The woman did not get more than three steps before the musket balls brought her and her child both down in the dust and blood. There were figures running everywhere, mostly Indians, firing at everything they saw. We saw one person down on his knees begging for his life. One Indian cut him open with a knife. I have never seen such butchery. One woman who stood beside me said she wished she were dead and in that moment a shot obliged her and she fell dead on the spot. I made a run for it and made it to the woods, though I had been shot twice and was losing blood. I had so much blood around me it ran down into my shoes. How I escaped that massacre I do not know. Most there were killed and some forty taken away prisoner, of which most died of their wounds, or later on from the long marches they were taken on. Mistress Rowlandson, however, I have heard survived. They are damnable beasts, Thomas. They are worse than that."

"My God, William, I had not heard this."

"But I have not sought you out for your sympathy, Thomas. That was years ago now. I sought you out because I had been told by some who knew you in the Narragansett country that you were living here and I remembered that you had training with me at Boston in the militia and you were then a very good shot with your musket."

"I still hunt fowl here with Jahleel Brenton on his estate. I can bring a bird down better than most."

"Since the burning of Providence Plantation many Rhode Islanders are willing to join the united colonies against King Phillip. I am recruiting here for a militia company to march with Captain Benjamin Church against Phillip, where he is hiding in the middle of his swamp, and make an end to that evil fellow. The swamp is his ally and we need a few men with good eyes and a sure hand to come with us and fight him, Indian style."

"I don't know, William. I am a man of peace, and my wife is a Quaker. I have a family here."

"And I had a family too, Thomas."

"I knew Phillip, once. I am not surprised."

"You know him!"

"Yes, I met him on my way here from Sandwich when he was about the age my son is now."

"That will make you invaluable to us, Thomas. You must come! These Quakers will not go to war, no matter what the provocation, and they are poor shots from sitting so long at their counting tables. But you, Thomas, we must have you with us."

"As I say, I am not a Quaker, but my wife is."

"What is your wife's name?"

"She was Master Peter Gaunt's daughter. You remember Peter, don't you?"

"Ah, yes, I do. His daughter's name was Mehitable. She was a very spirited girl, as I remember."

"Oh, no, Mehitable is here and married, but to another. I am married to his youngest daughter, Lydia."

"I don't remember her."

"Come home with me and we will all share stories about Sandwich."

"I would like to, Thomas, but we are urgently raising troops and hope to set out by week's end. I will come on Wednesday. I must recruit all the islanders I can. Come with us, Thomas."

"I must think about it. I am not a soldier."

"None of us are, but think of your family. These Indians will next come here. Think of your Lydia in the burned-out ruins of your home. Then tell me you will not come against them."

"I cannot say just now."

"You must, Thomas, we cannot succeed without you."

"I will then, William, I will."

"Good! We muster here on Thames Street near the Quaker Meeting House at sunrise a week from today. Come with a horse, a weapon, and whatever powder, shot, and food you have. God bless you, Thomas."

We parted in Thames Street and I walked slowly home. Lydia wept and begged me not to go, but I had lived too long an exile, not just from my land but from my responsibilities to my fellow man. Here was a clear and manifest danger to our lives. I could not stand the coward in the face of it. The Indians following Phillip might take Lydia's life, or my son Thomas's, or burn our house in Little Compton. I could not stand idly by while this madness raged. While Phillip lived, no Indian could be trusted and no white man safe in his bed. And who knows? Perhaps just by chance I might win a pardon from Plymouth for this service and could return to Cape Cod.

I could see Lydia's figure in the window, watching us as we mustered for battle. Whether she waved or wept I could not tell, but the slim light shape of her was there behind the glass. She sat faithfully in that window as long as I could look back and see her and she may have been there long after, for all I could tell.

I thought how proud Lydia must be, despite her Quaker scruples, to sit so long watching us march out.

35

IT IS AMAZING how life changes you. I am not the child I was in Sandwich — that little girl, with her romantic furbelows and desperate belief in the importance of everything. She is asleep somewhere inside me. This life of luxury and satisfaction Thomas and I have made seemed, until last Wednesday, all there was to life. I cling to it and all the friends we have made here, and to my sister, and to my son and his new wife and it seems it has always been this way. The candles of my life twinkle, the silver is bright, the crystal gleams, and the fire is warm. Our hands are full of gold rings, our ears full of music, our mouths full of the sweetmeats of this glorious place.

But one thing is not changed. It is the curse and joy of a woman. Why is it that way? We need the love of a man to fill the sails of our life. We measure ourselves, in some strange way, only by the image of us in his eye. Why do we live like that? Why is that so important? They could not care less about it, it seems. We wake in the morning to the thought of feeding him and fall asleep wondering what dreams that head which lies beside us has within it. Is it because it is so foreign? Is it because we are always mothers, somewhere in our souls, and they are our children?

That changes as time passes, but it is always there. I loved Thomas in the flesh, and as a fellow pilgrim, when we were young in that other world of my childhood, and now it is as if we see through each other's eyes. We are so incomplete when not together that I can be sitting deep in conversation with my sister and her friends, consumed with the makings and marrings of this place. Suddenly, there is a vacancy, as though some organ of my body were missing, because Thomas is not there. In my mind, I slip my hand into his arm, as we walk together on the quays, and I am complete again.

He is a strange man. In some ways clear as jell. In some ways sweet. Sometimes quiet and distant. When he is like that, I am sure he is brooding, but he assures me he is not. He seems not to need people as I do and is always searching himself for duties unfulfilled. Yes, there is the problem. I can live for myself, but strangely he cannot.

As I say, Newport is my reality now — such a sweet reality, and so full of fat and love that "my cup runneth over," with it and with this life with Thomas and our son, who is now at our property in Little Compton with his new wife. But Thomas brought home William Almy Wednesday night. I put a good face on it, but he had the smell of the past about him, and its bitterness was not a good condiment.

And now, you will not believe it, he has taken down his long gun from over the mantelpiece and that soft, happy, fat old man will go out and kill our friends the Indians in the forest. I cannot make myself say the words. Where is love in that? What fools men are. How can we love them so?

I sat in my best blue silk, even though it was summer, and looked out the double hung window in my sewing room onto the scene at the mustering ground: a crowd of old men playing at boys, measuring their weapons, smelling gunpowder and blood, and I could hardly see them for the tears. Why would they want to kill? Why could I not stop Thomas? What does he have to prove? After what we have been through, what contracts can he have unfulfilled to the other colonies?

I felt a knife of ice cut deep into my chest, into the lung itself, into the center of my being like a north wind in January. Nothing can wait for us in the forest now but disaster. I sat there long after they had marched out. They must have been to the ferry before I, at last, unfolded my hands and set my abandoned sewing aside. Nothing can come of this but sorrow and death.

36

WE WERE AN ill-trained and ill-matched group — mostly refugees from the Narragansett country and Providence Plantation and very few true Rhode Islanders. Many of them gave strange sidelong glances at my Quaker gray. I wondered as we rode if I had been wise and belonged among them. We crossed on the ferry and camped that night in the ruins of Providence Plantation. There it lay like the stubble of a newly burned corn field. We looked at it in amazement as we rode through it.

Those who had known it told us what a fine town it was. There was not so much pity among us as fascination that the Indians could do this to something that had seemed so permanent. All but Roger William's house had been burned and that old man still sat on his porch looking out as though all those houses were still around him. That was indeed a pitiful sight. I had seen the old man once before when he sailed all the way from Providence to Newport, alone in his skiff, to debate with the English Quaker Fox during that preacher's visit to the Newport meeting. But now he looked one hundred years older as he sat there: the only assurance that the town of tolerance and freedom he had dreamed into existence might rise again. Captain Church sat with him on his porch and they talked. I could think of nothing to say, and so I kept my distance.

I rode out the next morning with William Almy at my side for a very long day's ride to the outskirts of King Phillip's swamp. Rain was threatening and we knew that, rain or shine, there would be no footing for the horses in the swamp. There would be no way to be made for them among the trackless forest of small trees, and so we penned them in a farmer's field which still had its fencing up and selected some of our number to camp there with them and see that the Indians did not come around us and steal them, leaving us on foot. Most who won that duty looked relieved.

We had Praying Indians to guide us through the swamp to where we had been told Phillip lay with the last remnants of his army. We started that night on footpaths only the Indians knew, single file, Indian fashion. Our guides assured us we could reach the high ground in the middle of the swamp by nightfall. We could camp there, they told us, on the high ground and find Phillip in the morning. As we were a clumsy, noisy company, I expected an ambush at any moment. Although the narrow vistas out across standing water on either side seemed empty, we could only see about fifty yards at the most on either side. A large company of Indians could have shadowed us by sound alone and we not know it. Apart from the sounds of small animals and birds flushed by our approach, the swamp was silent and empty. We wondered aloud at last if anyone at all was there, or if our information had been faulty and out-of-date, but the leaders of the Praying Indians assured us that Phillip was there and urged us to be quiet. The oldest of the guides was an Indian called Alderman of the Awashonks and I tried to keep him in my sight as much as I could.

We made camp after nightfall on a ridge of high land. Pickets were put out along it, but as there were not many men likely to sleep that night they were not really needed. We made no fires. Captain Church had given the order that no man should speak a word. That silence among so many was an awful thing, like the quiet of some holy place, and made the night on that narrow hump of land above the musky-smelling swamp eerie indeed. Men would sit silently on the bank side with their guns at the ready, then start at the sound of something dropped in the camp as if it were a drum stroke or a musket shot that would wake the slumbering Indians we fancied were all around us as we lay in the very heart of our enemy's territory.

Those who had slept were quietly awakened at first light by a young man sent out from Church. He would put his hand over their mouth before he gently shook them so they would not groan and give us away. I could see him going from one to the other and when he came to me I simply put up my hand to show that I did not need his services.

A deep fog had risen in the swamp around us: thick near the water and thinner near the ridge.

As men went down off the hill crest in small bands they disappeared in it as though they were wading into water until it covered their heads.

Church was spreading us out to search across what our guides told us was a sort of large dry island in the middle of the swamp. The first to make contact with Phillip's men, if he should live to know it, was to discharge his musket, and the others would come running to the place.

I was in company with five or six. Among them were: the guide Alderman, William Almy, Caleb Cook, some other refugees, and one Indian I did not know.

We walked together, stealthily, step by careful step with our muskets always at the ready. The fog was so thick we could often barely see our neighbors. We had to quickly look down at the mat of dead leaves at our feet to check the footing and then up again, straining our eyes into the white fog for the enemy. We were climbing a slight rise when Alderman put out his hand, stopping us and pointing down at the ground. He ran his hand along the earth, bringing to our attention the stubs of burned pickets which had once been a stockade. They had been so recently burned there were some white ashes still clinging to them, but where this strange defense led to or came from there was no telling. Moving on up the rise the space around us seemed to be brightening, the fog growing less dense, letting us see all the company and to see that we were quite alone. We were in a clearing of beaten earth. Its size could be figured by the ghosts of trees on all sides in the mist but the fog made it seem much more vast.

A figure then started materializing before us in the mist. It was standing very still. We could not tell if it was an enemy or one of us at first and so Caleb signaled for us to hold our fire by dropping the point of his musket.

Just then, as though we were standing in a moving cloud, the mist opened and I said, "God save him! It is Phillip," for I recognized him.

It surely was. He was standing there in the open, naked to the waist, in his small breeches and moccasins. He had a pouch and powder horn as though he were waiting for us, but he had his musket crosswise in his hands at rest in front of him. On his face was a sort of strange grin as though he were daring us to face him off. We stood for some time like this as though we were in that dream world a snake makes for its prey before it strikes. Then Caleb Cook came to his senses, shouldered his musket, and pointed it point blank at Phillip. Phillip made no move but continued staring directly at him. Caleb fired, but it was a flash in the pan and a puff of white smoke passed away across the clearing, filling it with the smell of gunpowder. Caleb let the musket fall to the ground, putting his hands up to his face where he had been singed and blinded by the flash.

All this time Phillip had stood there unmoved, but now he began raising his musket slowly as though he had all the time in the world. He was still smiling and looked like a hunter who has been watching a foolish turkey feeding in a field. Now he does not want to alarm it with a sudden movement, but he will surely kill it. Only Alderman, looking upon this scene, had the presence of mind to raise his musket and let fire at Phillip. His gun had been double loaded and the shot spewing out of it tore a great hole in Phillip, and he fell like a stone to the earth with the same strange smile on his lips.

We turned and withdrew in disorder as though we had seen some infernal spirit struck, feeling it might rise again to pursue us in spirit form with its guts trailing on the ground.

Alderman called us to our senses as we reached the burned stockade. We all fell down behind its stumps at the ready for the other Indians we were sure must come on our heels. They did not, but they were there, as we could hear them crashing about in the forest near us.

We then saw a big fellow enter the clearing and go down on one knee by Phillip's body. This one called out, "Iootash! Iootash!" Alderman whispered that this was old Annowan, Phillip's great war captain, and he was urging his warriors to stand to it and fight stoutly. The battle was now to begin.

It was hardly a battle at all, for the outcome was never uncertain. The young braves came running from the trees shouting wildly. We fired from our cover and several of them fell. Those who remained fell back into the woods to regroup. We could hear Annowan shouting at them as we stood and reloaded. They ran at us again and we fired another volley. All who did not fall fled back into the trees and did not return.

My companions and some others who had come up at the sound of firing ran on after them across the open space and into the trees. I went out to the one I knew I had shot. He seemed so small and fragile in his nakedness. He was surely not older than fourteen and small for that. His tawny skin matched the curving light brown bed of leaves in which he lay as to be a part of them, or them a part of him. All about him in those leaves, in little pools and rivulets, his dark maroon blood had flowed and frozen. I then did a strange thing. I knelt down and kissed him on his soft child's cheek as I would have my son. I looked up to the branches framing the sky where the little birds were each making their small morning melodies. I knew a spirit had been breathed out of that wood on that morning and it would never return. I cried out to that empty sky, "What sin have I not sinned? What commandment have I not broken?" A passage from Leviticus caught in my mind: "And he shall bring his trespass offering to the Lord, unto the door of the tabernacle, even a ram for the trespass offering. And the priest shall make an atonement offering for him with the ram before the Lord for his sin which he hath done and the sin shall be forgiven him." I then dipped my hands down into the child's wounds where there was still warm blood and smeared it on my face and wept.

You will hear many stories about how the sachem Metacom was killed, but this is the true one.

When all Captain Church's men were gathered in the clearing, Church stood over Phillip's body and said, "What a doleful, great, naked, dirty beast he looks. For as much as he has caused many English to lie unburied and rot above ground, not one of his bones shall be buried." The company raised a cheer at that.

Church then called on one of the Praying Indians, Saconet, I think, to serve as executioner. This Indian made a sort of oration over the body, saying to the body as though it were listening, "You were a great man and made many afraid of you, but I will take your head," and he knelt down and cut Phillip's head off. The Plymouth men among us took this back as a trophy and set it up on a pike by the General Court. I understand it still stands there.

They then proceeded to quarter the body, as was the custom with traitors in England. It was the custom in England to hang these quarters at each of the corners of the wall of the traitor's town as a warning to others, but as Phillip had no village left in all that land they hoisted the grizzly burdens up into tall old forest trees about the clearing. As each piece of meat went up they cheered again.

I rode home without a word to William, as if I were a child with a shameful secret, running from the evidence of his mischief, hoping against hope no one could ever discover where the evidence of it is hidden.

37

WHEN COLD WEATHER came I fell ill with a cough and chills, as I often do. To cheer me up in those gray days Lydia accepted the invitation of my good young friend Jahleel Brenton for dinner at his home: Four Chimneys House. This was Restoration Day: the day set aside on the island to commemorate the restoration of King Charles to the throne of England. This day of thanksgiving for the end of the Protectorate had been set aside by Jahleel's father when he was governor, and so the family always gave a great entertainment for their friends on that day. Such an invitation was coveted, but for those who did not get it there was general merriment of other kinds. The day was a required holiday for servants, apprentices, and children and all the shops closed for the Restoration Fair at the Lime Rocks.

Now Jahleel was a young man, only slightly older than my own son, and very wealthy, but he had sworn to be a bachelor all his life. He had fallen in love when he was a child with his cousin Martha, but his father had declared the relationship too close in blood. He would marry no one else. The lady felt no such scruple and, rather than swearing to be a spinster all her life, she married and had several children. She came with her husband to Jahleel's parties and they were as warm as brother and sister.

Brenton's Neck is bounded by the Lime Rocks on the north. The rest of its two thousand acres is surrounded by the sea. In that vast area it has grassy hills, valleys, ponds, rocks, hemlocks, cedars, oaks, and great stands of chestnuts on its hill tops. All the walls around its fields are not of planks, but of cut granite. Its orchard trees were brought over from England. Two of the varieties of apple his father developed are the Rhode Island Greening and Yellow Russet which will keep for nine months in the barrel — as long as a baby will keep in the womb.

There is also a particular spot where you can call out toward the Lime Rocks and seven distinct echoes will come back to you. I have done that myself and so I know it is true.

Jahleel's father called the estate Hammersmith for his home in England and divided the land into two farms. Jahleel left the western farm uncultivated as a natural park, and through it he ran many lovely curving walks and paths all carefully laid out with gravel. It was a joy to walk there among the high grasses and blue flags. The point of land at the end of it was a mass of wild rose bushes and the most delicious whortleberries, blackberries, and wild strawberries. These were open to anyone who would sail across from Newport with a picnic lunch to pick them.

On the other farm he ran horses, cattle, and eleven thousand sheep. That was the sort of wealth he had. At one time he had more than one hundred people working on the land: among them everyone from stone cutters to his favorite shoe maker brought there from London.

On his beaches you might see teal, gulls, ducks, oldwives, and a bird we call the wamp which is like a duck, but with a longer bill, hovering around the rocks or floating on the sea. It was a rare day which did not have the sound of fowling pieces, and the sight of one of the dogs specially trained to bring the fowl back out of the water in their mouths.

There is a hill there called Wooly Hill, because near every spring the briars are strung with long white threads of wool that have been pulled from the coats of the sheep. At a distance you would think it is covered with some white flowering bush and when you come close you see it is hundreds of little white flags waving in the wind. Second to it in beauty is the Lily Pond where hundreds of old wild roses come all the way to the pond's edge, looking at themselves in its water where white water lilies float. Jahleel has set stone benches there, cut away the trees on one side to give a view of the Atlantic, and let its cool airs blow in the summer where a happy company can sit all the afternoon in conversation.

Jahleel also laid out cherry trees along one of the gravel paths and called it Cherry Neck after the old riddle: a wee wee man in a red red coat, a cane in his hand and a stone in his throat — tell me this riddle and I'll give you a groat.

The house was built by the Governor and called Four Chimneys House. It is one hundred and fifty feet square with a hall straight through the center sixteen feet wide. On its roof are railings, seats, and promenades. From these you can look down paths cleared of trees giving long vistas out to the sparkling Atlantic on one side and back to the blue bay on the other with the town of Newport on its edge like a toy town. Perhaps there will be white sails flying on the water, or some merchantman on a cloud of sail making for port. Behind, you can enjoy the green of fat hills that rise to make a close high horizon, as though that pleasant place was all there was to the world itself.

The house has large windows and seems wonderfully open. Its bare plank floors are always clicking with the feet of that large family and always full of guests.

At the dinner we would take there tonight, its heavy dark oak furniture, cut from trees on the estate and ornamented with many fat rings and fantastic faces, were groaning with good food, drink, and tons of heavy silver plate.

The rooms were a mass of silver candelabra with hundreds of tapers burning all at once, filing the rooms with a soft yellow light. It made all the ladies beautiful and Lydia most of all, as animated as she is and full of mischief and delight. Her serious sister makes a counterpoint, but just as full of life in her own way. The Brenton girls are thought great beauties in the town, but can not hold a candle to the Gaunts.

The meal started with sweet little sprats from Jahleel's own streams and ran on through eight courses to the chestnuts and pudding.

At one point Jahleel, John Rathbone, who had been overseer of his father's estates, Gideon Wonton, and I fell to talking about the Indian lands now opening up.

"It seems a shame that the poor devils cannot hold their land, but we will soon need it."

"They gambled and lost it," said John.

Jahleel listened for a time, then silenced us all with, "We have paid our price for the land. To some of us, it was a dear price. Some paid with their lives for it. When my father came here he had another son: my oldest brother John. I don't even remember him, but I have often heard my father speak of him with tears in his eyes in this very room. He sent John out to survey the wilderness and prepare a place for us there. I suppose he was a sacrifice to that land, our human sacrifice. That was thirty years ago and we have not heard a word about what his fate was, and no chance of ever finding out, I think. My father was sure he was killed, but I think he just kept on going through the dark forests and never knew where to stop. Now he is somewhere beyond the last white man's cabin and all his messages to us have been lost along the way before they could make it home to the island. He was our sacrifice. This family has made a sacrifice for the land. It is now ours by right."

When the meal was over and we had had our rum and tobacco, Jahleel went to the shutters and doors and threw them open to the black night. The candlelight within was so bright that it illuminated the outdoors with such a light that all the birds roosting in the nearby trees thought the sun had risen and began to sing. The whole company laughed and Jahleel said, "I could not have hired a better chorus for us in all of Newport. But I do know where we can find better entertainment. This is Restoration Day. Come with me, friends, and we will all go down to the fair at the Lime Rocks, waste some pennies, hear some music, see some strange sights, and see what trouble our maids and apprentices have gotten themselves into at the fair."

Horses were brought up for Jahleel's brothers and sisters. The girls had changed into their riding habits because it was their custom to ride down to the fair two by two, each brother with a sister. The horses were trapped out in gilt and ivory and the women's riding habits were imported from England and made of broadcloth hemmed up above the instep to show off their high-heeled shoes with silver buckles. They wore small jackets with tight sleeves and their collars turned back like gentlemen's coats, displaying satin vests, and they had matching headdresses made up of beaver hats with broad brims, and black ostrich feathers.

They rode on to the fair as an honor guard and we all followed on foot singing, laughing, and talking. There were great bonfires among the rocks and small boats running back and forth filled with faggots to keep them burning. We had missed the parade, but we were just in time to see the Restoration Day pageant carried in on a platform. On it was a man representing the old Lord Protector

Cromwell down on his knees, while just behind him stood a dark man dressed as His Satanic Majesty with one hand placed upon Cromwell's wig and the other uneasily brandishing a sword above his head. This masque was carried in by a great crowd of young men straining at its handles to hold it up. They were accompanied by the sound of kettle drums, hand bells, and fifes playing music both doleful and joyful. At intervals the stage would make a drunken stop, and when Satan had found his footing on it again he would declaim:

"Oh Cromwell, man! your time is come,
We tell it now with fife and drum;
And Satan's hand is on your head,
He's come for you before your dead,
And on his spear he'll throw you in
The very worst place that ever was seen,
For good King Charles is on his throne
And Parliament now you'll let alone."

Then all the apprentices cheered and the ladies laughed.

Lydia and I walked on down toward the beach where an old black man was playing his violin with great gusto.

The water was as black as coal with only the hint of the fires flashing on its surface and the steady shushing of the ripples on the sand. I knew the old black man. He had been a slave brought out of Africa on a slaver captained by a Newport man. As they crossed the Middle Passage this old man would sing. The sea captain so loved him for his sweet songs that he could not stand to part with him when he had him in Virginia. He bought him there and brought him back to Newport.

There were other tents set up on the beach with candles sparkling inside them and bonfires blazing in front of them. I was amazed to see my old Indian guide Alderman. I recognized him at once, even in the darkness, and introduced him to my wife. He was the proprietor of one of the tents, as it turned out, and there with his young crier advertising that for a penny you could go inside and see the relics of King Phillip who, as the crier said, "Like as Agog, was hewn to pieces before the Lord. So let all Thine enemies perish, 0 Lord!"

With great reluctance I went into the tent at Alderman's insistence. Indian relics were set up all around in the candlelight on boards, and a sad and dusty lot they were: an old leather shirt that may have been Phillip's, but which he surely did not wear at the time of his death as the young guide said, a pole with feathers on it which Lydia said might have been Missasoit's, the inevitable hatchet, a musket that I do think was Phillip's, and at last a nebuchadnezzar of dark brandy that the guide said contained the severed right bow hand of the sachem Phillip himself. The brandy gave the whole tent a festive smell it did not deserve.

The bonfires outside made the tent's sides throb with light, but it was not enough to see into the liquid. I knelt down and moved until the glass was between me and a candle flame. Now I could make it out. It was surely a hand, palm up, its fingers slightly opened in the brandy, as though it were offering me something, but it seemed much too small to be Phillip's hand — almost as though it were a child's hand. Then I felt quite ill and had to stand up and excuse myself. All of a sudden I knew whose hand it was. The hand had been at that battle, but it was not Phillip's. I felt lightheaded and had to rest my weight on Lydia's arm as we went up the hill to Thames·Street.

The next morning I could hardly get out of bed for the pains in my arm. News had come on the ketch *New Bedford* that my father was dead at Sandwich and with it came his bequest. He died a very old man and rich in money, cattle, and land, but he left to me, his oldest son, five pounds. Five pounds is what a wealthy man might leave to a servant, or have someone drop into the poor box on his death. That vindictive old man should have disowned me as I had thought he had, but instead, with his last spasm of life, he had cast the change out of his pocket at me to be the last lash of the whip on my back.

Lydia knew I was very ill, and after writing a will at my dictation she hired a skiff to take us both across the bay to Little

Compton where I might be with my son and his new wife at the last.

As we cast off from Easton's Wharf there was the soft sweet sound of a hymn on the still air:

How wondrous and great
Thy words God of praise!
How just King of saints,
And true are Thy ways!

Oh, who shall not fear Thee,
And honor Thy name?
Thou only art holy,
Thou only supreme.

To nations long dark
Thy light shall be shown;
Their worship and vows
Shall come to Thy throne;

Thy truth and Thy judgment
Shall spread all abroad,
'Til earth's every people
Confess Thee their God.

From the bay the new house looked very fine with its four gables watching us and the sun flashing in their glass. The young couple had been out on their lawn, and when they saw that the skiff was heading for their jetty, they both came down to welcome us.

Thomas has married a beautiful, dark-haired girl from Taunton named Sarah Richmond, the daughter of the iron maker whose industry has made that village famous.

As I took a hand up onto my son's jetty I wondered what that God who had once lived in Somersetshire would think of us here. I was filled with joy to be in Plymouth Colony again no matter what it might think of me. I remembered that it had been a simpler, quieter place where virtue once reigned.

Though it was only Little Compton, I felt that I was home at last.

I was very weak and still in great pain. They laid me out in a hammock hung between two large trees with a view of the bay and drew their chairs up around it while I got my breath again.

The evening was coming on very chill. Banks of fog were just forming, very slowly raising a barely perceptible thin blue fog from the water. An old orange ball of sun hung over the Narragansett, making the little ripples of that bay look like a pile of golden coins. And that is Newport, is it not? As I looked out at this sun the trees seemed like so many black bars, their long shadows reaching to us. Should you change a world when it is innocent and pure? Does any man have that right?

Somewhere, someone had cut a field of English hay and the air was full of the rich smell of the hay making: a smell of this new earth. It drew my mind back to a cabin standing alone in a field on Duxbury side, with new yellow thatch on its roof, and the people who lived there.

I am angry that Thomas died. I am angry that he left me a young widow. I am angry that I no longer have his income and will be dependent on my son and my sister. But I forgive him all of that. I loved him in every way a wife can love. God gave him to me and I do not question that gift.

When we were sure he was dead, I went down to the water's edge and took a shell out of my pocket I always carried there. I had a mind to throw it into the Narragansett, but in the end I could not. I just kissed it and put it back in my pocket.

AFTERWORD

The true name of the subject of this work was Thomas Burgess; although the name does appear as Burge in the court record of the case in Plymouth and occasionally in the records of the family in Cornwall. He was an ancestor of the author. Most of this work is based on historical fact.

The Burgesses were Cornish. One genealogy says the father of Thomas Burgess Sr., the Pilgrim, was mayor of Truro and our Thomas's grandmother was Elizabeth Pye. This is not, however, proven. There is some argument about the identity of his mother, Dorothy. A nineteenth-century genealogist found a marriage bond in Yorkshire for a Thomas Burgess and a Dorothy Waynes, but subsequent research has proven that couple died childless. One source thought she was the daughter of the Reverend Mister Phippen, driven out of his cure at the Church of Saint Mary Magdalen at Truro for Puritan leanings. On a trip to Cornwall this author found he had no daughter Dorothy, and that Dorothy was an almost unknown name in the duchy at that time, but a distant cousin of Elizabeth Pye in Saint Stephen in Brannel in his will mentions his granddaughter, Dorothy Pye, who would be the right age to be Thomas' mother. She would have been a Puritan and in a family frequently closely allied to the Burgesses by marriage.

The old sailor at the opening, John Cutting, was famous for carrying immigrants to the New World. He once knocked one of them down for calling one of his many ships "a ship of reeds." He finally settled in New England and died there.

Thomas' early memories of Saugus plantation are based on real accounts.

Elizabeth Bassett did meet Thomas when she was a child at Duxbury, and there were bastinados; the food, the house interiors, farming practices, and the clothes are all from contemporary descriptions, as they are throughout the book.

All of the people in Sandwich actually lived there and some of their personalities are based on how they came across in early records. William Wood did write the book attributed to him.

Thomas was called to the aborted war with the Narragansetts. The arms passed out by Edmund Freeman really belonged to him, and were as described from the Tower of London. The description of Boston is from seventeenth-century accounts, including the public houses and the social customs described. Even the ghost stories told by the hanger-on are ones current in Boston at the time. The sermon which so moved Thomas is a mix of contemporary sermons and the lines attributed to Puritans satirically by Ben Johnson in his play *Bartholomew Fair* from the same time period.

It is not documented that Thomas really stopped by Duxbury to propose to Elizabeth on his way back from Boston, but in the following year she and her widowed father and little sister did move to Sandwich. Her sister was not named Trial; that is a story from the Thayer family which this author could not resist using. The food and clothing at the wedding feast are correct for the time and place, as are the wedding customs, down to the scriptural passages embroidered on Elizabeth's undergarments.

The elder Thomas Burgess' spring where Lydia first sees Thomas is now the water supply for the town of Bourne, west of Sandwich. Lydia's father, Peter Gaunt, was an Anabaptist and a relative of his was the last woman burned to death in London, for harboring Quakers. All of the court cases mentioned as brought against him come from court records at Plymouth. George Barlow did take Peter Gaunt to court for not ringing the noses of his pigs and for the other charges mentioned.

Richard Bourne and Thomas Tupper became famous for their efforts to educate the Native Americans in the ways of their invaders. The matter of land ownership was a real problem for the Indians to grasp (as it may be to this day). The Kingdom of the Mashapee still exists on Cape Cod and this description of it is drawn from accounts and drawings of Native American settlements in the seventeenth century.

George, the sagamore of the Nauset, is based on a historical figure who did try to assimilate, with mixed results, and the mythology is drawn from ethnographic studies by the Smithsonian Institution. The mask is based on one the author saw in a collection of Native American art.

The Quaker lady, Mary Dyer, in the "Lamb's War," is a real person. Her style of preaching, confrontational manner, and dress are all drawn from early accounts of the Society of Friends missionary efforts in the Plymouth Colony. She was hanged on Boston Common. There is no record she visited Sandwich, but it is very likely, as that village became a hotbed of Quakers and she visited many of the villages in the Plymouth Colony. Modern Quakers will not recognize some of this and may even object, but their faith has evolved over the centuries to one that is not as militant as it was in the seventeenth century.

The oppression of the Quakers with particular savagery at Sandwich by Sheriff Barlow is documented, as are the Quakers' practices (including weddings without the benefit of clergy).

Mehitable Gaunt did not come into meeting naked, as she does here, but another Puritan girl did with the same result elsewhere in the colony, as described by Cotton Mather. Mehitable did marry John Easton, later to be governor of Rhode Island, and mentions "my sister: the widow Lydia Burgess" in her will. The Reverend Leverich did leave the town abruptly, never to return, at about the time the Gaunt children fled to Rhode Island.

The charges brought against Thomas Burgess by Elizabeth Bassett, and the verdict in this first divorce trial in the Colony, and probably in the country, are drawn directly from the minutes of the General Court of Plymouth.

The details of public whipping (including the good advice given Thomas by the Public Hangman) are based on real accounts of seventeenth-century whippings.

The author issued Lydia a slight reprieve: the historian of Sandwich said he was sure she was also whipped at Sandwich for her participation in Thomas' adultery.

There is no record of Lydia and Thomas being protected by the Wampanoag tribe, but the description of the dance is almost verbatim from an eyewitness account. All the characters in the tribe are based on real people in that tribe at that time, including Wassausman (the tutor to Phillip and his brother), who was educated at Cambridge and did affect the dress and speech of an English aristocrat. Sadly, the account of Wassausman's death is also historically accurate. This is what made it seem reasonable that he would have developed a love of angling while in England.

The descriptions of Newport, Rhode Island, are from seventeenth-century accounts, as are the trade and the places of business Thomas would have known well.

One of the Burgesses (very likely Thomas) served in King Phillip's War. The account of the last battle and the fate of Phillip is from an eyewitness account.

Jahleel Brenton's house did look as it is described, and the account of the celebration commemorating the fall of Cromwell and the restoration of Charles II is correct down to the words of the song.

Phillip's hand was displayed in a bottle of brandy around New England after the war and was widely thought not to be his. The child Thomas killed is not based on historical fact. Phillip's body was quartered and hung in the forest. His head was on display at Plymouth until it rotted away.

Thomas' father did leave him only five pounds in his will. The elder Burgesses are buried by the pond in Sandwich and are said to be the only Puritan graves of this age with markers surviving. Their daughter, Elizabeth, and her husband, Ezra Perry, are buried beside them. The Perrys had a descendant who became President of the United States: Franklin Delano Roosevelt. The elder Gaunts also spent the rest of their lives in Sandwich.

Thomas and Lydia's son was married to his first wife, mentioned here, but the author is actually descended from his second wife Martha (Wilbour) Closson. The Wilbour house still stands in Little Compton and all of the Burgesses of this generation can be found in the third row of graves out from the Congregational Church in the square of that village. It is very likely that Thomas did not become a Quaker because he is not listed in the records of the Quaker meeting at Newport. The Quaker Meeting House still stands in Newport, but is no longer in use.

Thomas may have died at his son's home in Little Compton (then in the Plymouth Colony and now in Rhode Island), but the speculation that he regretted the change his actions had helped to bring to the nation is pure supposition.